THE IMPERFECT GENTLEMAN

For all his infuriating faults, Peter Hawkins at least had always acted like a perfect gentleman toward Evelyn—until now.

Now, before Evelyn grasped his intention, he caught her roughly in his arms. The kiss that he pressed on her was savage. His mouth wholly possessed hers, and Evelyn felt herself drowning beneath its assault. Soon, his kiss was no longer brutal but strove to melt her with its heat. Then his lips left hers to travel the length of her throat until coming to rest on her frantic pulse. His teeth delicately nipped the flesh.

Evelyn had managed to resist Peter Hawkin's divine good looks, superb grace, flawless manners, and dazzling charm. But this was a new weapon in his siege of her single state—and she had to fight not only his startling new stratagem but her equally surprising urge to surrender . . .

SIGNET REGENCY ROMANCE

Miss Dower's Paragon

by

Gayle Buck

Ⓢ

A SIGNET BOOK

SIGNET
Published by the Penguin Group
Penguin Books USA Inc., 375 Hudson Street,
New York, New York 10014, U.S.A.
Penguin Books Ltd, 27 Wrights Lane,
London W8 5TZ, England
Penguin Books Australia Ltd, Ringwood,
Victoria, Australia
Penguin Books Canada Ltd, 10 Alcorn Avenue,
Toronto, Ontario, Canada M4V 3B2
Penguin Books (N.Z.) Ltd, 182-190 Wairau Road,
Auckland 10, New Zealand

Penguin Books Ltd, Registered Offices:
Harmondsworth, Middlesex, England

First published by Signet, an imprint of New American Library,
a division of Penguin Books USA Inc.

First Printing, July, 1993
10 9 8 7 6 5 4 3 2 1

Chapter One

Miss Evelyn Dower sat primly on the garden bench, her ruffled skirts spread about her ankles. Camomile blossoms clung to the hem of her skirt, adding their soft, clean scent to the fresh spring air. A warm breeze played in the new leaves in the tree above Miss Dower's head and caressed her face. She paid scarce heed to her delightful surroundings, however, as her attention was occupied to the exclusion of all else.

Evelyn's fulminating gaze rested on the two figures that approached her from across the lawn.

Her mother was escorted by a well-set young gentleman, who negotiated the way for himself and his companion with a feline grace and power. While the gentleman solicitously supported Mrs. Dower over the sloping ground, his magnificent leonine head was inclined attentively to hear her conversation.

As the two made their way closer to Evelyn's bowery seat, the gentleman sent several admiring glances in her direction. However, contrary to what might be expected of a young lady who found herself the object of a handsome gentleman's regard, Evelyn did not feel the least flutter of gratification.

On the contrary, Evelyn's frown intensified. The displeasure in her tawny eyes deepened when the gentleman caught her gaze. He had the audacity to smile at her. She caught her soft lip between her teeth and turned her head away in vexation.

Evelyn had known Peter Hawkins very nearly all of her life. As a young girl she had worshipped him, but she had never been bold enough to make her childish feelings known to him. And through the years, her feelings had not

changed in any degree. Not when she saw him again upon
his return from Oxford, nor upon his return from his travels. Rather, her emotions had been underscored by how the
quiet, reserved youth had grown to splendid manhood.

Only a few short weeks ago, Mr. Hawkins's present devotion would have driven the soft color of confusion into
her cheeks. She would have counted herself the most fortunate of young ladies and received his advances with all the
dazed happiness of any other lovestruck maiden.

However, that was all at an end.

On the very day that Evelyn was informed that Peter
Hawkins had been granted permission to pay his addresses
to her, she suffered a complete revulsion of feelings for the
gentleman. The circumstances of his suit precipitated this
state, for through them her pride had been trampled and her
affections had been callously discounted.

Even now, three weeks later, Evelyn could not forget
every moment of that humiliating interview with her
mother. Her thoughts turned inward as she remembered yet
again that particular evening, when she had received a summons that she was to come to her mother's sitting room before retiring.

Evelyn had entered the frilly room feeling only a mild curiosity. It was not unusual for Mrs. Dower to recall something of note that she wished to relate to her daughter from
the day's round of callers or some trivial household crisis.

On the evening in question, Mrs. Dower turned from her
mirror and exclaimed, "My dearest Evelyn, you shall never
guess! I have had such a day that I am left all in a whirl."

Evelyn sat down in her usual place in a wingback chair.
She regarded her mother with a genuine fondness and tolerance. "Indeed, Mama. Pray tell me, have the Reverend
Smythe's roses bloomed early this year?"

"Now you are funning me and you really must not. Why,
everyone knows it will be at least another month before the
dear reverend's prize blooms come into bud," said Mrs.
Dower.

"My pardon, Mama. Of course it was silly of me to think
it could be that which has put you into hoops. But do tell
me your news. I am always ready to hear your little anecdotes," said Evelyn with perfect truth.

She had long since learned to piece together the bits dropped by her mother's flighty tongue and she now held an emerging picture of the society which she had not yet entered that would have astonished Mrs. Dower by its accuracy. In fact, Evelyn had digested hints of some matters that would not in the ordinary way have come to the ears of a young lady who was just emerging from the schoolroom.

"I took tea with that horridly stiff Lady Pomerancy. Surely you know of her ladyship. She is grandmother to that handsome young gentleman, Peter Hawkins. How such a fine young gentleman could have survived tutelage under that one's stern nose, I cannot conceive," said Mrs. Dower, shaking her head at the mystery.

"However did you come to do such a thing?" asked Evelyn.

She rather unsuccessfully ignored the bump of her heart at mention of Mr. Peter Hawkins. She had fancied herself in love with him forever, it seemed, but it would not do to become so wrapped up in her fantasies that she forgot the truth.

He had taken no particular notice in her at all; at least, he had not until he had returned from the Continent. Then she had thought on one or two occasions to have caught a certain gleam in his eyes when she chanced to meet his gaze during Sunday services in the chapel, but she had never been certain that she excited more than a passing appreciation in the gentleman.

Whenever they met after the services or in the village, he was unfailingly polite and kind in his attentions to both herself and to her mother. There had been no distinguishable difference in his manners toward her than there was in the grave respect that he accorded Mrs. Dower.

It was the frustration of Evelyn's life, for even when she had been a small girl and he a grand three years older, he had treated her in just the same polite, distant, and considerate fashion.

"It is an odd thing for me to have done, is it not?" agreed Mrs. Dower. "However, Lady Pomerancy had sent me an invitation, which I felt I could not possibly ignore. She has always terrified me. I am in such a quake whenever we meet that she might find disfavor with my cap or ribbons or perhaps think me too terribly frivolous."

Evelyn laughed. "But you are terribly frivolous, Mama, you know you are!"

Mrs. Dower's anxious frown dissolved into a smile. "Yes, I know that I am, but that is not quite the same thing as being thought it by some crusty personage. You will say it is chickenhearted of me, dearest, but really, I have never been able to overcome my awe of such persons."

"Chickenhearted, indeed, but never mind. You are my own dear mama," said Evelyn, rising from her seat to bestow a kiss on her parent's cheek. Often she had wondered, as she did now, what it would have been like to have had a mother similar to everyone else's. She had never really felt like her mother's daughter. Instead, she had felt more like an aunt or an elder sister to Mrs. Dower.

Mrs. Dower had enjoyed a rather complacent existence, first as the petted daughter of a wealthy squire and then as the cosseted wife of a promising and rising politician. She had regarded her husband's untimely death—he had succumbed upon slipping on the cobbles in the rain and fatally striking his head—as unfortunate but not greatly grievous to her own pleasant pursuits of quiet entertaining, her shopping, her gardening, and, of course, the spoiling of her young daughter.

The girl's serious upbringing had been left to the nurse who had been engaged by the father and then to a governess, both of whom, fortunately, had been esteemable characters who recognized that little Evelyn Dower might have inherited her mother's lovely hair and features, but her character was very like her father's—questing, impatient, and quick. It had been they who managed to bring the girl to a recognition of her own gifts and to the beginning of an understanding of human foibles.

As Evelyn became older, she had come to regard her mother much in the same light as had her father, as someone to be indulged and to be amused by and perhaps to be a shade protective of. Evelyn felt she had nothing in common with her mother besides a physical likeness and a shared taste for romances. As she thought it, she said, "Shall I read to you this evening, Mama?"

"Oh, dearest!" Mrs. Dower blinked away sentimental tears. She was a somewhat scatterbrained, good-natured creature, generally considered to be still quite pretty though she was grown a little plump due to her indolent nature. She did not aspire to great passions or opinions, those being too fatiguing to maintain, but she did regard her sole progeny with loving fondness, and in the course of her daughter's growing up she had always kept her daughter's interests close to her heart. She smiled tremulously. "You are such a good daughter to me. I do not know how I shall go on without you, I truly do not. But I mean to do my best, so you must not be anxious on my account."

"Whatever do you mean, Mama?" asked Evelyn, startled.

"Why, haven't I said? What a perfect pea-goose I am, when *that* is what has put me in such a whirl!"

"What has put you in a whirl, Mama?" Evelyn inquired patiently, having long since learned how to deal with her mother's hyperbole.

"Your marriage, dearest Evelyn! It is all arranged, you see."

"My marriage!"

Evelyn regarded her mother blankly.

Mrs. Dower complacently patted her hair, very pleased with the reaction that she had garnered with her announcement. "I was quite as bowled out as you, I assure you. That is what Lady Pomerancy wished to discuss with me over tea. She has decided that you will make the perfect bride for her grandson, Peter Hawkins, and I was given to understand the plan suits him admirably. It is not wonderful?"

Mrs. Dower ended on a mingled note of triumph and congratulation. She was disconcerted when the stunned expression in her daughter's gold-brown eyes gave way to wrath.

"I am to wed Peter Hawkins?! And at Lady Pomerancy's bidding!"

Evelyn struggled to contain her feelings, but she could not help a burst of recrimination. "Oh, Mama, how *could* you?" She leaped up and took a hasty turn about the room.

Mrs. Dower's smile faltered. "But I felt certain that you would like it excessively, Evelyn. Why, you have been mad after young Peter since you were in pinafores."

Evelyn's face burned with indignation and embarrassment. She had not known before that her mother had gathered that much truth about her unspoken feelings. "Whether I was *mad* after Mr. Hawkins or not is quite beside the point."

"That is nonsense, dearest. I would not have agreed to the match otherwise, for I wish only for your happiness," said Mrs. Dower.

Evelyn's eyes were very bright. Pressing her fingers against her flushed cheeks, she cried, "Mama, can you not understand? It is not a proposal from the gentleman's *grandmother* that I wish to entertain!"

"Pray do not be silly, Evelyn. Of course it is not Lady Pomerancy who is to solicit your hand, but Peter Hawkins. I do hope that he'll do the romantic thing and go down on bended knee."

Evelyn recoiled. She had often dreamed of receiving an impassioned declaration that would fulfill all the romance of her soul. Now to envision Peter Hawkins going down on bended knee before her, because he had been urged to do so by his grandmother, struck her as a monstous ludicrousy.

At the sound of her daughter's wild laugh, Mrs. Dower cocked her head in concern and alarm. "Really, I do not know how you came to think such a thing. When I recall how many times Miss Phibbs assured me that you were admirably quick and bright of intellect, I cannot be other than bewildered now by your cloth-headed mistake. Even I am not so gooseish, my dearest one."

Caught between laughter and tears, Evelyn shook her head. "Dear Fussy Phibbs, I do miss her. Do not fret, Mama! It is all perfectly plain to me, never fear. I am to receive an offer for my hand from Peter Hawkins because Lady Pomerancy approves of the match."

"That is it exactly," Mrs. Dower nodded, much relieved.

Evelyn took another hasty turn about the bedroom, tossing over her shoulder, "I shall not receive him, Mama."

"Evelyn! Are you mad? Of course you must receive him!" exclaimed Mrs. Dower in acute dismay.

Evelyn faced her parent. Her face was white, only the glittering of her tawny eyes betraying color. "No, I cannot possibly. I am far too sunk by humiliation and pique to do so, you must see that!"

Evelyn saw that her mother was going to remonstrate

with her. "Pray do not think to persuade me to it, Mama! I have given you my last word on the matter. I shall not receive Mr. Hawkins."

"But you must! He is coming tomorrow to do the thing in a formal and proper fashion," said Mrs. Dower.

"Proper! Yes, indeed, Mr. Hawkins will certainly do all that is proper!" exclaimed Evelyn scornfully.

"Oh, my dear! Pray, pray—!" Mrs. Dower earnestly appealed to her daughter. "Do not speak in that fashion. You have just the look of your father about the eyes whenever he had worked himself up into one of his passions. It never did him the least good that I could see, for he set up the backs of perfectly credible personages and exhausted himself in the bargain. One is made so uncomfortable by such freakish tempers."

Mrs. Dower saw that her stricture was not having the salutary effect that she had intended. She reached out her hand to touch her daughter's muslin sleeve. "Dearest Evelyn, pray say that you will receive young Peter Hawkins. I gave my word to Lady Pomerancy, you see, and I very much fear she would speak to me in that positively cutting way she has when she dislikes one's little witticisms, and I know this would be a graver offense by far. Oh, Evelyn! I am begging you. Pray say that you will receive him! I do not insist that you accept his suit if it is repugnant to you, though I quite thought that—but not another word on *that* head shall you have from me. Only do, *do* receive him, at least!"

"I am sorry, Mama. But I cannot do so," said Evelyn.

Mrs. Dower dissolved into tears. But even so, she continued to present her pleas.

Evelyn was very fond of her mother and she was not entirely immune to Mrs. Dower's unhappiness. However, she remained firm in her decision and was in hopes of bringing her mother to a proper understanding of her feelings. But to all of her logical presentations, Mrs. Dower burst into fresh tears and took renewed recourse in her handkerchief.

Mrs. Dower's liveliest dread seemed to be what Lady Pomerancy would do, and nothing Evelyn could say could disabuse her of the notion that somehow Lady Pomerancy would ruin her social standing.

An hour after she had first entered the room and learned of her mother's astonishing settlement of her future, Evelyn realized that she was not making any ground with her persuasions. She broke off abruptly, saying, "Mama, it is obvious to me that you are too overwrought to discuss this matter with any rationality. Perhaps on the morrow, after you have had a night to sleep on it—"

"I shall not sleep a wink!" declared Mrs. Dower tragically, taking refuge again behind her thoroughly dampened handkerchief.

Evelyn sighed, "Nevertheless, I think it is best that we postpone further discussion until the morning. We are both tired and cross and have been unkind to one another." She bent to kiss her mother good night and left the room.

But the morning did not bring the agreement that Evelyn had hoped for. Mr. Hawkins sent in his card as the ladies were finishing breakfast, and Evelyn had the servant deny her to the visitor. Mrs. Dower made it plain that she was thoroughly unhappy and disappointed, while Evelyn attempted yet again to explain how her pride would not allow her to accept the manner in which Mr. Hawkins had been handed over to her.

Neither lady gave ground that day, or the next, or the next. A miserable fortnight passed during which Mrs. Dower resumed her tearful pleadings at every opportunity.

Finally, Evelyn could stand no more of the way that Mrs. Dower dragged herself about from room to room, sighing and sending reproachful glances in her daughter's direction. Mrs. Dower had even eschewed her usual social calls and denied herself to her friends, insisting to Evelyn that she was too heartsick to bear any entertainment and that she dreaded the possibility of receiving word of Lady Pomerancy's displeasure.

In the end, Evelyn reluctantly agreed to receive Peter Hawkins.

At once, miraculously, Mrs. Dower's tears dried, her woebegone countenance brightened, and she tucked away her damp handkerchief into her sleeve. "Now I may be comfortable again. You are such a good daughter to me, dearest Evelyn."

Evelyn eyed her parent in some resentment. A martial

light flashing in her eyes, she said, "I warn you, Mama! I have agreed to receive Mr. Hawkins, but that is all."

"Yes, dearest, I do understand," Mrs. Dower said reassuringly. "Now I shall just send round a note to Mr. Hawkins."

Evelyn sighed and shook her head, even as the smallest of resigned smiles touched her lips. It was useless to remain annoyed with her mother when that lady was completely oblivious to one's aggravation.

Chapter Two

Thus, Evelyn came to be in the garden reluctantly awaiting the approach of Mrs. Dower and Mr. Peter Hawkins. Ever since she had agreed to the meeting, she had had grave reservations of the wisdom of it. However, she had pledged her word and there was no possible alternative now, she thought, as the couple reached her. However, she had not bound herself to be pleasant.

"Oh, here you are at last, Evelyn. Only see who I have brought to see you," said Mrs. Dower.

Evelyn inclined her head in a manner reminiscent of an uppity dowager. With a cool smile, she gave two fingers to the gentleman and acknowledged his existence. "Mr. Hawkins."

The young lady's glacial tone could not be considered to be encouraging or welcoming, but, despite Mrs. Dower's patent dismay, Mr. Hawkins did not appear to notice anything amiss in his reception. He bowed gravely over Miss Dower's hand.

Evelyn was disgusted but unsurprised when the gentleman did not retain his hold on her hand for an inappropriate length of time, but instead immediately released her fingers. She certainly could not have expected anything more imaginative from a gentleman who had come to offer his suit in obedience to his grandmother's wishes, she thought waspishly.

Mr. Hawkins looked down into Miss Dower's lovely face, his gaze both searching and hopeful. "Miss Dower, I find you in pleasant surroundings, indeed. It is a fine day to be out of doors in all nature's new splendor."

Evelyn sniffed but did not deign to reply. At the last moment she had fled to the garden, preferring to receive Mr.

Hawkins there rather than in the small parlor. She had thought she would burst with her seething emotions, and even though she had ignored the beauty of the garden, it had nevertheless provided a soothing balm to her exacerbated spirit.

After throwing her daughter an anxious glance, Mrs. Dower said hurriedly, "Yes, indeed! The garden is already giving promise of the fine flowering to come. I am sure the good reverend has mentioned to me a score of times his opinion that it is to be an excellent year for his roses."

Mrs. Dower threw another glance at her daughter, taking particular note of the mutinous light smoldering in the girl's eyes. It obviously would be for the best to have the matter done with as quickly as possible, and she rushed on. "But we shall not spend another moment idling on about gardening, if you please, Mr. Hawkins, for I know that you are anxious to speak to dearest Evelyn on a particular topic. I shall step aside for just a few moments to give you privacy."

Mr. Hawkins looked faintly surprised and even a shade disapproving. "I am sure that is not at all necessary, Mrs. Dower. What I am come to say is most properly directed to Miss Dower in your presence."

Evelyn lifted a delicate brow, murmuring, "Come, Mr. Hawkins. Surely I am not so intimidating a personage as that."

Mrs. Dower uttered a soft murmur of distress.

Mr. Hawkins appeared taken aback. "Why, I had no such feelings at all, Miss Dower. Of course I would not think anything so disrespectful of one whom I hold in the most reverential regard."

"Very prettily said, Mr. Hawkins," said Mrs. Dower. Hidden from the gentleman in the folds of her skirt, she twitched her hand at her daughter.

Evelyn ignored her mother's urgent signal, and with a bright, brittle smile, she said, "Mercy, Mr. Hawkins. I am overcome, indeed, at such an exquisite compliment."

Mrs. Dower uncertainly eyed her daughter. All too readily she recognized the danger signals flying in her daughter's manner, and her heart bled for the poor unsuspecting gentleman. She wavered in her intention to leave the young couple alone. "I suppose—perhaps I shall do better to speak to the gardener another time."

"Pray do not put off your intention on my account, Mama," said Evelyn cordially.

Mrs. Dower sighed in defeat. "You shall call to me when I am needed, Evelyn dearest."

"Of course, Mama, though perhaps it will be Mr. Hawkins who shall feel in need of succor," said Evelyn.

Mr. Hawkins smiled. It was a smile of great charm, creating the tiniest quirk at one corner of his firm mouth.

Evelyn had once thought his to be the most fascinating smile in all England, and even now, at the height of her wounded pride, she found that she must harden her susceptible heart against it.

"You have a droll sense of humor, Miss Dower. I had not appreciated it before, I am sorry to say."

"Hadn't you?"

There was something in Evelyn's bright eyes and flippant voice that strongly reminded Mrs. Dower of her late husband when he had been in the throes of a towering temper, and that finally spurred her to action. With a hastily murmured word, she retreated in a most cowardly fashion.

"May I presume so far as to share your bench, Miss Dower?"

Evelyn inclined her head, still maintaining her haughty air. With magnificent indifference, she said, "As you wish, Mr. Hawkins." He seemed impervious to her snub, and to her fury seated himself beside her. Evelyn gave a faint sniff and lifted her nose as though she scented something faintly obnoxious. She stared straight ahead, presenting him with only her profile.

Mr. Hawkins cleared his throat, then said with a grave air, "Miss Dower, I am fully cognizant of the maidenly confusion a young lady of delicate sensibilities must feel upon entertaining an interview such as this. If your father had been alive, I would certainly have applied to him and therefore spared you the awkwardness of our present meeting. Indeed, that happy conclusion is what I had hoped for when Lady Pomerancy approached Mrs. Dower."

"Pray do not give it another thought, Mr. Hawkins. My mother persuaded me of the necessity of receiving you. I am quite resigned to it, I assure you," said Evelyn, bestowing upon him an artificial smile.

Mr. Hawkins appeared insensitive to her heavy insult. Instead, an expression almost of relief crossed his face. "I am happy to hear you say so, Mrs. Dower. I was afraid of offending you with my boldness."

Evelyn positively stared at the gentleman.

The thought crossed her mind that he was an idiot, but it was almost as instantly dismissed. Intelligence and humor enlivened his handsome contenance, while his vivid blue eyes regarded her with a smile in their depths. That left her with the uncomfortable suspicion that he was making game of her. "I assure you, Mr. Hawkins, I am not offended by your boldness," she said warily.

Mr. Hawkins's mouth quirked in its beguiling fashion. "I am glad of that." He gently took one of her hands and lifted her fingers in tender, reverential salute.

At the touch of his lips, Evelyn felt a tingling sensation that sped from the tips of her fingers to her heart. She snatched free her hand. Pink flags flew in her cheeks. She was furious with herself. How *could* she be so affected by this mawkworm, this handsome pattern card!

Of course, it was true that she had thought herself in love with him for years, and particularly in the past twelve-month. Mr. Hawkins was everything a young lady could desire in a gentleman. He was tall and well set-up, with a breadth of shoulder and an athletic build that were the envy of lesser men. His countenance was pleasant and his voice was pleasing to her ears. Whenever they had chanced to converse, she had been struck by his thoughtful intelligence.

If Mr. Peter Hawkins had applied to her under any other circumstances, she would gladly have accepted his suit and counted herself fortunate above all others.

However, that had not been her happy fortune. Instead, he had offered for her hand at his grandmother's bidding, thus killing any romantic standing that he had once held with her.

Mr. Hawkins apparently mistook the outward signs of her fury for maidenly blushes, for he said contritely, "I have presumed too much. I apologize for my forwardness, Miss Dower."

Evelyn all but ground her teeth. She did not look at him for fear he would read the contempt in her eyes too soon. She pleated her skirt between her fingers. Her voice trembled. "Mr. Hawkins, may we please come to the point of your visit?"

"Of course, Miss Dower. I understand completely your wish to be done with what must be a most uncomfortable business," said Mr. Hawkins. He gently recaptured one of her hands, forcing her to raise her eyes in a quick glance. "Miss Dower, I have conveyed a formal offer for your hand to Mrs. Dower. Your delightful parent has given me encouragement to hope that such an offer is not entirely distasteful to you."

Evelyn faced the gentleman seated beside her, intending to reject him without mercy. But when she met his eyes she found she could not be as brutal as she had intended. There was a shyness in his hopeful expression that made him look very much like an expectant puppy. Evelyn hesitated, then said quickly. "Mr. Hawkins, I do not think I can accept your suit." She drew back her hand and laced together her fingers in her lap. Despising herself for cowardice, she yet glanced up to gauge his reaction.

Mr. Hawkins appeared so crestfallen that she took even greater pity on him, though she did not understand why she should do so after being the recipient of such an insult. "Actually, I am not interested in anyone's suit at the moment. I—I am just come out of the schoolroom, you see, and I have not been presented yet . . ."

Evelyn let her voice trail off, wondering at herself. She had not meant to excuse her rejection in any way, and yet she had done so. She frowned, worrying at her lip as she reflected upon her inexplicable behavior.

"I understand you, of course."

Her eyes flew to his face. "Do you?" she asked, startled. How he could do so when she did not understand it herself was beyond her comprehension.

Mr. Hawkins smiled down at her, a little wistfully, she thought. "Your honesty does you much credit, Miss Dower," he said. "You have enjoyed a most sheltered existence. It is only natural that you should wish to try your wings and see a bit more of the world before entertaining such a serious suit. I should have thought of it myself. I respect your wishes, of course. Nothing more need be said at present. I shall take my leave of you now in hopes that I may call again at another time."

He had risen as he spoke and now he bowed formally to her. Mistaking her astonished expression, his mouth quirked a little. "Never fear, I shall not press you."

Mrs. Dower, who had been hovering anxiously in the background, took Mr. Hawkins's rising as her cue. She rushed over, already speaking before she reached the couple. "Oh, Mr. Hawkins! Surely you are not leaving us so soon. Why, I had quite hoped to be able to offer you some small refreshment."

Mr. Hawkins turned the charm of his smile on the older lady. "Perhaps another time, ma'am. I shall wait on you and Miss Dower again, I assure you."

He bowed to Mrs. Dower and the silent young lady who was still seated immobile on the bench. Then he walked away rapidly across the camomile lawn to disappear behind the green hedges that separated the house from the gardens.

Mrs. Dower turned with a hopeful expression to her daughter. She asked hesitantly, "How did it go, Evelyn dearest? Am—am I to congratulate you?"

"Pray do not be such a pea-goose, Mama. Of course I did not accept Mr. Hawkins suit," said Evelyn, more sharply than she had intended.

At the hurt in her mother's eyes, she relented. "I am sorry, Mama. I am in a beastly mood and all due to that mawkworm."

"Mawkworm! I would never describe young Peter Hawkins in such terms. Why, he is quite the handsomest gentleman in the neighborhood," said Mrs. Dower in liveliest surprise.

Evelyn shrugged her shoulders in scorn of such a frivolous assessment. "I do not know how else one would describe a gentleman who allows his grandmother to approve his bride! No, Mama, I have not the least feeling or respect for Mr. Peter Hawkins, and so I let him know."

"Did you, my dear?" asked Mrs. Dower doubtfully. "The

gentleman did not appear in the least put out of curl, as one
might have expected if he had been so abused. And he did
say that he would call again."

"Mr. Hawkins is merely all that is polite," said Evelyn
dismissively.

"Really, Evelyn. I am not used to such pertness in you.
One would think you had a score of suitors, all as good or
better than Peter Hawkins."

"Perhaps I shall have, Mama." Evelyn tilted up her chin
in an unconsciously challenging pose. "Why not, indeed? I
am considered to be passing fair and I am possessed of a respectable dowry. Why should I not attract a few eligible offers once I am out in society?" She curled her lip, casting a
glance in the direction that had been taken by Mr. Hawkins.
Under her breath, she muttered, "And offers that are not
urged by the gentleman's grandmothers, either."

"You are in a rare mood and no mistake. However, I
shall not say another word on that head as I suspect that it
would be of not the least use to do so! How like your father
you have become, and not once did I ever suspect it!"

Mrs. Dower sighed, but her next thought brightened her
eyes at once. "Though I must say, I am happy to hear you
say that you wish to be brought out. I had not thought you
cared overmuch for the notion before but perhaps now it
will be just the thing. Oh, I am persuaded it will be. Bath is
not London, of course, but it is a fair society nonetheless."

Mrs. Dower sat down on the bench, already beginning to
enumerate the pleasures in store for a young lady embark-
ing upon her first Season. She was soon quite happily resigned to the disappointment of the day, especially as she
tucked away into her memory the promise made by Mr.
Hawkins that he would call again. Perhaps once her daughter was exposed to other gentlemen she would come to see
just what a pearl Mr. Hawkins was among his peers.

Evelyn could not quite enter into her mother's plans for
her. There was something about the interview with Mr.
Hawkins that left her disquieted.

She had hoped to convey her displeasure and contempt
for his proposal through an exaggerated hauteur that was in
reality foreign to her nature. Indeed, she had intended to offend him so greatly that he would be so emboldened as to

refuse to comply with his grandmother's wishes and abandon any further pursuit of her hand.

However, she had the distinct feeling that she had missed an important nuance and that she had not come off from the meeting in quite the way she had wished. Nor, she suspected, had she conveyed to Mr. Hawkins her absolute and irrevocable rejection of his unflattering suit.

Chapter Three

Miss Dower's suspicions were correct.

On any other gentleman, her concerted effort to convey her displeasure and contempt would have served remarkably well. Any other gentleman would have realized his humiliation and mistake, and gone away with such a disgust of her that all notion of a suit was abandoned.

However, as Mr. Hawkins returned home, it was not disgust or humiliated anger that he felt.

Contrary to what Miss Dower had hoped, Mr. Hawkins was not at all affronted by the Turkish treatment he had received at her dainty hands. In fact, if anyone had expressed the opinion that he had been ill-used by the lovely lady, Mr. Hawkins would have been amazed.

He had had little experience with young ladies. He assumed that Miss Dower had behaved with quite proper reserve and diffidence upon receiving his declaration.

He did not dwell, therefore, on the manner in which Miss Dower had received him, but rather her rejection. He was deeply disappointed, naturally, but his disappointment did not encompass any sharper feeling of resigned discouragement such as might have been felt by a less-infatuated gentleman.

Instead, he gave a mental shrug and wondered how best to make an impression upon Miss Dower's as-yet untouched heart. Her desire to become comfortable in society before entertaining any suit was certainly not unreasonable, he thought. A lady had to have a certain amount of self-assuredness in order to play hostess to a new husband, and to carry if off well she needed first to learn how to deal with society.

He did not begrudge Miss Dower that experience; but

rather, he approved of her farsightedness. Miss Dower was sensible and intelligent, both of which were qualities that he valued.

Yet he had the disquieting notion that he was about to enter the lists in order to win his lady, and for that he felt the slightest sense of anxiety.

Mr. Peter Hawkins was still deep in thought when he returned home and gave over his hat to the butler. He picked up the few missives on the tray in the hall and flipped through them. One commanded his attention, pulling him out of his preoccupation, and he immediately broke open its seal. As he read its contents, a smile touched his lips.

His pleasant reflections were cut short when the butler informed him that Lady Pomerancy awaited him in her private salon.

Sighing, Mr. Hawkins nodded his acknowledgement and mounted the stairs. He would have preferred to have put off the visit with his grandmother after returning from his unlucky errand, but he knew that it was best to humor her ladyship.

He knocked on the door to his grandmother's apartments, and at a command to enter, he opened it.

"Peter, my dear boy!"

Lady Pomerancy peremptorily dismissed her maid. She was seated in her wheelchair so that the light from the window was cast behind her, leaving her sharp features partially in shadow.

"Grandmama." Mr. Hawkins advanced to catch hold of Lady Pomerancy's hands. Lady Pomerancy suffered to have her cheek kissed.

As he had anticipated, however, her ladyship's greeting was impatient. "Well, my dear?"

Lady Pomerancy indicated that he was to sit in the wing chair beside her.

Mr. Hawkins settled into the chair assigned to him. He knew quite well the subject of her abrupt query, and briefly, without elaboration, he said, "Miss Dower declined my suit."

Lady Pomerancy stared at her grandson for a long moment. Then she snapped, "What ails the girl? Is she simple?"

"On the contrary. Miss Dower is highly intelligent," said Mr. Hawkins.

"Then what is this nonsense about refusing your offer?"

"Miss Dower indicated a wish to be entered into society before she bound herself to any particular suitor. She felt that to go about in society would grant her a wider experience upon which to ground her decision," said Mr. Hawkins.

"Errant nonsense!"

Mr. Hawkins brushed a nonexistent speck of lint from his coat sleeve. "I thought the lady's reasoning quite sound."

"Do you indeed!" Lady Pomerancy said irascibly. "The girl sounds a perfect nodcock to me. Indeed, if she is anything at all like the mother, she undoubtedly has more hair than wit. She could not do better than to accept an offer from you."

Mr. Hawkins smiled at that. He regarded his grandmother with fondness, saying gently, "You are biased, ma'am. Admit it. You grudge me nothing in this world, and it annoys you when others do not do the same."

After a moment, Lady Pomerancy's fierce expression reluctantly lightened. She reached over a gnarled hand and briefly caught his fingers. "Aye, you are the light of my life. Of course I wish you to possess all that you desire." She let go of his hand and pounded the arm of her chair. "Drat the girl! Does she not realize that you are besotted with her?"

Mr. Hawkins was fairly certain that Miss Dower did indeed lack that perception. He said slowly, "I do not think the fact has any bearing at all on the matter. It is more a question of where Miss Dower's sensibilities may or may not lie."

Lady Pomerancy snorted. "Pah! What has that to say to anything! In my day, a young girl's future was arranged for her by her family and she was properly grateful to have it to be so. There was none of this misguided emphasis placed upon love matches that we see in these days."

Mr. Hawkins knew better than to remind his grandmother that her daughter, the lady who had been his mother, had been just so fortunate to have enjoyed such a love match. "I bow to your superior wisdom, ma'am."

Quick to catch his neutral tone, Lady Pomerancy regarded her grandson with a shade of suspicion. She smiled suddenly. "You are discretion itself, my dear. I know quite well what you are thinking, never assume that I do not. You are thinking of your own mother."

Mr. Hawkins bowed from the waist. A smile lurked in his eyes as he said, "I am an open book to you, I perceive."

"Oh, aye, as though I have not learned through the years to allow you the privacy of your thoughts." Lady Pomerancy snorted in derision.

Mr. Hawkins raised his brows in query. "I hope that I am not so rag-mannered as to refuse any reasonable question from yourself, my lady."

"Oh, you are never rag-mannered, my dear! I would not have borne that, you may be sure," said Lady Pomerancy, a glint in her eyes. "Only, there comes a certain expression into your eyes that warns off any intrusion. Even as a boy, you regarded any attempt to extract your reasonings as a violation, to be endured but resisted with a stubborn reserve that upon occasion I found to be most annoying."

Her ladyship's scowl was so ferocious that Mr. Hawkins laughed outright. "I see that I was a positive trial to you, ma'am."

"Aye, and you still are," retorted Lady Pomerancy, trying unsuccessfully to maintain her severity. Her voice softened. "The day you came to my care, I had little inkling then of the troubles that would thereafter beset me. Childish diseases and scraped knees and positive agonies of suspense until you had mastered the Latin verbs. Once you had the Latin, and the Greek, I breathed freer. I knew then that you had the proper turn of mind to match your physical prowess and that you had the potential to become the perfect gentleman."

Mr. Hawkins's mouth quirked in a lopsided smile as he regarded his grandmother. "I fear that I do not yet meet up to your high expectations for me, my lady."

"On the contrary. You have met and surpassed all my expectations for you, Peter. The years of tutors and fencing and dancing masters were a sound investment. The education at Oxford that you received deepened an already well-informed understanding, while the grand tour which you undertook smoothed the last rough edges of your character to a pleasing, yet sober, patina of sophistication." Lady Pomerancy gave a sharp nod. "Indeed, I could not be more pleased with you, Peter."

Mr. Hawkins was overcome. These were high accolades indeed from the stern lady who had been the guiding force of his formative years. He reached over to lift his grandmother's misshapen fingers to his lips in grateful salute. Quietly he said, "I know full well that I could not have had a better guardian than yourself, ma'am. It was not an easy task to take on the upbringing and education of a five-year-old boy."

Lady Pomerancy shrugged. "I saw my duty, however. Was I to leave my orphaned grandson to the casual offices of my brother, Horace? That wastrel, that womanizer! Why, if you had not died of neglect first, you would have attained manhood with just as little notion of propriety and moral fortitude as that gentleman holds. No, I would not have it, even though Horace offered to take you on. Horace felt obligated, of course, since your father had been his heir."

Her ladyship reflected for a short moment. "I must give him credit for that much, I suppose, though I don't doubt he would have regretted it within the hour. He was always one to speak first and to think last."

Mr. Hawkins smiled at this sharp analysis of his great-uncle, who was an extremely selfish gentleman beneath a bluff and good-natured exterior. "No, I would not have fared half so well at the viscount's hands," he agreed soberly.

"No. Nor would you have flourished in Lord Waithe's household," said Lady Pomerancy. She said loftily, "I do not dislike my son-in-law. However, it has been my regret for these several years that his lordship lacks a certain quality that I deem essential in the well-rounded gentleman."

Since Lady Pomerancy's irascible opinion regarding the Earl of Nottingbook's limited intelligence had been openly and often expressed, Mr. Hawkins had little difficulty in interpreting her ladyship's meaning. However, Lady Pomer-

ancy's reference did recall to him the short note that he had
received. "By the by, I have had word from Percy. He
wishes to come down from London to visit with us. I trust
that will not put you out, my lady?"

"You must have whomever you wish, Peter. By all
means, let Percy rusticate with us," said Lady Pomerancy
cordially. "However, pray do not expect me to bestow a
perpetual smile or nod on your cousin's rattle-pated prattle.
He is as cloth-headed as his father and sports-mad, as well.
I shall not pretend to you, or to that nodcock for that matter,
that I enjoy constant babblings about this race or that."

"Percy mentioned nothing about a race, ma'am, so you
may rest easy," said Mr. Hawkins soothingly.

However, there was such a pronounced twinkle in his
eyes that it made Lady Pomerancy slant a shrewd glance at
him. "Then it is hunting or fisticuffs that brings him, for I
am certain that it is not my company that he seeks out."

"You are perfectly right on all counts, ma'am, as always," said Mr. Hawkins politely.

"Aye, I do not doubt it in the least," retorted Lady
Pomerancy. "The pair of you share at least one quality, my
dear. Percy also is the politest of creatures when it suits
him."

"My cousin goes in abject terror of your frowns,
ma'am," assured Mr. Hawkins.

"Does he, indeed." Lady Pomerancy was openly pleased.
"Percy has a degree of intelligence I had not heretofore suspected. Of course you must have him here, my dear. I will
not have it said that I turned away any member of my family out of sheer prejudice, however justifiable."

Mr. Hawkins rose to his feet. He bent to kiss her ladyship's cheek. "I shall write Percy at once and relay your
kind forbearance, my lady."

"Rogue." Lady Pomerancy waved him away, hiding the
pleasure that she took in his fond salute. "I cannot conceive
what it is that you have found in Percy besides an amusing
rattle-pate."

"No, I do not suppose that you do," said Mr. Hawkins,
declining to enlighten her, just as he had chosen not to do
years before.

He would never tell her of the misery he had endured at

Oxford before he had been befriended by his cousin, Viscount Waithe.

Awkward and shy when he found himself in the company of his contemporaries for the first time in his sheltered existence, his exceptional reserve had marked him as an outcast amongst his youthful peers. He had excelled from the first in his studies, which had but further served to alienate him from less intellectually minded young gentlemen, and made him the object of cruel ridicule. Even now, it would have wounded his grandmother to know of it, or that she had erred in keeping him so close as she had.

It had been Percy who had broken the near-unbearable misery of his existence. They had found common ground on the cricket field. Peter had never played the game before, but he was quick and strong and before the game was done he and Percy had discovered in one another a mutual love of athletics.

The fact that they were cousins was a minor revelation. Viscount Waithe, the elder by two years and an upperclassman, did not usually mingle with those in a lower form. However, he made an exception with Peter Hawkins, and fairly soon his patronage served to ease his cousin's life. For that careless gesture of friendship, Peter had always been grateful.

Their meeting was not such a coincidence as might have been supposed, for all the aristocracy sent their sons to either Cambridge or Oxford. What had been amazing was that they had not recognized one another before. However, the explanation lay in Lady Pomerancy's having chosen to remove herself and her small grandson from the evil influences pervading London, most specifically the wayward sway of certain members in her own family. As a consequence, Peter had grown up with very little contact with any of his relations. After leaving Oxford he had made a conscious effort to meet each member and come to know something about them.

Lady Pomerancy knew well the expression in her grandson's eyes. He would reveal no more than he wished. She sighed. "Very well, then. I shall continue to accept your cousin Percy on that much alone, for I know you to be an excellent judge of character. I shall even be pleasant toward him, so he need not stand in terror of my disapproval."

"Thank you, Grandmama. It is all that I ask, and more," said Mr. Hawkins.

He would have left her then, but she stayed him a moment longer. "Shall you press your suit with the Dower chit?"

Mr. Hawkins smiled at Lady Pomerancy. The twinkle in his eyes became once more pronounced. "You have taught me that a gentleman is true to himself, my lady. Can I do aught else?"

Lady Pomerancy hid her smile behind her hand, before saying, "I am well answered, indeed. Go away now and send my maid in, for I wish to rest. Later I shall talk with you more on the subject and you may tell me what you wish me to do, for you know that I will assist your cause in whatever capacity that is within my power."

"I do know it." Mr. Hawkins smiled and exited the room, quietly closing the door behind him. He conveyed her ladyship's message to the maid, who had been waiting for just such a summons.

As he traversed the hall and returned downstairs, a frown knit his well-formed brows. He knew what he desired. He also knew that Lady Pomerancy was as good as her word. Her ladyship would help him attain the connection that he wished above all others.

However, what he did not know was how to impress a sensitive and innocent young lady's heart so that she returned his own reverential love for her in fullest measure.

Peter was uncertain whether he was capable of launching the sort of flirtation or courtship that seemed now to be required of him. He was under no misconceptions as to how Miss Dower's advent upon Bath society would affect his chances with her. The young lady was a beauty and she was of good family, besides being known to be well dowered. She would have enough admirers of adroit address that must surely throw his own poor talents into sharp relief.

He had never been one to 'dabble in the petticoat line,' as some of his acquaintances referred to the art of flirtation and conquest. The thought of a casual relationship had always been repugnant to him. His upbringing had imbued

him with a reverence and respect for the feminine sex that
had become an ingrained part of his character. He could no
more have brought himself to basely seduce a woman than
he could have committed an act of immolation upon himself.

There had been opportunities, of course, and he had not
always refrained. Even now, the memory of a certain lady
had the power to bring the burn of shame to him. He had
met the lady in Italy while on the grand tour. She was older
and more worldly-wise, and he had been dazzled as much
by her beauty as by her sharp wit.

At the time he had no notion how he had come to share her
bed, but now in retrospect he recognized that she had been the
seducer and he the seduced. However, to his mind that neither
expiated him nor excused his gross misconduct. He at least
had the satisfaction of knowing that he had not been entirely
lost to his own ideals. He had made an honorable offer for
her. It had been received with sheer amazement, and then was
gently rejected. The lady had regretfully pronounced their
idyll at an end, and he had never spent another moment in her
company.

The experience of his grand tour had tempered his naiv-
ité and had made him more comfortable in society, as well.
When he returned to England, he took apartments in London so that he could mix with those friends he had made at
Oxford and afterward.

Yet still, he never forgot the roof that had sheltered him,
nor the redoubtable lady who had so clearly seen her duty
toward him, and so he spent much of his time in Bath.

For Peter Hawkins, his real home was at Lady Pomerancy's place in Bath. Even though she had made over the
town house and estate to him upon his majority, so that in
reality it was his own roof, he still thought of it as first and
foremost to be her home, and so he phrased his courteous
inquiry whether she would mind having company that was
more of his liking than hers.

Recalled to thoughts of his cousin, a smile lifted the cor-
ners of his mouth. Mr. Hawkins went into his study to dash
off a note assuring Viscount Waithe of his welcome.

Chapter Four

Evelyn did not anticipate that Mr. Hawkins would come to call again very soon after the freezing manner with which she had treated him. Nor did she believe, after reviewing their interview over and over in her mind, that, however much her heart had led her to soften the blow, any gentleman could actually take her rejection in other than final terms.

The thought was not altogether a satisfying one. Despite the wound to her pride and her indignation over the origin of the offer for her hand, she discovered to her dismay that Mr. Hawkins was still set firmly enough in her affections that she almost wished that he was too dense to have taken affront at her rebuff.

However, she had intended to offend him so greatly that he would refuse to accede to his grandmother's wishes, and she could not imagine how her purpose could possibly have been overlooked by any gentleman that had the least amount of wit.

Evelyn sighed, frowning a little as she went downstairs to join her mother at tea. She had thought of little else over the intervening day since the occasion of Mr. Hawkins's visit. She still felt anger, but it was now tinged with regret for what might have been.

As she approached the drawing room, she gave a small shrug. It would certainly not do to brood overmuch about the matter, for it was done with and over. She was not likely to see Mr. Hawkins again except perhaps in passing at chapel or at a social function, she thought.

Evelyn was not well enough acquainted with Mr. Hawkins to have developed an appreciation of the hidden depths of his redoubtable character. Therefore, when she

went into the drawing room and the gentleman who had occupied so much of her thoughts rose at her entrance, Evelyn
was very much surprised. She stopped short, transfixed by
amazement as her startled gaze met Mr. Hawkins's slightly
smiling eyes.

Evelyn recovered quickly, hiding the dismay that she
felt. The smile she managed was polite and stiff. She went
forward to greet him, extending her hand. "Mr. Hawkins.
How unexpected."

Mr. Hawkins briefly took her hand in his warm clasp.
His vivid blue eyes smiled down at her in a friendly fashion. "I found Mrs. Dower's previous kind invitation to take
tea one that I could not for long resist."

Mrs. Dower expressed more pleasure than Evelyn felt
capable of summoning up for the occasion. "Isn't it a
lovely surprise, Evelyn? I must tell you, however, that I did
not expect you just today, Mr. Hawkins. Otherwise I would
have made certain that we had something more substantial
than cake and biscuits, for I know that gentlemen, particularly large gentlemen, like to take their fill whatever the
time of day."

"Really, Mama," murmured Evelyn, faintly embarrassed
by what she perceived to be her mother's unfortunate ten-
dency to speak whatever was on her mind. She sat down
beside her mother behind the table that held the tea tray,
and Mr. Hawkins returned to the wingback chair which he
had previously occupied.

Mr. Hawkins turned his attention to his hostess. His eyes
twinkled. Without glancing in Miss Dower's direction, as
though he had not heard her interjection, he said gravely,
"Indeed, ma'am, that is quite true. I have never known it to
be otherwise."

Mrs. Dower smiled on him. She privately thought that
Mr. Hawkins was one of the handsomest gentlemen she had
ever beheld, as well as one of the prettiest behaved. It was a
pity that her daughter did not agree with her. "You shall not
be made to suffer, Mr. Hawkins," she said cordially. "I
shall ring for sandwiches to be made up at once."

"It is not necessary, ma'am. I shall be quite content with
the cake, I assure you," said Mr. Hawkins.

"But I insist, sir!"

"I do not wish to put you to such trouble, Mrs. Dower," said Mr. Hawkins.

Evelyn allowed a small smile to curve her lips. It reassured her that her previous reading of Mr. Hawkins's character had been accurate, after all. Naturally this most proper of gentlemen would do the polite thing, which was to aver his complete contentment with the tea already prepared.

With a shade of malice borne out of her pique and embarrassment, Evelyn added her own mite to the discourse. Tossing a glance in the gentleman's direction, she said, "Mr. Hawkins is obviously unwilling to put out Cook, Mama."

"No such thing! It will not put anyone out in the least. It is what we pay the woman for, after all," said Mrs. Dower, rising. Instantly Mr. Hawkins leaped to his feet out of respect.

Mrs. Dower smiled approvingly at him as she crossed the room to give a vigorous tug to the bellpull. There was no answer to her summons, and with a frown, Mrs. Dower said, "How very odd! I wonder whether the bell is broken again. I shall just step out for a moment to relay my request. Mr. Hawkins, do pray excuse me. Evelyn, you must not wait to pour the tea. I shall be only a moment, I promise you."

Mrs. Dower left the sitting room.

After a brief pause, during which his grave glance met Evelyn's eyes, Mr. Hawkins resumed his seat. Evelyn quickly averted her eyes and instead turned her attention to her duty as hostess. "Tea, Mr. Hawkins?"

"Thank you, yes, Miss Dower."

Mrs. Dower had left the door to the sitting room open, and Evelyn could hear her mother's voice in the distance. Nonetheless, she felt distinctly uncomfortable to be left alone in the company of the gentleman whose suit she had rejected not twenty hours before. She occupied herself with the teapot to disguise her sudden attack of nerves. After pouring, she glanced at her silent guest. "How do you prefer to take your tea, Mr. Hawkins?"

She discovered that it was a mistake to meet his eyes. As Mr. Hawkins indicated his preference, he smiled at her. Her heart uncomfortably contracted and Evelyn quickly looked away. She added the small amount of milk to his tea that he had requested and offered the cup to him.

As he took it, their hands brushed, and the feathered touch of his fingers electrified her.

Evelyn felt the flush of heat in her face. Annoyed with herself, she poured her own tea in unseemly haste and splashed it. She snatched at a napkin to mop up the evidence of her discomfort, and in the process overset a small basket of fruit.

Evelyn was mortified. Angry tears came to her eyes. She would have given anything not to have made such a thorough idiot of herself in front of this particular gentleman. Surely he must be laughing under his breath at her expense. After the manner in which she had treated his suit, she could scarcely blame him if he should now enjoy her discomfiture.

The napkin was taken gently out of her hand.

"Allow me, Miss Dower."

Evelyn looked up quickly. She met Mr. Hawkins's eyes with defiance. "I am not generally so clumsy, sir," she said, daring him by her tone and by her expression to contradict her.

"I am certain of it," he said gravely. He made short work of setting the tray to rights.

Evelyn would have been astonished and not a little dismayed to have known how accurately he guessed the extent of her discomfort, and how well he judged her for what he assumed to be a manifestation of her sensitive nature. It was only natural that a well-bred young lady should feel uncomfortable at being left alone with a potential suitor, he thought.

Mrs. Dower bustled back into the sitting room. "We shall be served directly, Mr. Hawkins, for it will take Cook but a moment. I do hope that you will forgive me for leaving you in such an abrupt fashion."

Mr. Hawkins had risen at once at the older lady's entrance. Now he sketched a slight bow as he waited for her to reseat herself. "Of course, ma'am. Pray do not spare another thought on it. Miss Dower was charming company and has kept me very well entertained."

Evelyn flushed again, but in fury. She could not believe

the audacity of the man in making game of her clumsiness. When she chanced to meet her mother's inquiring glance, she said frostily, "Indeed, Mama! Mr. Hawkins was kind enough to help me with the tea. Do you wish to take a cup?"

Mrs. Dower's brows puckered slightly. She wondered what had taken place while she was out of the room. Her daughter was obviously much annoyed. "Thank you, my dear. Two lumps only, if you please. I find that I do not quite like my tea so sweet in the warmer weather that we have been enjoying this past fortnight."

She turned to their guest. "Mr. Hawkins, I trust that dear Lady Pomerancy is well? I have not seen her ladyship since I last took tea with her. I hope that she is not suffering a renewed bout with her joints?"

"Unfortunately, yes, Mrs. Dower. However, her ladyship remains in her usual strong spirits, and as you mentioned, the weather is becoming warmer, so that I am persuaded that she will quickly come about again," said Mr. Hawkins.

"Dreadful to suffer so. My own dear father was afflicted in just such a way. I recall quite vividly how the pain so reduced his temper that we all ran in terror of his awful rages," said Mrs. Dower.

There was an instant of awkward silence. Feeling constrained by civility to do so, Evelyn sent a conciliatory smile toward Mr. Hawkins. "It is difficult to imagine Mr. Hawkins running in terror of her ladyship."

"On the contrary, Miss Dower," said Mr. Hawkins with the faintest of grins. "Mine is a most sensitive nature. I assure you that I am easily cowed."

The gentleman's teasing manner caused Evelyn to arch her brows. "Are you indeed, Mr. Hawkins? Certainly *I* would not have thought it."

He looked on the point of a retort, which Evelyn awaited with lively interest.

But before Mr. Hawkins could reply, Mrs. Dower interjected, having belatedly realized that she had made a faux pas. "I do apologize! I never meant for a moment to imply that Lady Pomerancy was of a freakish temper. Though her ladyship is somewhat severe, I would not precisely term her to be so *cross* that—"

"Mama, perhaps you should have one of the biscuits," said Evelyn in a determined fashion, offering the tray to her mother.

Mrs. Dower, whose percipience was not great, nevertheless realized that her daughter was attempting to distract her from her course of conversation. Thoroughly dismayed, she said, "Oh dear, I have put my foot in it, haven't I?"

Her contrite expression was such that Mr. Hawkins laughed.

Evelyn regarded him in amazement as he replied in all apparent good humor, "Not at all, Mrs. Dower."

Evelyn, who had formed the opinion that he was dreadfully starched up, had already bristled in defense of her dear but foolish parent. It took her very much by surprise when her intervention was not needed. Her brows knitting, Evelyn studied Mr. Hawkins with renewed interest and a trace of bewilderment from over the top of her teacup. Her preconceived notions of his character had been thrown off balance once again.

The door to the sitting room was opened. A footman entered laden with a tray of sandwiches, which he deftly set down before the ladies.

"Oh, here it is at last! May I tempt you, Mr. Hawkins?" Mrs. Dower asked, indicating the tray. She was gratified when the gentleman made a generous selection.

Mr. Hawkins sampled a sandwich. "You must convey my compliments, ma'am. This is indeed a repast fit for a large, hungry gentleman."

Evelyn choked on her tea. Her indignant eyes met Mr. Hawkins's bland expression. He was shameless, she fumed.

Completely oblivious to undercurrents, Mrs. Dower was emboldened by the gentleman's graciousness to confide in him something of her concerns. "Actually, I should not dare to say anything to the point at all, for I am petrified of her ladyship. How does she look at one! I feel no more than a fidgety schoolgirl brought up before the matron."

"My grandmother cultivates a stern exterior but I assure you that her heart is very soft, indeed," said Mr. Hawkins.

"Well, certainly there is no one who could be better expected to know," said Mrs. Dower with a dubious tone.

Evelyn perceived it was again time to rescue the conversation in order to spare them all any further inadvertent embarrassment. Ruthlessly she changed the subject. "Mr. Hawkins, you were in London before coming down to Bath, were you not? How could you bear to tear yourself away from the beginning of the Season? I would have thought Bath was rather staid compared to the entertainments to be found in the city."

Mr. Hawkins smiled, appreciating Miss Dower's obvious desire to protect her parent. "While it is true that I enjoy the Season's offerings, I always take pleasure in returning to Bath for I count it to be more my home than anywhere else since my childhood was spent here. As you can surely understand, Miss Dower, I hold my grandmother in considerable affection and I visit her as often as she allows me to. Lady Pomerancy scolds me if I am too long away from London, however, for she deems society the proper milieu for any unattached gentleman." His rueful smile invited them to share in his amusement.

Mrs. Dower obliged him by laughing even though she was unclear exactly what it was that she was supposed to be amused at. However, she knew very well that gentlemen liked their little jokes to be appreciated and so she nodded. "Quite true."

Though Evelyn had also smiled, her attention was caught by the implication of what Mr. Hawkins had said. "I assume then that you will be returning to London quite soon," she said, raising a brow in delicate inquiry.

Mr. Hawkins's smile gentled. He said quietly, pointedly, "I have no such plans, Miss Dower."

His clear blue eyes caught her glance, and held it for several moments. Time stretched. Evelyn realized belatedly that she was staring. Quick color entered her face. She bent her head and pretended to be absorbed suddenly with choosing a small apple from the fruit bowl.

Mr. Hawkins continued as though there had not been that amazing moment of communication. "I am awaiting the arrival of my cousin, Viscount Waithe, who will be staying with us for several days. So you see, Miss Dower, I am not the only London gentleman who finds something of interest in Bath."

"It is the fisticuffs match, of course," said Mrs. Dower, nodding.

"What did you say, Mama?"

Mrs. Dower met her daughter's astonished gaze with an apologetic glance. "I am sorry, my dear. I should have recalled it earlier, I know. I always tell Evelyn every interesting tidbit that comes to my ears, you see, Mr. Hawkins. I heard of the match whilst visiting with the butcher this morning. Mr. Gumpner is a very talkative gentleman. So interesting, the things he knows."

"Mama, really," Evelyn murmured, dismayed, throwing a glance in the direction of their guest. She knew all too well that gossiping with tradespeople was frowned upon, and she prepared to shield her mother from disapproval.

Contrary to her fears, however, Mr. Hawkins but laughed. "Yes, I fear that it is the fisticuffs match that brings the viscount," he admitted. "We gentlemen are notorious for our vulgar tastes in entertainment, I fear."

"Oh, I don't know. There is something peculiarly appealing about the masculine sports, I have always thought," said Mrs. Dower. "My late husband was himself very fond of the 'rough-and-tumble' as he called it, and I never thought him more handsome than when he returned from a bout at the saloon, still flushed and possessing that martial light in his eyes." There came a faraway expression into her eyes and the slightest of smiles touched her lips.

Mr. Hawkins appeared a good deal astonished by Mrs. Dower's reminiscence, but he made no comment upon it. Instead, he turned and engaged Evelyn in polite conversation. The conversation did not again stray from general topics before Mr. Hawkins finally rose to take his leave.

Evelyn felt a sense of letdown as Mr. Hawkins made his excuses. However, she smiled politely and said what was expected of her. It was not that she felt inclined to keep the gentleman with them any longer. On the contrary, she was rather relieved when at last the door closed behind him. Yet there was something that seemed missing to her.

Evelyn reviewed the visit in her mind.

Mr. Peter Hawkins had been all that was kind and agreeable. He had been considerate and forbearing toward her mother when that lady had unthinkingly insulted Lady

Pomerancy's redoubtable character. He had not put forth a single opinion that one could have taken exception to, nor reparteed one of her own statements in a lively fashion. All in all, with the exception of that one striking glance that he had leveled at her, Mr. Hawkins had been an extraordinarily boring guest to tea.

Evelyn realized that had been the trouble. Mr. Hawkins had committed the unpardonable sin. He had not shown the smallest hint of partiality for her, even when her mother had absented herself those few moments from the sitting room. Instead, he had put himself in the least romantic light by indulging in desultory conversation and had ended by expressing his pleasure in their company.

Mrs. Dower had been speaking at some length before Evelyn became aware that her mother was discussing their departed guest, and that her mother's opinion very nearly echoed her own.

"So kind, so proper—the perfect gentleman. Do you not agree, Evelyn?"

"Oh, yes," Evelyn sighed. "Yes, I most certainly do."

It was an incredibly lowering reflection.

Chapter Five

The Pump Room was well crowded when Evelyn and her mother entered through its august portals. The elegant columned room was a gathering point for Bath society, even for those who did not take the healthful waters. An orchestra played in the balcony, providing a nice counterpoint to the myriad conversations going on all sides.

Evelyn had always enjoyed accompanying her mother to the Pump Room. It was a pleasant excursion into the society that she had not yet entered, and invariably she heard or saw something that interested her.

As usual, Mrs. Dower saw several acquaintances, and she paused many times to exchange greetings and small conversation. She made a point of bringing Evelyn to the attention of all they met, to that young lady's astonishment. The dowagers and matrons responded with a friendly scrutiny of Evelyn and issued kind invitations to the Dower ladies for whatever functions that they were getting up.

Evelyn snatched at a quiet lull in their social progress to say in a low voice, "Must you put me forward in such a way, Mama? I have known most of these people all my life, after all."

"But you are coming out now, Evelyn, and this is simply one way of notifying everyone of the fact," said Mrs. Dower. Her gaze traveled beyond Evelyn and she smiled and put out her gloved hand. "Oh, Mr. Hawkins. Good morning, sir."

Evelyn turned her head and met the gentleman's gaze. There was an expression of approval in his eyes as his glance swept her appearance before returning to her face. Knowing that she looked her best in a new straw bonnet and a blue morning dress trimmed in satin ribbons, Evelyn responded without thought to his obvious admiration. She smiled shyly at him, thinking how well he looked in a morning coat with plated buttons and pantaloon trousers.

Then she abruptly recalled that he had offered for her because he had been told to do so. Her smile faded to little more than a polite expression.

Mr. Hawkins was not unaware of the sudden clouding of the warmth in her eyes, but he pretended otherwise. He bowed over each of their hands in turn. "Mrs. Dower, Miss Dower."

Evelyn murmured a greeting, very much on her dignity now that she had remembered the insult he had dealt her. She was prepared to pull her hand free if he took the slightest liberty. But he did not, instead letting go of her fingers immediately so that she had nothing to object to in his attentions. The gentleman was impossibly infuriating, she thought crossly.

"Have you come to take the waters?" Mr. Hawkins asked.

"Oh, no. I fear that I cannot like the stuff, you see. It quite escapes me why everything that one is supposed to take for one's health is always so foul-tasting," said Mrs. Dower.

Mr. Hawkins smiled and agreed. "I personally would not willingly choose to drink something tasting of sulphur, but many are convinced that but adds to its healthful properties. I am on the point of fetching a glass for Lady Pomerancy. However much she detests the water, she still reluctantly follows her physician's orders."

"Quite admirable for her ladyship, I am sure," said Mrs. Dower. "Oh, there is Lady Pomerancy, sitting close to the hearth. It is terribly drafty in this high room, is it not? I myself never come without a shawl—she has seen us." The last was said with a strong overtone of consternation.

"We must go over and pay our respects, Mama," Evelyn said. She smiled again at Mr. Hawkins, discreetly nudging her mother's elbow.

"Oh yes. Of course we must." Mrs. Dower did not sound particularly enthusiastic, and in fact there was such an expression of dismay in her eyes that Evelyn could not but feel sorry for her.

"I shall join you presently," said Mr. Hawkins. He sauntered off in the direction of the pump where there was a
short line of the fashionable waiting to receive their dose of
health.

Mrs. Dower looked wildly about. "Do I see Aurelia by
the window? Why, I do believe that must be her. I shall just
go over and—"

Evelyn caught her mother's elbow. "No, Mama. We
must speak first to Lady Pomerancy. You know that we
must. She has waved at us, and Mr. Hawkins knows that
we have seen her."

"But I do not wish to speak to her ladyship. Oh, Evelyn,
why ever did you turn down Mr. Hawkins's suit? Lady
Pomerancy must be so very angry with me," said Mrs.
Dower.

"Mama, we shall not discuss that again, if you please,
and especially not here. As for speaking to Lady Pomerancy, if you do not do so you will be giving her the cut direct. How do you suppose that will affect her temper?"

Mrs. Dower turned startled eyes on her daughter. "Oh
my! I had not thought—! Evelyn, how terrible *that* would
be! How very glad I am that you are with me, you cannot
conceive. Yes, by all means let us go greet Lady Pomerancy. She cannot exactly *eat* me, after all."

Evelyn laughed at the almost forlorn note in Mrs.
Dower's voice. She squeezed her mother's hand. "Never
mind. I shall be with you."

"I do not know that is such a good thing, for she must be
ever so much angrier at you than she is at me," said Mrs.
Dower, sighing.

Evelyn ignored this observation and inexorably led her
reluctant parent over to the lady who awaited them.

Lady Pomerancy was seated in her wheelchair as though
it were a throne from which she presided over a royal court.
Her posture was regal, and the piercing expression of her
pale eyes was discomfiting. She held out her hand to Mrs.
Dower. "Well, ma'am? My grandson had told me that you
have been somewhat out of curl. I trust that you are in the
way of better health?"

Mrs. Dower flushed guiltily, aware that Lady Pomerancy

was alluding to her previous unavailability to all of her visitors. "Oh, yes. A trifle only, I assure you."

Lady Pomerancy smiled faintly, immensely satisfied at the ease with which she had reduced the woman. She turned her sights on the younger lady. "I have not seen you in a great age, Miss Dower. You have improved vastly, I must say. I recalled you as a thin girl, all matchstick arms and legs. I was much surprised to hear my grandson describe you as otherwise."

Evelyn smiled, deliberately attempting to be at her most charming. She knew very well that Lady Pomerancy had seen her at chapel on any number of occasions through the years, though that lady had recently not attended as often as had been her former want. "I suppose that is why one is not allowed out of the schoolroom until one acquires a certain age. I hope that you are well, my lady?"

"Very well, thank you," said Lady Pomerancy firmly. Her eyes traveled past the ladies, and a softened light entered her austere glance. "Ah, here is Peter at last with my first water. Thank you, my dear." She stoically drank from the glass that her grandson had presented to her.

Mr. Hawkins nodded pleasantly to the other two ladies while he watched Lady Pomerancy drain the glass. With sympathy, he asked, "Do you truly wish a second glass?"

Lady Pomerancy grimaced. "Pray do not tempt me, sir. You are well aware that I am ordered to take the customary three glasses, even though I detest drinking it."

"I will bring back the second glass with all due speed," Mr. Hawkins promised.

"Detestable man! Get on with it, then," said Lady Pomerancy irascibly.

Mr. Hawkins left on a laugh, the empty glass in hand.

Mrs. Dower, anxious to be gone from her ladyship's proximity, decided that she had sufficiently discharged her duty. "Oh, I have just seen an acquaintance of mine, my lady. I hope that you will not think I am abandoning you, but I really should greet her before she gets away."

"Of course you must," said Lady Pomerancy agreeably.

Mrs. Dower looked immensely relieved and began to take her leave.

Evelyn made her excuses as well, but Lady Pomerancy

caught her by the wrist. Evelyn glanced down in surprise.
There was unexpected strength in the old, twisted fingers.

"Miss Dower, you may keep me company until my
grandson returns," said Lady Pomerancy.

"I—I believe that my duty to my mother must be foremost, my lady," Evelyn said, taken off guard.

"Mrs. Dower is perfectly capable of traversing the room
without your youthful support, my dear. She ain't yet in her
dotage," said Lady Pomerancy with an arrogance quite ir-
refutable. She fixed her eyes on Mrs. Dower. "Leave the
girl with me, ma'am. I assure you that she will be perfectly
chaperoned while in my charge."

"Quite so. I could not think otherwise," said Mrs. Dower
unhappily. With a helpless glance for her daughter's appalled expression, Mrs. Dower made good her escape.

Once they were alone, Lady Pomerancy released the girl,
disdaining to rely on that means of restraint. She fixed Evelyn with steely eyes. In an interrogating tone, she asked,
"Well, girl? What have you to say for yourself?"

Evelyn felt her eyes widen with startled surprise. She
stammered, "My lady?"

"Pray do not play the nodcock with me. Come girl. We
haven't much time before someone comes to interrupt us. I
understand that you have rejected my grandson's suit," said
Lady Pomerancy.

Evelyn flushed. Her eyes sparked with annoyance and
angered pride. Lady Pomerancy had no right to question
her at all, let alone in such a setting. However, she was no
shrinking miss to grovel before the old woman's glower,
and she held her head high. "Yes, ma'am. I have."

"Do you dislike him?"

Lady Pomerancy was treading increasingly dangerous
ground.

With an attempt at politeness, Evelyn smiled. "My lady,
I do not believe that this is the time or the place to discuss—"

"A straight answer if you please! Do you dislike my
grandson?"

Evelyn tightened her lips, recognizing that Lady Pomerancy had no intention of being diverted. "Very well, my
lady, since you insist. I do not dislike Mr. Hawkins."

"Then why have you not accepted his offer, Miss Dower? You do not appear to be a stupid girl. Quite the contrary. Certainly you must understand the advantages of the match," said Lady Pomerancy.

"Of course I do." Evelyn realized that she had just given Lady Pomerancy more fodder for her cannon, and to forestall her ladyship's next obvious question, she said quickly, "However, there are reasons which make it impractical for me to accept any offer at this time. I wish to become familiar with society and to meet several other eligible *partis*."

"Ah, yes. My grandson very carefully explained it all to me," said Lady Pomerancy. She made an impatient dismissive gesture. "Nonsense, all of it. That might wash in London, but not in this society. We've a surfeit of retired admirals and meek parsons, but precious few eligible titles. No, I suspect that you are playing some game of your own with my grandson, my dear. Pray do not allow your fanciful notions to cloud your judgment for too long. My grandson is patient, but he is also a gentleman ripe for the altar. He'll not wait on you forever."

Evelyn was made so furious by this extraordinary speech that if she had replied as she desired, she feared she would give grave offense. She bit back the hasty retort that she would have made, struggling to find something less combustible to say. It was just as well that she held her tongue, for a moment later Mr. Hawkins returned with her ladyship's second glass of water.

He glanced at Evelyn's carefully expressionless face and lowered eyes. A small frown came into his eyes. He turned to his grandmother. "Here is your water, my lady. I hope that I did not keep you waiting too long."

"Not at all. Miss Dower and I have enjoyed a comfortable gossip." Lady Pomerancy took the glass but made no immediate move to drink the water it contained. Instead, she stared balefully at it. "Vile stuff. It is hardly worth the hope that it will do one good."

Mr. Hawkins smiled down at her. "It is worth it to me, my lady."

Lady Pomerancy glanced up quickly. A reluctant smile tugged at her withered lips. "You were always one with just the right word," she said approvingly. She waved her hand in an imperious fashion. "Go away, the two of you. If I must drink it, I prefer not to have others hovering about to watch my agony. Peter, take Miss Dower on the promenade. I shall do very well by myself, you know."

Mr. Hawkins laughed. "Your wish is my command, my lady."

Evelyn started a little at his statement, and her eyes flew to his face in a searching glance.

He did not appear to notice, but merely offered his arm to her. "Miss Dower, will you do me the honor?"

As much as she disliked to fall into Lady Pomerancy's machinations by even that much, Evelyn felt that she had little choice but to accept his escort. She certainly had no desire to remain in the old lady's company and be subjected to more impatient interrogation.

She nodded at the glass in Lady Pomerancy's gnarled hand. "Your health, my lady," she murmured, and had the satisfaction of seeing a flash of annoyance in the elder lady's eyes.

Mr. Hawkins led her off.

"Oh, there is my mother by the window. She will be wondering where I have gotten to," said Evelyn brightly. She quickly realized that Mr. Hawkins was not going to take her broad hint when the gentleman steered her in the opposite direction. She looked up at him. "I should prefer to be returned to my mother's chaperonage, sir."

"In good time, Miss Dower." He glanced down at her, a faint smile quirking his mouth. "I realize that it is unbearably rude of me not to accede instantly to your wishes, Miss Dower. You have my leave to bite off my head at your convenience."

Evelyn's sense of the ridiculous was reluctantly roused, and she chuckled. "Thank you, Mr. Hawkins. I do appreciate the offer," she said, her ill feeling toward him lessening.

They walked in companionable silence for a few minutes.

"You must not let my grandmother tease you, you know. She means well, I assure you. She is naturally quite concerned about my affairs, perhaps even overly so at times," remarked Mr. Hawkins.

Evelyn threw a quick glance up at him. "Indeed! One would never have guessed it," she said in a marveling tone.

Mr. Hawkins grinned, which so startled her that she lost her hold on her returned sense of ill usage. "I am glad that you can take it in that spirit, Miss Dower. It says much for your own sense of humor and compassion."

Evelyn had had no intention of creating such an erroneous impression in the gentleman's mind. On the contrary, she had wanted him to be acutely aware that she had been outraged and displeased by Lady Pomerancy's delvement into a matter that should never have concerned her ladyship to such a great degree at all.

Yet, however much she wanted Mr. Hawkins to understand that, she was reluctant to disabuse him of the pleasant picture that he had formed of her character. Evelyn sighed. It was all so very difficult.

She attempted to make some sense of her confused feelings. "Mr. Hawkins, I find this whole business to be rather awkward. It has caught me so at a disadvantage that I discover myself entertaining quite unworthy thoughts, as well as making statements that I later regret for their stupidity."

"I think I understand. Believe me, it was never my intention to place you in an untenable position," said Mr. Hawkins, frowning.

"Do you understand? Do you truly?"

Evelyn stopped and turned toward him, her hand slipping from his arm. She searched his face before she shook her head. "I do not think that you do, sir. Or otherwise you would never have made the offer in quite the manner that you did."

Mr. Hawkins appeared startled. "My dear Miss Dower, I do not take your meaning at all. What is it that you are trying to convey to me?"

Evelyn smiled a little sadly. "If you need ask me, Mr. Hawkins, then how can I possibly explain it to you? No, I suspect that would but humiliate us both. I—I think it best that we leave off this subject. Would you be so kind as to return me to my mother, sir?"

Mr. Hawkins regarded her for a short moment, an unhappy expression in his eyes. "Miss Dower, if I have offended you in any way—"

"Not at all, Mr. Hawkins. How could you think it?"

He saw that there was nothing more to be said. With a bewildering sense of defeat, he offered his arm to her again. "Very well, Miss Dower. I shall be happy to lend you escort back to Mrs. Dower's side."

There was not another word exchanged between them as they retraced their steps.

Mrs. Dower greeted their appearance with pleased surprise. "Evelyn, and Mr. Hawkins! Why, this is nice. But where is dear Lady Pomerancy?" She looked around as though expecting that lady and her chair to materialize behind them.

"Her ladyship tired of my company and sent me off with Mr. Hawkins," said Evelyn with an attempt at a smile.

"Oh, I am certain she was no such thing, for you are never boring, dearest," said Mrs. Dower with an arch glance upward at Mr. Hawkins. However, for once her dependence upon that gentleman's exquisite manners was disappointed, for he did not catch up her broad hint.

Mr. Hawkins merely smiled and bowed. "I shall leave you now, Miss Dower. My grandmother will be waiting for me to fetch her last glass of the water."

Evelyn inclined her head, but she did not raise her eyes. "Of course, Mr. Hawkins."

Mrs. Dower made one last attempt. "I trust that we shall see you at tea again, sir?"

Mr. Hawkins glanced at Miss Dower's averted face. "You may depend upon it, ma'am."

When Evelyn's glance flew up to meet his, his mouth quirked. He said quietly, "I do not give up so easily." He bowed again and walked away.

When the gentleman was out of earshot, Mrs. Dower at once rounded on her daughter. Her eyes sparkled with satisfaction. "Evelyn! Did you hear? Mr. Hawkins remains determined to press his suit."

Evelyn made a small, tired gesture. "It scarcely matters, Mama, for I shall not entertain it."

Mrs. Dower's face fell. Without heeding their surroundings, she said clearly, "Well! You are certainly the oddest girl. Any other young lady would be in high alt at such a compliment."

A couple of ladies who stood nearby sent curious glances in the direction of the Dower ladies. Evelyn realized that she and her mother were engaging interest, and well aware of how indiscreet her mother's tongue could become, she said desperately, "Mama, could we not return home? I believe I feel the headache coming on."

At once Mrs. Dower was all solicitude. "I shouldn't wonder at it. You have had a harrowing time of it, indeed, what with your scolding from Lady Pomerancy and now from myself. And of course, there was Mr. Hawkins as well! I do understand, completely, believe me. I shall accompany you home and myself prepare a cloth for your head."

Chapter Six

Evelyn made a determined effort to put Peter Hawkins out of her mind. It was more difficult than she had hoped, since Mr. Hawkins came to tea that week on three separate occasions. On those days that he did not appear, there was a civil note conveying his apologies.

Reading one of these notes, Mrs. Dower remarked, "Such a remarkably civil young gentleman. I am really quite impressed with Mr. Hawkins." She eyed her daughter, who was calmly matching embroidery yarns, and said hopefully, "Do you not wish to encourage him just a little, Evelyn?"

"No, Mama, I do not," said Evelyn firmly. "Mr. Hawkins may be all that is exemplary, but I do not find him in the least romantic. The gentleman who finds favor with me must be able to sweep me off my feet."

"My dear child, how very extraordinary of you! I had thought you to be quite practical, just like your dear papa. He did not care in the least for such things, calling it all nonsense and worse, besides. I had not realized that you were so very like me," said Mrs. Dower wonderingly.

Evelyn was not certain that she cared for this comparison, for though she loved her mother dearly she nevertheless thought of Mrs. Dower as somewhat foolish and scatterbrained. "I do not think it in the least impractical to look about for a gentleman for whom I have a decided preference," she said stiffly.

Mrs. Dower hastened to reassure her. "No, indeed! Why, that is exactly what I did. I refused ever so many offers before I accepted your father. He was so handsome and so very clever. Of course I did not discover until much later how uncomfortable he could make one."

Evelyn's attention was truly caught. She looked up from the spread of colored thread in her lap. "What do you mean, Mama?"

Mrs. Dower waved her hand in a vague manner. "Oh, it was that side of his nature that always remained completely foreign to me. He was often utterly consumed by politics and other such things which I have never thought to be of much interest. You will not remember, of course, but there was always such a swirl of drama about him! He felt things so strongly. You have no notion how often I cringed at what was said about your papa by various personages." Mrs. Dower shuddered as she recalled. "Quite, quite uncomfortable, I assure you!"

"Is that why you removed permanently to Bath after Papa died?" Evelyn asked.

"The society was easier, you see. I was always more comfortable in Bath. One was not as likely to run into one of your dear papa's antagonists just as one was beginning to enjoy oneself at dinner or on the dance floor," said Mrs. Dower apologetically. She gave a little shrug. "Besides, Bath is so much less expensive than London. However frivolous I may seem, I do understand how to manage an allowance, and I knew that I would be quite run off my feet if we remained in London. I did not wish to be obliged to dip into the portion that your father settled upon you, dearest."

Evelyn returned to her task, and with exaggerated deliberation she chose some yarns. She did not pay as much attention to her mother's last revelation as she might have done at another time. "I had not previously known that you were so unhappy with Papa," she said quietly.

"Unhappy!" Mrs. Dower exclaimed, astonished. She looked at her daughter, suspecting that the girl was playing off one of her funning tricks. But Evelyn appeared perfectly serious, and she exclaimed, "No such thing! Why, wherever did you get such an odd notion? Really, Evelyn, how you do catch one up and put a meaning that one never intended to one's words."

Evelyn was taken aback. "But, Mama, you have just been saying how awful London was for you because of Papa's connections."

"That was quite a different thing altogether!" said Mrs. Dower emphatically.

When Evelyn shook her head, she regarded her daughter somewhat pityingly. "My dear Evelyn, you are so very young. I do hope that given a little time you will learn to discern the chaff from the wheat."

With that obscure remark, Mrs. Dower rose, announcing her intention to see to the next week's menus. "For what with your coming out in a few days' time, I must make certain that Cook understands what will be required of her when we begin to entertain." She left the sitting room.

Evelyn was left to ponder her mother's meaning, a faint frown gathering her brows. She felt that she had been rebuked in no uncertain terms, but she had little inkling what her true offense had been. She had never paid great heed to anything that her mother ever said, having learned at an early age that Mrs. Dower's remarks were not of the most profound nature, but this particular time there had been an unusual perceptivity in her mother's eyes that had startled her.

After a few moments of reflection, however, she shrugged away the odd feeling that her mother had truly been trying to convey something momentous to her and turned her full attention to her dull task. She worked over the yarns, matching shades and colors, and that was how she was occupied when a visitor was ushered in.

The young lady was rather tall with a graceful carriage. She regarded Evelyn with slightly raised brows, and her green gaze was amused. "I did not know you were of such a domestic bent, Evelyn." She sauntered forward, dragging off one of her supple gloves.

Evelyn laughed. "You know very well I am not! It is for Mama, of course."

The young lady flashed a smile. She stretched out her browned hand in greeting. "Of course. Good day, my dear. How do I find you?"

"Well enough, Pol." Evelyn shook her friend's hand, as always tensing her own hand against the other girl's hard grip. "Pray do sit down. I am going out of my mind with this, as you may well imagine." Her friend accepted the invitation and gracefully sank down on the settee beside her.

Evelyn nodded at the other's somewhat worn but well-fitted riding dress. "I see that you have just come in. What goes on up at the manor?"

"The squire is hard at it this fine morning, which is the reason you see me now," said Miss Woodthorpe, peeling off her other kid glove and smoothing both between her fingers. Considering a moment, she said meditatively, "My parent is very dear to me, but on occasion he tries my patience most effectively."

"Oh dear! I do hope that the squire calms down soon. I know that you do not particularly care to come into town on such a fine day," Evelyn said sympathetically.

Miss Woodthorpe shrugged. "It is of no consequence. An hour or so given to calling on friends and the discharge of a few errands will stand me in good stead. The squire will have exhausted his spleen by the time I return, and then he will be manageable again."

Evelyn laughed, shaking her head at her friend. "How you can remain so cool about it all, Appolonia, I have never quite fathomed. I know that I should not be so collected if I were in your shoes. But then I have never had brothers, nor a father since I was a girl, so I have not the practical experience, have I?"

A smile hovered about Miss Woodthorpe's full mouth as she regarded her younger friend. "One usually needs more than just a bit of experience to handle the male of our species, my dear. I believe it is a rare talent to be able to do so. Men are very like horses, I have found. One learns to handle both, or neither. A pity that I have never discovered a gentleman possessed of the proper combination of raw spirit and ability."

"Oh, Pol! You could have accepted any one of a dozen offers this past year and more," said Evelyn.

"True, but none of my suitors proved enough of a challenge for my abilities," said Miss Woodthorpe. When Evelyn laughed, she said with her characteristically quick smile, "But enough about my affairs! What is this prattle that has come to my ears of your coming out?"

Evelyn laughed again, her eyes sparked instantly by mischief. "I apprehend that Mama has been busily engaged in spreading the news. It is quite true. Mama is launching me into society, in a quiet fashion, of course. I am to gain a little polish and dash whilst I mull over the eligible gentlemen at large."

"What delicious fun. I shall naturally do all that is within my power to guide into your sphere those gentlemen most likely to put an offer," said Miss Woodthorpe.

Evelyn grimaced slightly. "Thank you, but no. I know just the sort you have in mind for me, Pol."

Miss Woodthorpe gave a deep, throaty laugh. Her green eyes were alight with amusement. "No, I suppose you would not be taken with the horsey set," she agreed. "Though I must tell you, I have seldom seen a better instinctive seat than you possess. If you could only overcome that absurd fear of yours for jumping fences."

"As I recall, I acquired that fear when your brother John slapped the rump of my mare before I knew what he was about," Evelyn retorted.

Miss Woodthorpe frowned. "Yes, it was very bad of him. I dressed him down severely on the spot, but of course you would not recall that since you were knocked senseless. John was quite remorseful when he saw how badly his little prank had ended."

"Yes, I know. He has told me so over and over again. It has been months now. Can *you* not persuade him that I have forgiven him?" Evelyn asked on a mock-plaintive note.

Miss Woodthorpe laughed again, but she shook her head. "Of course I will not. Were I to do so, he would become just as careless and unthinking as before. As it is, he is learning to accept the feel of the bridle that his own conscience has become. I say leave it well enough alone."

"Poor John!" Evelyn said, laughing, and Miss Woodthorpe joined in.

The door to the sitting room opened, and Mrs. Dower entered, accompanied by another young lady. Mrs. Dower started speaking before she cleared the threshold. "Evelyn, only but see whom I discovered in the hall coming to call on us. Our dearest Abigail! Her mother has sent us a basket of her delightful jams. You must thank her for us, Abigail. I, for one, am very fond of her offerings."

"I shall certainly do so, ma'am," Miss Abigail Sparrow said.

Mrs. Dower exclaimed anew when she saw that Evelyn was already entertaining a guest. "Apollonia, my dear! No one informed me of your arrival. Has your mother come with you?" She looked around as though expecting Mrs. Woodthorpe to appear out of the woodwork.

Miss Woodthorpe was quite used to Mrs. Dower's reasonings. "No, ma'am. I rode in with Toby, my groom. However, my mother sends her regards. She knew that I meant to call on you and Evelyn."

Miss Sparrow had advanced to give greeting. "Evelyn, how happy I am to see you." She exchanged a warm hug and a few words with Evelyn before she turned her mild blue eyes to the other young lady, who was now regarding her with a slight smile.

Miss Sparrow's greeting to Miss Woodthorpe, though gracious, lacked the same warmth as that which she had bestowed upon Evelyn. "Apollonia, I am glad to see you, too. I hope your family is well?"

"We are none the worse, Abigail," Miss Woodthorpe said wryly. "I trust that the reverend has recovered from his malaise?"

Miss Sparrow smiled and nodded her gratitude for the kind inquiry. "Yes, thank you. Papa is perfectly stout now. Mama and the rest of us were quite anxious for a time, but our fears have been completely laid to rest, thank God."

Evelyn was well aware that these best of her friends had never truly developed a deep affection for one another. Miss Woodthorpe's forthright manners and the consuming passion she had for animals and the land often put her at cross-purposes with Miss Sparrow, whose sympathies could always be counted upon to side with humanity. The young ladies were physical opposites, as well. Miss Woodthorpe was a striking brunette of willowy and athletic grace. Miss Sparrow appeared fragile in both stature and temperament, but her blonde prettiness and sweet expression hid a surprising amount of will.

"Abigail, pray do make yourself comfortable. Mama, I understand from Pol that you have been telling everyone of my come-out?"

"Of course I have. Why, if I did not, and at such short notice, too, there would not be upward of half a dozen personages at our first dinner party. I know that I may count upon the Woodthorpes and Sparrows, at least," said Mrs. Dower, seating herself beside Miss Sparrow on a second settee.

All three young ladies laughed.

"I suspect that you may count on a few more to attend than just our respective families," Miss Woodthorpe said.

"Of course you may! You and Evelyn have ever so many friends and acquaintances. I am certain it will be a most horrid squeeze," Miss Sparrow said warmly, lightly touching the older lady's hand.

"Thank you, my dear, I am sure," said Mrs. Dower, gratified. "I do not anticipate a *squeeze,* for after all we are not in London, but I do hope that the numbers will at least prove to be respectable."

"I hope you mean to invite Lady Pomerancy and Mr. Hawkins. The attendance of a London gentleman can but add a certain cachet to the occasion and I am certain that I do not need to tell *you,* Mrs. Dower, that her ladyship's approval must go far in making the evening a success," said Miss Sparrow.

Evelyn threw a fleeting glance at her mother, and Mrs. Dower at once seemed to find inordinate interest in the edging of lace at her cuff. Evelyn awaited her mother's reply with interest.

"Oh, indeed! I have sent round an early invitation to Lady Pomerancy, and it is my hope that her health will permit her to attend. As for Mr. Hawkins, I believe that he has already accepted," said Mrs. Dower, still avoiding her daughter's eyes.

"I was not aware that you had begun the invitations, Mama. You should have told me, for I would have been most happy to help you address them," said Evelyn fiendishly.

Mrs. Dower fidgeted a little. "Oh well, I have not precisely *begin* them. It was only that I wished Lady Pomerancy to have advance notice, for I know that her ladyship must pick and choose the functions she means to attend in order to conserve her energies," she said. "And I could not very well send an invitation to Lady Pomerancy without including Mr. Hawkins in it, could I?"

Evelyn bent her head, ostensibly so that she could peer closer at two similar yarns, but in actuality to hide her disrespectful expression.

"Very proper and considerate," Miss Sparrow said, nodding.

Evelyn looked up, still smiling, but she said nothing. She knew very well that her mother had gone to lengths to be certain that Mr. Peter Hawkins would be in attendance on the evening of her come-out. Mrs. Dower had not pressed her very hard lately to reconsider Mr. Hawkin's suit, but she knew that lady too well not to realize that her mother meant to do her utmost in promoting the match.

Chapter Seven

"I suppose, then, that we shall also see Mr. Hawkins's guests at your dinner party," said Miss Woodthorpe.

The other ladies looked over at her in surprise.

She regarded them all with a lifted brow. "Have none of you heard, then?"

"I heard the bells announcing an arrival, but I had no notion who it might be," said Miss Sparrow. "And no one that I have spoken to this morning knew any more than I."

"But perhaps that is understandable, for the gentlemen must only have arrived a little while ago. I met their carriage on the road into Bath. It seems that we shall have three London gentlemen circulating among us this spring. Mr. Hawkins has apparently invited his cousin, Viscount Waithe, and another gentleman to stay," said Miss Woodthorpe.

"We knew that the viscount was expected. But who was the other gentleman?" asked Evelyn curiously.

Miss Woodthorpe shook her head. "I do not know, and naturally I did not fall into conversation with the gentlemen. We merely exchanged greetings. However, I recognized the viscount from his previous visit a few years ago, and I naturally assumed that his companion was also either a relation or a friend of Mr. Hawkins's."

"But this is marvelous news!" exclaimed Miss Sparrow.

Her large blue eyes sparkled in anticipation as she turned to her friend. "Oh, Evelyn, you shall have such fun. I envy your coming-out when we have such exalted company. There were not such gentlemen about when I entered society last year, I vow. Perhaps I may persuade Mama to allow Maria to make her bows also. She is perhaps a bit young, but it is not often that our own cadre of gentlemen is added to in such a fashion, and certainly no one can deny the possibility of attracting the attention of a well-bred gentleman is enough to tempt even the most devoted of mothers."

Since all there knew that Miss Sparrow was the eldest of five daughters and was herself but recently affianced, none found anything of surprise in her statement. The good reverend and Mrs. Sparrow would naturally wish to establish all of their daughters well and as quickly as possible as the girls came of an age for marriage so that their younger sisters would not be put to any disadvantage.

"Indeed, I shall speak to your dear mother myself and offer my services as chaperon if she should so wish. I am not so ungenerous as to wish Evelyn to sew up all of the eligible gentlemen into her own circle of admirers," said Mrs. Dower with instant sympathy.

"Really, Mama!" exclaimed Evelyn, even as her friends laughed.

"Oh, but it is quite true. No one will be able to hold a candle to you, Evelyn," said Miss Sparrow. She shook her head, smiling a little. "I fear that I am a disloyal sister, indeed, when I say that poor Maria will be quite overshadowed. But it cannot be helped, and who is to say that Maria will go over quite well once you have accepted an offer?"

"Indeed, and it is my hope that Evelyn shall do that very thing soon after her come-out," said Mrs. Dower with a meaningful glance at her daughter.

"Oh stuff! Perhaps I shall not accept an offer at all, while Maria will speed her way to the altar," said Evelyn, misliking both her mother's broad hint as well as the intimation that she must accept a suit before the younger Miss Sparrow had any hope of contracting an eligible offer. She had never been particularly vain about her attributes but had merely accepted her good fortune for what it was. It bothered her when others assumed her appearance should entitle her to exceptional treatment.

"Oh, I do not think it likely. Truly I do not! Why, you are ever so pretty, in an unusual style, and quite clever, too. I shall expect the gentlemen to positively flock around you," said Miss Sparrow.

"Do you think so, indeed?" asked Evelyn meditatively. A

wicked sparkle came into her eyes. "I wonder if I shall care for it?"

Miss Sparrow shook a slim finger at her. "Now you are funning with me, I know! But I shall let you have your little joke. We shall see who has the right of it, will we not? You are already beside yourself with curiosity over the viscount and this unknown gentleman. Confess it, Evelyn!"

Evelyn only shook her head, laughing. "Not I!"

Miss Woodthorpe had listened silently to the conversation, only smiling now and again, but now she added her own observation. "The gentleman driving the carriage was a veritable whip, and the team he drove was the most splendid I have ever seen. I imagine that he must arouse some interest among our young aspiring sprigs, if not with you, Evelyn. As for the viscount, as I recall, his lordship was very prettily behaved and rather well formed of countenance."

"I, too, recall his lordship upon the occasion of his previous visit. A vastly handsome young gentleman, I thought, but quite sports-mad, of course. He is here for the fisticuffs, you see. I shall send a note to Lady Pomerancy that the gentlemen are naturally to be included in the invitation to our little dinner party," said Mrs. Dower. Her expression became faintly anxious as she reviewed in her mind those arrangements she had already settled on. "I do hope that it will not be considered too provincial an affair for the dashing young blades. One cannot hope to rival London entertainments, after all. Perhaps I should speak again to Cook regarding the menu."

"I am certain that it will all be quite as it ought," said Evelyn reassuringly.

"Yes, indeed. Why, everyone knows you for an excellent hostess," said Miss Sparrow.

Mrs. Dower was exceedingly gratified by this and said so. "You are a dear, dear girl, Abigail. You quite put my mind to rest. Though one cannot but wonder whether music—but I shall not think about it another instant. It will be a splendid evening, I am positive of it." She ended on a hopeful note, obviously attempting to convince herself.

Miss Woodthorpe cast a curious glance at Evelyn. "How

did you learn of the viscount's intention to visit Bath, Evelyn?"

"Mr. Hawkins mentioned it when he took tea with us," said Evelyn casually. She was quite aware that her friend's mild question disguised a sharp interest, for Miss Woodthorpe was possessed of a keen intelligence.

Miss Woodthorpe said nothing. Instead, she raised a slender brow to provide silent exclamation to her thoughts. Evelyn returned her friend's level glance, but did not oblige Miss Woodthorpe's curiosity.

However, Mrs. Dower was not so reticent. "Such a gentleman! I vow, I have never been more impressed by anyone's excellence of manners. Mr. Hawkins has sent round a note of apology whenever he has been unable to join us, for it has become quite an established thing that he should call on us."

Evelyn unconsciously put up her chin, a certain sign of challenge to those who knew her. "Mr. Hawkins has a decided preference for Mama's notions of proper tea," she said lightly.

"I did not know that you were so well acquainted with Mr. Hawkins," said Miss Woodthorpe, a lazy note of amusement in her voice. Her green eyes sparkled as she discerned the slight grimace that crossed Evelyn's face.

"No, nor I," said Miss Sparrow. "I don't believe I have myself spoken to him above half a dozen times since his return to Bath, even though he always stops to speak with Papa on Sundays after chapel."

"That is just like him. Every time he comes to tea I am struck anew by his exquisite sensitivity toward one," said Mrs. Dower, nodding.

Evelyn pretended to ignore the speculative gleam that had entered even Miss Sparrow's eyes. "Mr. Hawkins is a most proper gentleman," she said with dignity. She bent her attention to finishing up the sorting of the embroidery yarns, then almost thrust them toward her parent. "There, Mama! You may begin your next project whenever you wish."

Though she accepted the yarns, Mrs. Dower could not be diverted by something so mundane. "Indeed he is! I could not hope for better company for Evelyn. His exquisite manners, his pleasing countenance and bearing—why, I think Mr. Hawkins quite dashing in all respects."

"Oh, my," murmured Miss Sparrow, throwing an interested glance at her friend. What she saw in Evelyn's expression caused a small knowing smile to come to her lips. Gently teasing, she said, "Perhaps we shall see you engaged sooner than ever we expected."

Evelyn threw an annoyed glance in her mother's direction. "Stuff! Mama may have succumbed to Mr. Hawkins's charming manners, but I assure you that I have not done so. Mr. Hawkins may be a paragon, but he is definitely not the gentleman for me. I am heart-whole and so I shall remain for a while yet."

Miss Woodthorpe began to pull on her gloves. "Be that as it may, my dear, I would urge you not to toss aside Mr. Hawkins as a candidate quite so heedlessly. He is a gentleman of untested mettle and, I suspect, one of surprising strong will. Apply the spur warily, for without proper care that sort can give one an unexpected toss."

She stood up and smiled at her companions. "I have kept my groom and the horses standing too long. I must be off if I am to be back in time for tea."

The ladies all said good-bye as Miss Woodthorpe took her leave.

When she was gone, Mrs. Dower shook her head. "I cannot but blame the squire."

"For what, Mama?"

"Why, for naming his daughter after a horse, naturally. Apollonia! Is it any wonder our poor Miss Woodthorpe speaks in such an odd fashion? Really, what was that nonsense about spurs and such? I did not in the least comprehend it," said Mrs. Dower, frowning.

Evelyn exchanged a tolerant glance with Miss Sparrow. "Never, mind, Mama. It was just Apollonia's way."

"I, too, must be on my way, for I have a few errands to accomplish before returning home for luncheon. I had wondered whether you might like to bear me company, Evelyn, if you also have errands," said Miss Sparrow.

"I had intended to purchase some ribbons to refurbish an old bonnet," said Evelyn, nodding. "I'd like nothing better than to accompany you, Abigail."

"Perhaps you might then return with Evelyn and take luncheon with us?" Mrs. Dower suggested. "I should like someone's opinion on the new mutton that Cook is experimenting with today. One should never serve an entrée at a dinner party until it has been previously approved by several personages, you know."

"I am sorry, but I cannot. Mama would wonder if I stayed away," said Miss Sparrow. "After luncheon, we are to visit with some of the sick and Mr. Applegate comes to supper this evening, besides, so you see that I must return as quickly as possible if we are to accomplish everything."

"We shall not urge you, then. I am certain you have any number of things you wish to see to after your visits are made this afternoon," said Mrs. Dower. She had instantly understood the most important point. "How well I recall that time flies swiftly when one is anticipating one's betrothed to come to call!"

Miss Sparrow blushed and smiled shy agreement. "Oh, indeed."

"If you will wait but a moment for me to put on a pelisse, Abigail, I will walk with you," said Evelyn. Miss Sparrow agreed to this and Evelyn turned to her mother. "Have you any commissions for me, Mama?"

Mrs. Dower considered for a moment and finally shook her head. "I cannot think of a thing, though I am certain as soon as you walk out the door I shall recall any number of items. My mind is all taken up with the dinner party, you see, for despite Abigail's kind words I cannot escape the lowering feeling that I have forgotten something. No doubt it will prove to be a paltry affair in the eyes of the London gentlemen."

"Nonsense, Mama. It will go off in splendid style just like all of your entertainments. Lady Pomerancy herself will not be able to find a single item to fault," said Evelyn.

"Lady Pomerancy!" Mrs. Dower's eyes widened. "Good gracious, that is something else to plague me. I have forgotten that great chair of hers. Evelyn, I cannot possibly serve dinner in the upper room! We shall never get her ladyship abovestairs."

Evelyn recognized a valid point, but the solution seemed

readily apparent. "We shall simply have her ladyship carried up the stairs."

Miss Sparrow shook her head with the slightest of frowns marring her smooth brow. "Oh, I don't know that that will do at all, Ev—"

"Carried! I wish I might see it. One shudders to think of the look in her ladyship's eyes that such a suggestion must conjure up," said Mrs. Dower, giving a realistic shudder.

"Mama, do not fret so, I pray you. I am certain that everything must turn out for the best," soothed Evelyn.

"Indeed, ma'am. Everything does work out to its best advantage," said Miss Sparrow.

"Well, there you are quite wrong, my dears. One can never leave such a thing to chance," said Mrs. Dower, unexpectedly firm. "Your dear father never understood it, Evelyn, and many times I was put to positive *extremes* of ingenuity to snatch an affair from complete disaster." Mrs. Dower gave way to her anxiety and wrung her hands. "Whatever shall I do about Lady Pomerancy's chair?"

Evelyn saw that it was useless to remonstrate with her mother. Therefore she merely repeated her intention to go purchase some ribbons and kissed her inattentive mother on the cheek.

Miss Sparrow trailed Evelyn out of the sitting room, glancing back in concern at Mrs. Dower, who had accepted her leave-taking in an abstracted manner. "Evelyn, perhaps you should stay with your mother for a little while. I will soon be headed home, in any event, and—"

"It wouldn't be the least use if I did so, Abigail. You know that it wouldn't. Mama will not hear a word that I say while she worries at the puzzle she has set for herself."

"Yes, of course you are right. And I am certain that the dear lady will manage to work it out to her satisfaction," said Miss Sparrow, her natural optimism rising.

"Of course she shall," Evelyn agreed. "I shall look for something in the shops to divert Mama's thoughts, besides."

Miss Sparrow applauded this laudable intention. "Oh, that will be just the thing, I am sure of it."

Accompanied by her friend, Evelyn went upstairs to change into an outfit more befitting a shopping excursion.

Chapter Eight

Evelyn and Miss Sparrow left the town house in Queen Square and set out on foot. Evelyn's maid followed the young ladies so that after they had parted ways Evelyn would not be unaccompanied upon her return home.

Miss Sparrow's first stop was to an apothecary's shop to purchase several items that would be required during the visits to the sick that she and her mother would make later in the day. She also had on her list sundry other items to purchase, as well as commissions for the chandler and the butcher.

When the young ladies emerged from the butcher shop, where Miss Sparrow had left her order and had elicited the promise that it would be delivered for her, her basket had obviously become weighty on her arm. Evelyn's maid offered to carry the basket, but Miss Sparrow smilingly refused. "You would spoil me, Milly, for you must know that I am quite used to carrying my own basket."

The ladies proceeded to the milliner's establishment, where Evelyn chose and made her purchase in such short time that it was still early. Miss Sparrow suggested that they might browse for a while. "For you must know that I rarely peek into any shops with which I do not have business," she said, almost wistfully.

"Oh, yes, let's. It is so much more amusing when one is with a friend," said Evelyn, handing over the carefully wrapped lengths of ribbon to her maid.

It was a lovely spring day and Evelyn and Miss Sparrow enjoyed walking slowly past the various shop windows while exchanging comments on the displayed wares. Twice they could not resist a closer look at the tempting offerings and they slipped into the establishments, though never to actually make a purchase. Evelyn, and Miss Sparrow in particular, understood the limits of their funds.

At length, Evelyn noticed a clock in one shop window. She pointed out the advancing hour. "Perhaps we should turn back at once, so that you will have ample time to reach home before luncheon."

Miss Sparrow was unwilling to call an end to the leisurely promenade so soon, for it was a rare treat to be able to enjoy herself without also having to discharge some responsibility or other. "I do not think Mama will be very anxious if I am a very little later than I anticipated. Let us continue to the end of the street before we return."

Evelyn agreed to it and they walked on. However, when they came opposite the lending library, Evelyn's eyes lit up. "Oh, do let us go in!"

Miss Sparrow was reluctant. She knew that her friend was an avid reader and that it would be difficult to tear Evelyn away once she began browsing. "I shall certainly be late for luncheon if I allow you to persuade me."

"I promise you that I shall not spend one moment longer than I must. But I should like to find something for Mama. She does so enjoy for me to read to her in the evenings," said Evelyn.

Miss Sparrow hesitated, then sighed. "Oh, very well. Just this once, and for Mrs. Dower's sake. But I warn you that if you take root I shall be forced to leave you for pruning!"

Evelyn laughed and reiterated her promise. However, once inside among the books on the shelves, the familiar spell quickly came upon her and if it had not been for reminders from both Miss Sparrow and her maid of the waning hour, she might have remained an indefinite time.

"Oh, very well. I see that you have even Milly conspiring against me, Abigail, so I must surrender," said Evelyn.

"At last, and with such a gracious manner," said Miss Sparrow with gentle sarcasm.

Evelyn laughed and carried her choice of four volumes to the front.

Miss Sparrow picked up one of the books and read the title on the spine. She made the slightest grimace. "A romance, I see. Really, Evelyn, how can you choose to fill your clever mind with such unsavory tales?"

"Mama particularly likes them," said Evelyn, with a flash of mischief in her eyes. She knew that her friend was well aware that she was a passionate *afficionado* of romances on her own account.

Miss Sparrow threw her a disbelieving glance. "Oh indeed, and you naturally suffer through them the best you can."

Evelyn laughed. She tapped the last slim volume. "A treatise on ancient Greek civilization. Surely that is learned enough for your taste, Abigail?"

"Barbarians, but admittedly the Greeks contributed to certain philosophies and art forms," said Miss Sparrow with a sniff.

A particularly wicked gleam entered Evelyn's tawny eyes. "Yes, indeed. There is the stoic, for instance, and we must not forget the influence of Hippocrates upon our men of medicine. Why, we have but to look about us to see their strong influence on our own architecture. Where would we be without Doric and Ionic columns, and of course the Corinthian. I wonder, can our so-called Corinthian gentlemen be deemed to be aping the Greeks?"

Evelyn continued to deliver herself of a discourse in pompous fashion until they had emerged from the lending library and she had successfully reduced her friend to laughter.

Miss Sparrow threw up a pleading hand. "Very well, very well! Your arguments have left me all but reeling. Pray do not trot out more examples, for I assure you that I am wholly convinced."

"You are not convinced so much of the Greek contribution to the world as you are that you cannot abide further lecture from myself," said Evelyn.

Miss Sparrow agreed to it, saying, "I shall inform Papa that I have already had my dose of philosophy for the week, and a vile one it was, too!"

"It was not as bad as all that, surely!" Evelyn protested.

Miss Sparrow assured her that it was, even as a martial light leaped into her eyes. "And I am quite convinced that much of what you claimed as originating with Greek literature is surely erroneous, for I recall Papa commenting once that the Greeks were still barbarians when the Hebrews were composing poetry."

"I had no notion that you were such a bluestocking, Abigail," said Evelyn wickedly.

Miss Sparrow at once denied the charge. "Surely if anyone may be called a bluestocking, it is yourself, Evelyn! You are forever toting about some book or other."

"But I read romances, which you have assured me are not at all proper fare for a quick mind," said Evelyn.

Miss Sparrow was momentarily taken off guard, but she rallied quickly and retorted with gentle insult. Evelyn answered, equally good-natured. As the young ladies slowly walked back up the street, the maid trailed behind, chuckling over their amicable wrangling.

The young ladies formed a pretty contrast, one a diminutive blonde and the other a striking redhead, and more than one head turned to follow their progress. Two gentlemen in particular took note of them.

"Miss Dower, this is fortuitous, indeed."

The young ladies paused to see who had thus addressed Evelyn.

A fleeting frown entered Evelyn's eyes, which was as quickly veiled. She smiled politely at the gentleman who had accosted her and offered her hand to him. "Mr. Hawkins, what a surprise. Are you doing some shopping as well?"

Mr. Hawkins shook her hand and released it circumspectly. "No, actually. It is my cousin, Viscount Waithe, who was in need of a few items. Lord Waithe, Miss Dower. And this delightful lady is Miss Sparrow."

Viscount Waithe also shook Evelyn's hand, but he did not so quickly release it.

He nodded in Miss Sparrow's direction, but though he smiled at both ladies the admiration in his eyes was plainly reserved for Miss Dower. "Alas, I was foolish enough to come down from town without my valet, and so I discover myself bereft of combs and brushes. It quite escaped me that I should bring such mundane items, for they always seem to be where one needs them without a thought bestowed upon them."

Evelyn laughed, quite taken with the viscount's wry confidence. She was also flattered by his patent admiration and gently, so as not to give offense, she withdrew her fingers from his light clasp. "Indeed, I quite see how one could easily forget. But I thought all gentlemen allowed their valets to pack their cases for them?"

Viscount Waithe leaned forward in a conspiratorial fashion. "It was to be a lesson, you see. I meant to be quite self-sufficient, just to show the old Turk that he was not indispensable." He straightened, laughing at himself in a self-deprecating manner. "I am quite rolled up, however, and I fear that I shall be forced to send for the man before the day is out. It will make him quite insufferably smug, of course."

Evelyn laughed again, delighted with his lordship's sense of the ridiculous and his easy manners. As the viscount turned to Miss Sparrow and addressed a pleasantry to her, she swept him an interested glance. His blond good looks and his athletic figure were set off to advantage by a flaw-lessly tailored coat and form-fitting pantaloons tucked into gleaming black Hessians. She thought it was easily seen that Viscount Waithe and Mr. Hawkins were related. They shared similar features and coloring. Though his lordship's countenance did not possess the same strength of character as his cousins's, nor was he as tall as Mr. Hawkins, Viscount Waithe was still one of the most fashionable gentleman Evelyn had ever seen and decidedly one of the most attractive.

"If you ladies have no objection, I am certain that I speak for both my cousin and myself in requesting your permission to accompany you on the remainder of your errands," said Mr. Hawkins, his smile one of winning charm.

"I stand ready to carry whatever number of awkward parcels that you may acquire," said Viscount Waithe, bowing to both ladies.

"Thank you gentlemen. But with my errands done, I am due to return home," said Miss Sparrow.

"I, too, have quite completed my purchases and I am now on my way home for luncheon," said Evelyn. Though her smile was impartial, her glance strayed shyly to the viscount. "But perhaps, if you should like it, you might call late in the week to take tea with me and my mother?"

"Splendid notion, ma'am. I cannot think of anything I

would like better," said Viscount Waithe quietly. He took Evelyn's hand once more and briefly brushed his lips across her gloved fingers.

"We shall certainly come to tea, Miss Dower," said Mr. Hawkins. "Perhaps on Thursday, if that is convenient?"

"That will be quite nice," said Evelyn, smiling.

"We shall look forward to it then," said Mr. Hawkins. "Might we escort you ladies to your respective addresses?"

But Miss Sparrow declined this suggestion. Evelyn followed suit, sensing that her friend's sense of propriety was already shocked that she had solicited the gentlemen for tea. The gentlemen said a few other things and then they took leave of the ladies.

Miss Sparrow waited only until the gentlemen were out of earshot before she began to scold. "Evelyn! How could you behave with such boldness? I am persuaded that you must have given Mr. Hawkins and his lordship a most improper notion of your manners."

"It was really quite reprehensible of me," Evelyn agreed readily, already realizing that she had been somewhat bold before a gentleman whom she had just met. "I should have advanced a rather vague invitation and let it rest on the hope that Mr. Hawkins would bring the viscount with him when next he decided to call. I truly did not take time to reflect, Abigail."

At the perturbation in her friend's eyes, Miss Sparrow's heart softened. "Oh, *I* fully realize that, Evelyn. However, you must learn to be more circumspect. It is all very well to be free and easy in your manners to those of us who have known you all of your life, but you simply cannot do the same with gentlemen such as Mr. Hawkins and Viscount Waithe. They are used to quite a different society than ours, and the singular partiality of your glances for his lordship could so easily be misinterpreted for other than naive innocence."

Miss Sparrow smiled gently as the color rose in Evelyn's face. "Oh yes, it was very noticeable that the viscount made an impression upon you. As you did upon him."

It had not occurred to Evelyn before, but she thought it would be wonderful if Mr. Hawkins could see that other gentlemen admired her, and quite without the prodding of their respective grandmothers. She turned a hopeful expression on her friend. "Did I, indeed?"

Miss Sparrow laughed, but shook her head. "I fear so. You must not let it turn your head, however. I believe gentlemen are often taken by a pretty countenance, and just as quickly they grow bored. You are just coming out so you cannot be expected to understand such things as yet, but— *do* you understand at all what it is I am saying, Evelyn?"

The last was said with a quick glance of concern. Miss Sparrow had not been out so long herself that she perfectly understood all the nuances, and she felt herself to be somewhat at a loss in guiding her even less experienced friend.

Evelyn thought about some of the things that her mother had relayed to her over the years. She rather suspected that Miss Sparrow would be shocked at how much she understood of worldly matters, and so she confined herself to expressing her appreciation for her friend's genuine concern. "I do thank you for explaining it all to me, Abigail. I promise you that I shall do better in future."

Miss Sparrow smiled, relief apparent in her eyes. She had discharged her duty not too badly after all, she thought. Her mother could be proud of her daughter. "Good. Now I really must be going. I have tarried too long already. Mama must have started to wonder what is keeping me."

"Give my fondest regards to your parents and your sisters," said Evelyn.

Miss Sparrow promised to do so and hurried away, her heavy basket swinging from her arm.

Evelyn stood a moment, to all intents absorbed in watching until Miss Sparrow had turned the corner, but her thoughts were actually far from measuring her friend's progress. She remarked happily, "Mama will be very pleased when I show her the romances, Milly."

"Yes, miss," said the maid tolerantly. She thought that she knew better than to believe it was romance between the two book covers that had brought the blush of roses into her young mistress's cheeks. "Here, let me carry those heavy things, miss."

Evelyn willingly gave the books to her servant's care. She hurried home, anticipating the astonished and gratified expression that must possess her mother's face when she informed Mrs. Dower of the exalted company that was to call later in the week.

Chapter Nine

A splendid and sumptuous tea had been prepared and was spread on the sideboard. Mrs. Dower had made certain that there would be everything that must be pleasing to the gentlemen's palates. The cold collation of cut meats and cheeses was set off by various sandwiches and a generous choice of fruits, jellies, tarts, and biscuits.

Mrs. Dower sent a practiced glance over the offerings. "Quite nice, indeed. I do not think we shall have cause for any complaint."

"Decidedly not, unless one of the gentlemen suffers from the gout," said Evelyn.

"Now you are funning with me. I know quite well that the viscount is not above a year or two older than Mr. Hawkins, and he is scarcely out of shortcoats," said Mrs. Dower.

Evelyn laughed at the wide exaggeration. "And what of me, Mama?"

"A veritable babe in arms," said Mrs. Dower. "Or is that a babe in the woods? At all events, it is really quite exciting that you are not yet officially out and already you have attached two such fashionable admirers. Shall you accept an offer from Viscount Waithe since Mr. Hawkins does not appeal to you?"

"It is too early to say, surely! I have scarcely spoken more than a dozen words to his lordship, after all," said Evelyn flippantly.

"Oh, as to that, what matters a few words or more? All that is needed is a little encouragement in the proper direction." Mrs. Dower unnecessarily straightened the lace at her cuff, humming a little.

Evelyn regarded her mother with a gathering of foreboding. "Mama, I mislike it excessively when you begin to hum in just that fashion."

"Why, do you not like music, dear? How very odd of you," said Mrs. Dower.

"Mama, pray give me your word that you will say nothing that—"

"Well, really, Evelyn!" Mrs. Dower turned a wounded expression on her daughter. "The way you look, one could almost suspect that you do not place the least trust in me."

"I am sorry to wound you, Mama, but I *have* known you to utter the most embarrassing things," said Evelyn apologetically.

"Yes, well, I promise you that I shan't do so today," said Mrs. Dower. She patted her daughter's arm, giving Evelyn a fond smile. "I am quite up to snuff with the gentlemen, my dear, never fear. You may rest easy on that head."

Evelyn was not at all reassured, and demanded, "Mama, *what* do you mean to do?"

"Nothing so very awful, Evelyn. It is but a mother's duty to encourage her daughter's suitors. You may safely leave it in my hands, dearest," said Mrs. Dower.

"But that is precisely what I cannot do, Mama!"

Evelyn would have pursued the matter, but to her distinct dismay at that moment the gentlemen were announced.

Throwing Evelyn an arch glance, Mrs. Dower rose to greet them. "Mr. Hawkins, how happy I am to see you. I am always glad when you come to call," she said. "I have been thinking that we have become such good friends these last few weeks."

Mr. Hawkins bowed over her hand. He said with a smile, "I could not ask for a warmer welcome, ma'am."

He turned toward Evelyn and she saw that his eyes glinted with speculative humor. "I know that I am fully as welcome with you, Miss Dower."

Evelyn would not allow his gentle dart to raise a retort from her. Her company manners were better than that, she hoped. She smiled winningly at him. "Of course, Mr. Hawkins. How could it be otherwise?"

Mr. Hawkins chuckled quietly. "Mrs. Dower, allow me to introduce to you my companions. My cousin, Viscount Waithe, and Sir Charles Reginald."

Mrs. Dower regarded the third gentleman with astonishment. "Why, I had no notion that we would be so honored, Sir Charles. I am so glad that I had Cook arrange such a very large tea. There was some question in my mind, you see, but there! It only proves that one should always plan in a generous fashion."

Sir Charles smiled down at his hostess and delivered himself of a flowery compliment. "I am not at all surprised by your superior perception, ma'am. Such a lovely lady could scarcely be otherwise."

Mrs. Dower acknowledged the gentleman's gracious words with approval and then introduced Evelyn to the gentlemen. "You and Mr. Hawkins are old friends, Evelyn, so I need not say more there, and of course you must recall Lord Waithe. Sir Charles, my daughter, Evelyn."

Sir Charles raised Evelyn's fingers to his lips for a brief salute. "Miss Dower, it is a pleasure to discover such a rare and beauteous flower." There was an enigmatic expression in his glance for her that at once established an aura of intimacy between them.

Evelyn was disconcerted by Sir Charles's singular style. She acknowledged his gallantry with a slight blush and murmured greeting before she turned her head to smile at the other two gentlemen. "Of course I recall the viscount. I am glad to be able to further my acquaintance with you, my lord. I consider myself fortunate to have met you so soon after your arrival, for Mr. Hawkins told us but a few days ago that you would be coming to visit him here in Bath."

"I am more glad than I can say that I have done so. Bath is quickly proving to be of more interest than I had ever anticipated," said Viscount Waithe. His admiring smile gave his words a meaning that could not be misunderstood.

"We do enjoy a lively society," Mrs. Dower agreed, seemingly oblivious to her daughter's heightened blush. "Do make yourselves comfortable, gentlemen." She requested that the attending footmen serve from the trays while she occupied herself with the pouring of the tea.

For the next hour, Evelyn thoroughly enjoyed herself. It was an enlightening and heady experience to be the recipient of the gallantry of three fashionable and completely eligible gentlemen. However, she knew enough of the ways of the world to be careful that she did not favor one gentleman over any other. She had often heard how disastrously such public preference could affect a lady's reputation, particularly that of an unestablished miss. It was one of those helpful insights that she had gathered from her mother's light gossip about friends and society.

Other callers chanced to stop in and graciously acceded to Mrs. Dower's urgings to take tea. Among them was a retired admiral who had long been a great admirer of Mrs. Dower. When the elderly gentleman realized that Miss Dower had come of age to receive gentlemanly compliments, he also added his mite.

"We'll soon have your pretty head turned, my dear," the admiral chuckled, nodding in approval at her high color and sparkling eyes. "In no time at all those maidenly blushes will be replaced with a coquettish air."

"I trust not. You must not listen to this old reprobate, my dear," said a lady, one of two of Mrs. Dower's contemporaries who had come to visit.

"Mustn't I?" Evelyn asked, laughing a little.

"Indeed not! Nothing is more devastating to a young lady's reputation than to come to be considered a flirt. Those sorts do not make successful marriages," agreed her companion, sipping delicately at her tea.

Since Evelyn knew that both ladies had never married, it crossed her mind to wonder whether each had suffered that very ignoble fate. Her glance inadvertently met that of Mr. Hawkins. The amusement in his eyes told her that he knew very well what she had been thinking. That perception had the startling effect of making her want to laugh. Her voice trembled with the restraint that she exercised upon herself. "I am certain that is so, ma'am. I shall try to heed your excellent advice."

The ladies were most gratified and confided to Mrs. Dower that she had a very prettily behaved daughter. "Indeed, dear Mary, it is particularly gratifying to observe a young lady who is modest and maidenly in the presence of gentlemen," said one.

"Oh, yes. So often our misses are encouraged by such obvious attentions to behave distressingly forward," said the other.

"I flatter myself to think that Evelyn is levelheaded enough to weather the admiration of any number of gentlemen," said Mrs. Dower. "Why, Mr. Hawkins has shown the most marked preference, but Evelyn remains quite true to her strict upbringing."

"Indeed!" As one, the two ladies turned bright speculative glances on Evelyn and Mr. Hawkins.

Evelyn's cheeks burned at her mother's indiscreet utterance. She chanced to meet Mr. Hawkins's eyes at that moment. His brow was raised and there was a peculiar wryness to his smile.

Evelyn decidedly turned away from Mr. Hawkins to address the viscount. "My lord, I have not been to London since I was a small child and therefore my memories are from the childish viewpoint. Tell me, is Astley's Circus as fine a spectacle as it seemed?"

"Quite, Miss Dower! And perhaps it is even better than you recall. There is a melodrama now and quite rousing it is, I assure you," said Viscount Waithe enthusiastically.

"Oh, I should like to see it."

"I would do anything in my power to make you happy, Miss Dower," said Viscount Waithe, smiling at her. "An excursion to Astley's it is, then!"

Evelyn blushed, most pleased by his lordship's patent admiration. It was a pleasant novelty to receive such open regard from a gentleman. On the thought, her glance slid briefly in Mr. Hawkins's direction. Certainly that gentleman could take a lesson or two from his cousin. "If my mother and I am ever in London, I shall hold you to that invitation, my lord!"

One of the maiden ladies also directed a question about London entertainments to Viscount Waithe, and he turned courteously to her. Not by expression or demeanor could it be inferred that he was reluctant to give up his conversation with Miss Dower to another of the party.

Of all the gentlemen, Viscount Waithe was the most obvious in his attentions toward Evelyn. Though his lordship was too well bred to neglect the others of the company, his large blue eyes strayed often to Miss Dower's face, and it could be noted that he was particularly attentive whenever she spoke.

Sir Charles made a lazily amused, low-voiced comment on the fact to Mr. Hawkins. "Our Percy appears to be well smitten."

Mr. Hawkins was initially surprised by Sir Charles's observation, but he became thoughtful as he watched Viscount Waithe's manner. Firm in his own pursuit of love, he had forgotten how easily his cousin fell into infatuation. It had never occurred to him that one of his rivals for Miss Dower's affections could be the viscount.

Mr. Hawkins glanced in Miss Dower's direction. She appeared perfectly at ease with Viscount Waithe's sallies, and there seemed to be a good deal of favor in her expression when her gaze rested upon his lordship's countenance, but she did not appear to be dazzled by him. Nor, when she turned to Sir Charles to acknowledge one of his elegant compliments, did she appear to be particularly stricken by his dark, saturnine good looks.

Mr. Hawkins was particularly glad of the last, for he knew Sir Charles Reginald to be an excessively charming companion to the ladies. The gentleman's address was exceeded by none, and his talent for penning romantic sonnets had gained him entry into more than one London lady's boudoir.

If Miss Dower was indeed proof to these two formidable rivals, Mr. Hawkins took hope that he might yet have the advantage with her. Of course, it remained to be seen what rivals might appear once she came out. Mr. Hawkins would wager, however, that there were few Bath gentlemen who could hold a candle to the gentlemen then present in Mrs. Dower's drawing room.

Tea ended with all present expressing their pleasure in the past hour, and the callers took leave of the Dower ladies. As Evelyn bade the London gentlemen good day, she felt the most curious sensation, as though she were floating on air.

When the door had closed on the last departing guest, Evelyn spun spontaneously about the drawing room. "Oh, how wonderful it was!"

"I am happy that you enjoyed it, my dear. I, too, am immensely satisfied and I quite look forward to your come-out," said Mrs. Dower. "Even though you insist that you will not have Mr. Hawkins, I am persuaded that there will be at least one gentleman who will *sweep you off your feet!*"

Evelyn laughed gaily as she recalled how the viscount had lingered over his good-byes. She might still harbor the thread of a *tendre* for Mr. Peter Hawkins, but perhaps it might unravel a bit quicker now that there were others to claim her attention. "Indeed, Mama! I begin to think so, too."

"Viscount Waithe indicated that he should like to call upon us again," said Mrs. Dower with a sly glance.

"Yes, I do believe his lordship did mention something of the sort," Evelyn said in her demurest tone.

"You shan't comb the wool over my eyes, young lady. As I told you, I am quite up to snuff," said Mrs. Dower. "Now tell me directly, which of the gentlemen did you prefer? I thought the viscount very pretty-behaved, but Sir Charles has such a way about him that—. Why, here I am rattling on in fine style and you are not saying a word."

Evelyn laughed, shaking her head. "No, and I do not intend to do so. I am not such a goosecap as to give you cause to leap to unwarranted conclusions."

"You are the most provoking creature, my dear," Mrs. Dower observed. "But I shall watch most carefully which gentleman receives your preference the next time that they come to tea, I promise you."

Chapter Ten

As it chanced, the gentlemen did not return for tea again that week. Mr. Hawkins sent a brief note of apology, promising that they would call on Thursday next if that was amenable.

"Depend upon it, there is some sort of sporting event," said Mrs. Dower knowledgeably.

Evelyn was disappointed, but not as much as she might have been if her thoughts had not begun to turn on the coming-out party that her mother had arranged for her.

When Mrs. Dower announced that she had indeed engaged musicians for the evening's entertainment, Evelyn was delighted. "Oh, are we to have dancing?"

"Of course we are. Depend upon it, the younger set will think it frightfully dull otherwise. And music is always a pleasant counterpoint to the conversation of those of my generation," said Mrs. Dower sagely.

"You are not so aged that you could not still dance, Mama," said Evelyn teasingly.

Mrs. Dower agreed, somewhat wistfully, but said, "I shall do my duty, though, and take my place with the matrons, for I would not have it said that I was so taken up with my own pleasures that I neglected the proper direction of my daughter's come-out."

Evelyn wrote out the gilt-edged invitations from the closely written guest list that her mother had provided, and as she did so, she became impressed with the extent of her mother's acquaintance. Evelyn realized that she had underestimated her mother. Mrs. Dower might be thought frivolous and scatterbrained, but she was also an astute participant in society.

Mrs. Dower declared that Evelyn would have a gown

very different from her usual style for her come-out. "You are no longer a child, dearest, and certainly it must reflect that," said Mrs. Dower.

Her mother's emphatic opinion caused Evelyn to await the delivery of the completed gown with scarce-contained anticipation. When it arrived and was lifted out of the box, the white tissues that had separated its folds floating away to the floor, Evelyn drew in her breath. She had never seen anything so lovely. It was a costly confection of pale blue silk.

"Will miss be wishing to try it on?" asked the maid, a note of teasing in her voice.

"Oh, yes, Millie!"

When Evelyn had on the gown and turned to the mirror, she was stunned by her reflection. Her image was no longer that of a fashionable young miss, but that of a sophisticated woman. The silk shimmered at the curve of her breast and thigh when she moved. Evelyn had never given much thought to her well-rounded bosom, but the low décolletage of the gown suddenly centered her attention. "Oh my."

"Indeed." Mrs. Dower frowned thoughtfully at the revealing neckline. "It is cut a bit tight, do you not think so, Millie?"

The maid coughed. "It does give one notice of the young lady's rising hopes, ma'am."

Evelyn chose to ignore her maid's sly comment as beneath her dignity. She tugged lightly at the neckline, to no avail. "I cannot think how the seamstress came to make such a mistake after having taken my measurements."

"I do wish you to appear out of the schoolroom, Evelyn, but that décolletage is inappropriate. We shall have it altered, only a very little, and you shall not appear quite so daring," said Mrs. Dower.

"I own, Mama, I should feel more comfortable," said Evelyn, again giving an ineffectual pull to the tight neckline.

On the eve of the coming-out party, it quickly became apparent that the function boded to be well received. As the Dower ladies stood together at the entrance to greet their guests, Evelyn began to realize that those who had received invitations were nearly universal in their attendance.

Mrs. Dower was moved to say, with justifiable pride, "It is shaping up to be a very respectable event, after all. You shall not lack for attention this evening, dearest."

Evelyn's heart fluttered with unexpected trepidation. However, nothing in her demeanor or in her countenance betrayed her initial nervousness. Her confidence could not be entirely shaken, either, not when she knew that the pale blue gown that so graced her slender figure was also the perfect compliment to her burnished hair and cream complexion. She appeared lovely and composed, while her manners inspired the approval or admiration of those she greeted.

Mrs. Dower also looked at her best gowned in a rich robe of gold crepe. She wore a small feathered turban in acknowledgment of her responsible role, but there was nothing of the bored matron in her manner. She greeted each of her guests with delighted warmth, which faltered only a little when Lady Pomerancy arrived.

Uncertain as Mrs. Dower was of the old lady's mood, she was somewhat tentative in her greeting. "My lady, how very happy I am that you have been able to attend."

Lady Pomerancy's eyes snapped with errant humor. "I cannot conceive why, for you are trembling like a blancmange at sight of me. Come to tea tomorrow. I should like to talk privately to you."

Mrs. Dower assured her ladyship that she would be delighted to do so, though her expression would not have led anyone to believe the truth of her words.

Lady Pomerancy snorted before she turned her eyes on the younger lady. "Well, girl, you have entered society at last. I trust that it shall meet all your expectations."

"I doubt it not in the least, my lady," said Evelyn with a small smile.

Lady Pomerancy stared at Evelyn for a moment, attempting to put the girl to the blush. Her ladyship gave a sharp nod when Evelyn steadily returned the unnerving appraisal. "You'll do."

Lady Pomerancy had dispensed with her wheelchair for the evening. She was instead leaning heavily on a cane and the arm of her grandson. She turned her head to Mr. Hawkins. "Peter, I am tired of standing about. Find me a chair."

"I shall do so at once, ma'am."

Mr. Hawkins smiled and said a few words to his hostess and Miss Dower. His eyes lingered appreciatively on the younger lady before he guided his grandmother off in search of a suitably placed chair. They were flanked by a stalwart footman and her ladyship's maid, the latter carrying her mistress's cushion.

Once Lady Pomerancy had been settled with a small circle of friends, with her ever-vigilant maid and the footman in attendance, Mr. Hawkins was released from his duty.

He immediately set out to seek Miss Dower, only to discover that she also had dispensed with her duty in the receiving line. Not unexpectedly, he found her to be the center of attention amongst several of the guests.

Evelyn had gathered a circle of admirers from among the gentlemen. Her tawny eyes sparkled and her color was becomingly high at the compliments that she accepted. The ready laughter sprang lightly from her lips, and Mr. Hawkins had no difficulty in discerning that she was thoroughly enjoying herself.

He cast a swift critical glance over the other gentlemen surrounding Miss Dower. With the exception of Viscount Waithe and two or three others, there were none that he deemed to be of much competition. Most were very young gentlemen, but amongst the admirers were several graying heads as well. Mr. Hawkins recalled that the Bath population numbered an unusual number of retired admirals and clergymen. He grinned to himself, thinking that perhaps his own powers of address were not in any danger of being outshown, after all.

A small stringed orchestra struck up, signaling that dancing was to be the order of the evening. A wave of expectation raced over the company. Young ladies waited breathlessly to be led into the first set of a country dance that was forming. It was always an anxious moment, for no one cared to be left sitting next to the wall when there was dancing.

Miss Dower, at least, would have no lack of partners, for

Mr. Hawkins could already hear the appeals of her admirers. He started forward, to put his own bid for the lady's hand for a dance.

"Good evening, Mr. Hawkins."

Mr. Hawkins turned. He immediately recognized the lady who had addressed him, but he was less certain of the identities of the gentleman and the young lady with her. "And to you, Miss Sparrow," he said with a polite glance for her companions.

Miss Sparrow brought to Mr. Hawkins's recollection her betrothed, a worthy gentleman by the name of Fiddle, and her sister. The younger Miss Sparrow blushed fierily when she was addressed and was obviously painfully shy in a gathering.

Miss Sparrow gently suggested that perhaps her betrothed might find a lemon ice for her sister. The gentleman's face registered surprise. "I know that Maria would adore such a high treat, sir," said Miss Sparrow with a meaningful look at Mr. Fiddle.

"Of course, my dear. With the greatest of pleasure," responded Mr. Fiddle, his momentary amazement giving way almost immediately to polite convention. With greater presence of mind than his benign countenance suggested, Mr. Fiddle took the younger girl off.

Miss Sparrow glanced up at her tall companion with a small smile. "Maria's come-out is such a short time away that it was thought there would be little harm in her accompanying me this evening. Mama would have accompanied Maria herself, but one of our younger sisters has the toothache and is very fretful. However, Mama had complete confidence that my chaperonage would do as well. The Dowers have been our good friends for many years, after all, and may be depended upon to have a respectable gathering."

"I am certain that you may rest easy, Miss Sparrow," said Mr. Hawkins. He wondered what the lady could possibly have to say to him, for her maneuver to have him alone had been obvious. He did not have long to wait.

Miss Sparrow fell silent for only a moment before saying hesitantly, "May I request a favor of you, Mr. Hawkins?"

"Certainly, Miss Sparrow."

She smiled up at him, but with a question in her eyes. "You do not yet know what I would ask, sir."

"I can hardly be so ungallant as to regard your unspoken request with suspicion," he said with the quirk of a smile.

Miss Sparrow laughed. The reservation in her eyes completely vanished. "Perhaps you should, though, for what I would ask is rather indelicate. It concerns Maria, whom I care for very much, and I would not ask at all except that I know you to be a true gentleman. Mr. Hawkins, I would be very obliged if you would aid my younger sister to overcome her retiring manner in company. I—I do not mean for you to hang upon her sleeve or anything of that sort, of course, but—"

"I understand perfectly." Mr. Hawkins smiled down at the lady reassuringly, thinking that she had the air of a small anxious hen with one chick. "I was once myself terrified of society. It is the worst feeling imaginable. I have every sympathy for Miss Maria, believe me."

Miss Sparrow smiled her gratitude. "Thank you, sir. I had hoped that I might find a sympathetic ear in you. You seem to engender trust, as I could certainly see when Evelyn and I chanced to meet you and the viscount."

"Miss Dower has an open and engaging manner," said Mr. Hawkins.

Miss Sparrow's blue eyes suddenly sharpened on him, becoming very earnest in expression. "You must believe me when I say that I have not known Evelyn to be so easy in her manners with any gentleman before."

Mr. Hawkins recognized that Miss Sparrow was attempting to correct any erroneous conclusions about Miss Dower that might have been drawn by himself or Viscount Waithe. It said much of the quality and depth of the friendship that was enjoyed between the young ladies. "I assure you, Miss Sparrow, I have nothing but the utmost respect for Miss Dower. On the contrary, as I come to know her, I am increasingly aware of her fine qualities. As for his lordship, you may rest easy there as well. I suspect that Lord Waithe has been greatly impressed by Miss Dower's attributes."

"Yes, so I, too, have noticed."

Miss Sparrow nodded at the coterie that was protesting the good fortune of one of their number, who was leading a laughing Miss Dower out onto the floor. "Evelyn is quite the belle with the gentlemen this evening. I had told her how it would be, of course. I do not think that it will be long before we hear the announcement of a betrothal." She looked up in time to catch a glimpse of an odd expression in her companion's eyes. It was so quickly gone that she thought she must have been mistaken.

"Perhaps not, indeed," said Mr. Hawkins in a noncommittal voice.

Mr. Fiddle returned with Miss Maria and the offering of a lemon ice for his betrothed. "I did not forget that you, too, enjoy such refreshment, my dear," he said gruffly, with almost an embarrassed air.

Miss Sparrow accepted the ice with blushing pleasure. She had not often in her life had her partialities catered to in such a fashion. The expression in her eyes was shyly adoring as she looked up into her betrothed's face. "Oh, thank you! Of course it is just what I most desired."

Mr. Fiddle turned red about the ears with gratification.

Out of politeness, Mr. Hawkins remained with the trio for a few minutes. He deliberately directed some of his comments to Miss Sparrow's young sister and encouraged her whenever she managed a strangled word or two. It was not long before Miss Maria had forgotten her tongue-tied awkwardness with him and began chattering happily about the party.

"It is beyond anything great! I have never before attended such a fashionable squeeze," she confided, her blue eyes sparkling with awe.

"You will be enjoying many more such functions in future," said Mr. Hawkins, smiling at the girl's naive breathlessness.

Miss Maria's eyes rounded. She glanced swiftly at her sister for confirmation. "Shall I really, Abigail?"

Miss Sparrow also smiled, her amusement accompanied by a fond glance. "Indeed you will, Maria. I shall inform Mama about your progress this evening and I am certain that she will give her consent to your attending a few more small parties such as this."

"Miss Sparrow, if you would not object, I will introduce Miss Maria to a particular lady known to me who may be

depended upon to take her under her wing," said Mr.
Hawkins.

"Of course, Mr. Hawkins," said Miss Sparrow. There
was a slight intonation of surprise in her voice, but she did
not appear to be alarmed by his suggestion, but merely en-
joined her sister to watch her manners.

Mr. Hawkins led away Miss Maria and brought her to
the notice of a matronly acquaintance whom he knew
would treat the shy young miss with kindness. He had met
the lady, an acquaintance of his grandmother's, in the
Pump Room, and during their brief conversation he had
learned all the news about the lady's two stalwart sons. He
had thought it would be a good thing if Miss Maria was to
become acquainted with a few young gentlemen around her
own age so that she could begin to feel more confident on
her own in mixed company.

His obligation to Miss Sparrow fully discharged, he
began to mingle again among the other guests. Though he
smiled and held polite conversation with several personages, he was ever alert to the possibility of catching Miss
Dower between partners in order to solicit her hand. It was
undoubtedly too late to be favored with a dance, but he
hoped that she had not yet been asked for dinner.

Miss Sparrow's earlier observation was never far out of
his thoughts. He found that it perturbed him to hear that
Miss Sparrow, who was obviously a close friend, could
predict with such certainty that Miss Dower would soon be
betrothed.

Perhaps he was too complacent in concluding that he had
little to be anxious about in presenting his suit to Miss
Dower. He had assumed that because he was not a callow
youth nor an octogenarian he would be one of the most
likely gentlemen to catch her interest. Yet what did he
know of a young lady's preferences, and particularly of
Miss Dower's?

Certainly it did not appear that she felt any lack for his
company, he thought, a shade grimly. Miss Dower had not
been given a single moment off the dance floor. The instant
one set ended, a new partner appeared at her side and swept
her back as the music again struck up.

As he watched the activity of that evening, he became

even more convinced that he had allowed his confidence to betray him into complacency. Miss Dower appeared impartially appreciative of the attentions that were paid her. He could not assume that she would not do the same with himself.

Mr. Hawkins discovered that a streak of jealousy was stirred in him whenever he witnessed Miss Dower bestow a smile upon another gentleman. Though never having experienced the emotion before, he had no difficulty in identifying it. It did take him by surprise, however. He had not thought himself capable of such a base emotion, especially in connection with the high regard that he held for Miss Dower. He knew that it was unworthy, but he could not shake himself of it.

Even more than jealousy, however, he felt a stab of unexpected fear. He feared that the gentlemen he had dismissed so perfunctorily might appear quite different in the estimation of a young lady of untouched heart.

Mr. Hawkins's perturbed thoughts were not aided when Sir Charles came up beside him.

"The little Dower is quite the flame for the moths this evening. And with some reason," commented Sir Charles, his dark eyes on the lady in question.

Mr. Hawkins glanced sharply at his friend. "Do not tell me that you are infatuated."

Sir Charles smiled. He gave the slightest of shrugs. "Unlike Percy, I never fatigue myself with such all-consuming emotion. However, it cannot be denied that Miss Dower possesses an intriguing beauty. Perhaps it is worth pursuing." He looked at Mr. Hawkins, his hooded eyes gleaming. "You do not dance, Peter?"

"I have not the desire," said Mr. Hawkins shortly.

Sir Charles nodded. "True, it is an exertion like any other. The effort hardly outweighs the energy one must put into it. Yet, it does have worth, for the ladies, for some peculiar reason known only to themselves, set store by a gentleman's talents in that direction. At any rate, it seems to greatly appeal to Miss Dower."

"Miss Dower is naturally like any other young lady just out," said Mr. Hawkins.

"It is your thought that she might eventually become

jaded by the exercise? I do not agree, my friend. Miss Dower is a lively beauty not easily contained. As such, her favor must naturally fall upon a gentleman of social address and grace who can lavish these attentions upon her. This society boasts few gentlemen of our caliber, but I do not rule out the energy of these youthful sprigs, nor the entice-ment that wafts about a dodder's bank account. It is not un-known for the older gentleman to possess the dashing young beauty and show a tolerant face at her subsequent in-discretions."

"Have done with your philosophizing, Charles. It sets my teeth on edge," said Mr. Hawkins abruptly.

Sir Charles sighed. "How extraordinary that one so un-flappable as yourself can admit to excess imagination. You are excessively bad company this evening, Peter. One must in truth wonder why." With a mocking smile, he excused himself.

Mr. Hawkins nodded. He was not at all put about at his friend's departure. If the truth were told, he was relieved. He had not cared for Sir Charles's observations. They had tallied uncomfortably close with his own and only served to underscore his sudden doubts about his chances with Miss Dower.

Chapter Eleven

If Mr. Hawkins could have but known it, his fears were very nearly groundless. Though Evelyn was thoroughly enjoying the admiration of several assorted gentlemen, her eyes strayed more than once after a certain tall figure.

When Evelyn had greeted Mr. Hawkins in the receiving line, she had been struck at once by how elegant he appeared. The exquisite cut of his dark evening coat had magnificently set off his broad shoulders; his stark white cravat flattered the line of his firm jaw and deepened the tan of his face; his silk waistcoat mutely testified to the expanse of his chest; and his close-fitting pantaloons emphasized the long, clean length of his limbs.

Evelyn had felt her pulse leap in response to the sheer virile masculinity that he embodied. It was a pity that Mr. Hawkins was too passive to determine upon his own bride because otherwise he was everything that she had ever dared to hope for in a gentleman.

An admiring glint in his eyes had told her that he was at least as impressed with her own appearance. She had seen when his glance lingered on the intriguing neckline of her gown before rising to her face. She had hoped that she had not betrayed her perception by too obvious a blush.

She had expected Mr. Hawkins to pay court to her at least once, if for no other reason than it was the conventional thing to do upon a lady's come-out. She could always depend upon Mr. Hawkins to behave with perfect propriety, she thought with an inner smile. Her confidence had been further underpinned by that singular appreciation that she had seen in his eyes. Evelyn awaited him with close-held breath, wondering whether he would unbend enough to compliment her on her fine appearance. Despite other claims of her, she unobtrusively managed to keep watch for Mr. Hawkins's approach.

However, Mr. Hawkins had not instantly sought her company. He had instead stood about talking with her friends and then had taken Maria Sparrow off on his arm. Maria Sparrow, who was still in the schoolroom! Evelyn could scarcely believe it. Why, it was a positive insult to be thought of as of less importance than a schoolroom chit. After that upsetting sight, she had not glanced again in Mr. Hawkins's direction.

Even as she laughed and danced with several partners, she inwardly fumed over the insult that she perceived for herself. Once again, Mr. Hawkins had dealt in an awkward manner where she was concerned. What was more, he did not grant her the courtesy of letting her convey her displeasure to him.

The gentleman was positively impossible, she thought, not really certain what she desired most. The opportunity to give Mr. Hawkins the set-down that he so richly deserved would give her considerable satisfaction. But she was as strongly tempted to prove to him that she was worthy of more than his grandmother's recommendation as a bride. She had a heart, and she had a right to be wooed. Anyone with the least intelligence could certainly see that others agreed.

As she was escorted from the floor yet again, Evelyn thanked her partner.

"The pleasure was mine, I assure you, Miss Dower," he said, leading her toward the chair that she had scarce occupied all the evening.

Evelyn glanced up into the gentleman's face, making a laughing rejoinder as she turned away. As she did so, she practically collided with a second gentleman. Embarrassed, a swift tide of color sweeping her face, she attempted to disentangle herself. "Oh! I do beg your pardon!"

Sir Charles steadied her with a hand under her elbow. He smiled down, his eyes lingering on the soft flush in her cheeks. He said softly, "My fault entirely, Miss Dower, I do assure you. I was in hopes of soliciting your lovely hand for this next set."

Evelyn was acutely aware of the intensity of his dark gaze. It inexplicably unnerved her, even as on the first occasion that she had met the gentleman. "Sir Charles, I—"

"Miss Dower is fortunately my partner this set." Viscount Waithe's voice was cheerful as he appeared beside them. He grinned at Sir Charles in a friendly way, but with a determined glint in his eyes. "Take yourself off, sirrah."

Sir Charles bowed. "I must yield the field."

His glance caught Evelyn's, entangling her in its power. Her heart missed a beat.

"This time," he said silkily. He sauntered off.

Evelyn turned almost with relief to the viscount. At least she knew where she stood with his lordship. "My lord."

Her expression was such that Viscount Waithe raised his brows. "What is it, Miss Dower? You appeared a little uncomfortable just now with Sir Charles."

"I find Sir Charles somewhat . . . overpowering," she admitted.

Viscount Waithe laughed as he led her onto the dance floor. "Yes, so he can be to those who are less well acquainted with him than his intimates. Sir Charles is even something of a legend in some circles."

Evelyn was made curious. "Sir Charles a legend? How do you mean, my lord?"

"Well, as you may have readily observed, Sir Charles is what is known as an Exquisite. I do not think I have ever seen him with a hair out of place or with a crease in his coat," said Viscount Waithe.

"But that, surely, is not the stuff of legends," said Evelyn.

The movement of the dance separated her from the viscount and when they came together again he had obviously thought over her observation. "It is Sir Charles's way with horses more than anything else, you see. He is a consummate whip," he said.

"Oh well then!" said Evelyn on a laugh. "Sir Charles must definitely meet my friend, Miss Woodthorpe, for I am certain that there is nothing she admires more in a gentleman than a proper understanding of horseflesh. I shall introduce them at the first opportunity." She smiled warmly at the viscount. "You must meet her as well, my lord, for she is quite one of my dearest friends. I know that you shall like her."

"I will be honored," said Viscount Waithe, smiling down

at her. His thoughts had nothing to do with the pleasure of becoming acquainted with Miss Dower's friends, however.

Standing off to one side in order to observe the country dance, Mr. Hawkins could readily interpret the expression that he glimpsed on the viscount's amiable face. His mouth tightened momentarily, before he gave a barely perceptible shrug of resignation. He had not really expected his road to the winning of Miss Dower's heart to be an easy one, after all. His cousin's newfound infatuation was simply part and parcel of the whole.

If he was fortunate, and he had always thought of himself as being so, the viscount would follow his habitual pattern, and the present feverish infatuation that his lordship felt for Miss Dower would swiftly cool to friendly indifference. That would be the least complicated outcome in regard to the viscount.

Unless, of course, Miss Dower was inclined to take Viscount Waithe's present devotion in too serious a vein.

In that instance, Mr. Hawkins thought that even at the risk of encroaching upon his friendship with his cousin, he must try to somehow turn the viscount's thoughts elsewhere. If he did not, then his lordship's furious flirtation would more than likely burn itself out at cost to Miss Dower's sensitive heart. Mr. Hawkins felt that if it was in his power to do so he would shield her from such disillusionment, but at the moment he did not perceive what he could do.

"Mr. Hawkins, such a prodigious frown! I do hope that you do not find the evening disagreeable."

Mr. Hawkins turned to find his hostess surveying him with a somewhat anxious expression. He smiled, effectively lightening his countenance. In an expression of ruefulness, he said, "Not at all, Mrs. Dower. It is only that I seem to be neatly cut out each time I detect an opportunity to pay my compliments to the lady whose evening it is. I shall confide in you, ma'am, that I have hopes of persuading Miss Dower to accept my escort in to dinner."

Mrs. Dower smiled up at the gentleman's twinkling eyes. "It is very bad," she agreed. "You are, after all, quite one of our favorite acquaintances." She lowered her voice in a conspiratorial fashion. "Leave it to me, Mr. Hawkins."

The set was at that moment coming to an end. Mrs.

Dower slipped her hand into Mr. Hawkins's arm and urged him forward to intercept her daughter and the viscount as they left the floor.

"Oh, Lord Waithe! There you are. You must forgive me for not visiting with you already this evening. Pray, will you be so kind to allow me to make up for my deficiency by adjoining with me to the refreshments? I discover that I am parched with thirst," said Mrs. Dower.

"Certainly, ma'am," said Viscount Waithe courteously.

In almost the blink of an eye, Mrs. Dower had whisked the viscount off, leaving behind with Mr. Hawkins the laughing admonition to see that her daughter was well looked after.

"I assure you that I shall do my utmost best, ma'am," he said on the ghost of a laugh. He was still smiling when he looked down at Miss Dower. "At last I have the opportunity that I have been awaiting all evening, to tell you how very lovely you are tonight."

Evelyn blushed, caught by surprise at the unexpectedness of his gallantry. She wondered at his unusual forwardness as she met his intent glance. "That is a vastly pretty compliment, sir."

"But only the first of many, if you will but consent to do me the honor of joining me for dinner," he said.

Evelyn hesitated as the unbidden thought came to her mind that Lady Pomerancy must surely have coached him for days in just how best to approach her. But perhaps she was not giving the gentleman credit when it was due. Perhaps, she thought, perhaps he had not needed any prodding in this instance.

"You do not yet have a dinner partner, Miss Dower, I hope?"

"No, but—" At his quizzical look, Evelyn gave a small laugh. She yielded to the curiosity that had risen in her at his invitation. What lady could reject the prospect of being paid court. "Thank you, Mr. Hawkins. I would be delighted with your escort at dinner."

With a lopsided smile, as though he had guessed the reason for her reluctance, Mr. Hawkins offered his arm to her. Accepting it, Evelyn allowed him to lead her into the dining room.

Chapter Twelve

Mrs. Dower had rejected the notion of a formal table and had instead arranged that the room adjoining the small ballroom to be set up with several seatings and a buffet supper, so that as her guests were inclined to do so they could adjoin to the impromptu dining room where they could be served in intimate groups. The result assured an air of comfortable intimacy to the large gathering and was greatly admired, as was evidenced by various comments that could be overheard.

If Mr. Hawkins hoped to enjoy something of a tête à tête with Miss Dower, his ambitions were speedily dashed.

Miss Sparrow and her sister Maria were already seated at one table, the remains of their supper evident on the plates before them. Miss Sparrow, espying Evelyn and Mr. Hawkins, immediately waved them over.

"Do join us, Evelyn! Mr. Hawkins, surely you have met Miss Woodthorpe and her brother, John?"

Acknowledging Miss Sparrow's greeting and Maria's shy smile, Mr. Hawkins glanced at the other two occupants at the table. Seated beside Miss Woodthorpe was a gentleman whose youthful countenance bore a strong resemblance to the lady's own. "I have not previously had that pleasure, no."

"Miss Woodthorpe and John are two of my particular friends," said Evelyn, glancing up at her escort's face.

She felt a half beat of disappointment when his expression did not reflect some annoyance that he was not to have her company to himself. Evelyn inwardly sighed, knowing it would hardly have been in character for the gentleman to be so rude as to reveal any such thing in light of her declaration.

Instead, Mr. Hawkins said all that was pleasant as he seated her at the table. Then he inquired after Evelyn's preferences and excused himself to go fetch a plate for her and himself.

Evelyn watched him go, and when she turned her head back to her friends, she discovered that Miss Sparrow and Miss Woodthorpe were both looking at her with varying degrees of amusement in their expressions. "I shan't hear a word from either of you," she said defensively.

"I would not dream of it, Evelyn," said Miss Woodthorpe.

"Nor I," said Miss Sparrow gravely, then marred her solemnity by the lightest of laughs. "I do think Mr. Hawkins is the dearest of gentlemen, however. The lady who entertains his suit will be exceptionally fortunate."

"Oh yes, indeed. He is ever so kind. I should like to marry him myself," said Maria with a vigorous nod.

"What a thing to say! Why, you're just a baby," said John Woodthorpe in surprise.

Maria threw a mutinous look at him. "I am quite sixteen and very nearly out. And I have already been assured that I have the admiration of two gentlemen, at least."

John Woodthorpe made a derisive sound.

Maria flushed. "It is true! Mrs. Culpepper's sons paid me the most lovely compliments."

"Ned and Robert Culpepper? Are you daft? Why, they are the greatest gudgeons alive. I shouldn't want *my* sisters to receive their attentions," said John with brutal honesty.

Maria burst into tears. "Oh, you are horrid, horrid!"

At once, Miss Sparrow put her arms about the younger girl, speaking to her soothingly. "Never mind, Maria. I am certain the Culpeppers are as esteemable as one could wish. Young gentlemen often speak critically of their peers, never meaning the half of what is said."

"Well, I like that!" exclaimed John indignantly. "I have been truthful as can be."

"John, that is quite enough," said Miss Woodthorpe.

The young gentleman appealed to his sister. "Well, but it is true! You know it is. Ned and Robert have always been pattern cards of the stiffest respectability and jobbers to boot."

Miss Sparrow rose, her arms still about her sister's shoulders so that she drew the weeping Maria from her chair as well. "I think that I shall take Maria upstairs for a few moments to compose herself. It has been such a very exciting evening. Evelyn, if Mr. Fiddle should return before I do, will you tell him where I have gone?"

"Of course I shall," said Evelyn sympathetically.

Miss Sparrow smiled at her gratefully and led her sister away.

Miss Woodthorpe gave her younger brother a rakedown for his indiscretion. "Whatever your own feelings, John, you should not have paraded them so emphatically. I do think that Maria is owed an apology."

"Yes, of course," he muttered. He jerkily excused himself, his thin face flushed, and went off.

Miss Woodthorpe coolly looked over at Evelyn and raised a slender brow. "Well, the sensitive topic of Mr. Hawkins was conveniently passed over, was it not?"

Evelyn spluttered on a laugh. "Yes, perhaps it was," she owned. "But I shan't say more than that, Pol."

"I did not expect that you would," said Miss Woodthorpe imperturbably.

Mr. Hawkins returned, accompanied by Viscount Waithe. Evelyn introduced the viscount to Miss Woodthorpe and explained the sudden lessening of numbers of their party. The remainder of dinner was very pleasant and uninterrupted except for Mr. Fiddle's reappearance. Once apprised of the situation, however, that gentleman went off again in search of the Misses Sparrow.

Evelyn did not expect that Mr. Hawkins would claim her company further once dinner was done with, but he surprised her again by requesting her hand in a set.

"If you wish it, Mr. Hawkins," she said.

"I wish for nothing else but this particular honor," said Mr. Hawkins gravely.

Evelyn was aware at once of Miss Woodthorpe's amusement and the viscount's slight frown. She knew that Mr. Hawkins's statement had fueled her friend's speculations, but there was nothing that she could do to remedy the impression. As for Viscount Waithe, though his expression was pleasant and gave no further hint of his thoughts, Evelyn suspected that he felt somewhat abandoned. She was confident, however, that Miss Woodthorpe would keep Viscount Waithe sufficiently entertained, and she went away in good spirits with her hand laid on Mr. Hawkins's elbow.

Evelyn discovered that Mr. Hawkins was a superb dancer. "You astound me, sir. Is there no end to your perfections?" she asked.

Mr. Hawkins looked down at her and gave her a smile of such dazzling charm that she blinked. "I do believe that is the first compliment that you have ever paid me, Miss Dower."

"Oh no, surely not," said Evelyn, her color heightening.

"I assure you that it is. I hope to elicit several more accolades from you before the Season is finished," said Mr. Hawkins, still smiling.

There was a certain warm intensity in his gaze that made Evelyn's heart flutter. "I believe it is the lady who is generally thought to harbor such hopes," she said.

"But you are an unusual lady, Miss Dower, as I trust that you will acknowledge one day," said Mr. Hawkins quietly. "I have never laid my heart at the feet of any other."

Evelyn stiffened in his arms. Her eyes flashed at him. "Indeed, sir! I can well imagine that you have not, if her ladyship had anything to say of the matter."

Mr. Hawkins appeared a good deal astonished. "What do you mean, Miss Dower?"

The music came to an end. Evelyn instantly moved apart from him. "I believe you know very well, Mr. Hawkins. And I assure you that I wish no part of such a scheme. I am sorry to wound you, Mr. Hawkins, but I could never accept your suit knowing what I know."

She started to turn away, but she was caught fast by her elbow. She looked up, astonished that the correct Mr. Hawkins would so detain her. She was even more surprised by the grimness of his expression. "Sir!" she directed a meaningful glance down at his fingers clasped about her arm.

"I apologize for my heavy-handedness, Miss Dower. However, I should like to hear what it is that you say you know," he said. He gestured courteously with his free hand, as though requesting her company, but the pressure of his fingers left little doubt in Evelyn's mind that he was quite determined that she accompany him.

Evelyn threw another glance up at his profile when she realized that he was drawing her over to a settee against the wall. She could scarcely believe that this most proper of gentlemen would actually dare to defy convention in even such a small matter.

"Pray be seated, Miss Dower."

Evelyn sat down, perforce because she did not wish to make a scene, but she sat bolt upright with her hands held tight in her lap. Her eyes lowered, she said, "I do not wish to discuss this matter with you, Mr. Hawkins."

"Nevertheless, Miss Dower, you may begin with your reference to my grandmother. That is apparently the crux," he said quietly.

Evelyn rounded on him, stung out of proportion by his reasonable tone. "How could it be otherwise, sir? I was never more insulted in my life. And that you fell in with her ladyship's suggestion with the greatest of indifference—! I suppose it would not have mattered if I had been squint-eyed and possessed of a madwoman's temperament, as long as I had Lady Pomerancy's stamp of approval!"

Mr. Hawkins regarded her with the beginning dawn of understanding, which became swiftly intermingled with amusement. "My dear Miss Dower, I assure you that was not quite the way things proceeded."

Evelyn was further incensed by the springing of laughter into his eyes. "Oh, naturally not! I imagine that her lady-ship had only to present to you how very *proper* such a match would be," she retorted.

Mr. Hawkins had the audacity to laugh.

She rose hastily from the settee. "Excuse me, Mr. Hawkins. I must not neglect my mother's other guests." She swept past him, her head held high.

Evelyn's wrist was caught in a gentle yet commanding grasp. Evelyn was consternated as she turned to face the gentleman. More and more Mr. Hawkins was surprising her, throwing her increasingly off balance. "Unhand me!" she hissed softly.

"I do not think so, Miss Dower. You have thrown a hard

accusation in my teeth. I ask that you do me the courtesy of finishing this conversation," said Mr. Hawkins. "Pray sit down again, Miss Dower."

Evelyn regarded him with some resentment. She glanced down at the imprisoning fingers about her wrist. "I have little choice but to do so, it seems."

Mr. Hawkins smiled slightly, even regretfully. "Believe me, this is not my usual style."

Evelyn resumed her place on the settee. She lifted a significant brow as he let go of her. She rubbed her wrist, though it felt not so much pained from his fingers as it did branded. "No, it is not, Mr. Hawkins. I am profoundly shocked, I assure you."

"No more than I, Miss Dower. I was not aware of several things about myself until this evening," said Mr. Hawkins reflectively. At her look of impatient confusion, he smiled. "Forgive me, ma'am. I digress to little purpose, it seems. Pray continue. You were on the point of explaining your aversion to my suit."

"How could it be otherwise, Mr. Hawkins? A lady prefers to know that she is the gentleman's choice, not the object of a proposed marriage of convenience," said Evelyn tightly, not looking at his face.

There was a short silence. When she dared to glance up, it was to meet a contemplative regard from his blue eyes. Evelyn felt herself flush. "I am sorry to put it so baldly, sir."

"I am glad that you did so, Miss Dower." Mr. Hawkins was silent a moment, then sighed. "Miss Dower, I wish to assure you that it has ever been my choice to court you."

Evelyn was discomfited. "I did not mean to imply that you did so under false pretenses, Mr. Hawkins."

"No."

She looked up quickly. The expression in his eyes was somber. The amazing thought came to her that she could have been mistaken. Perhaps he did care for her.

Evelyn bent her head, feeling more vulnerable than she ever had. Carefully she pleated her skirt. "I—I wanted only to be assured of your true regard." With shortened breath she awaited his reply. Surely with such blatant encouragement he would declare himself.

"Quite."

"Oh!" Bitter disappointment flooded her, dashing her trembling hopes. Evelyn sprang up. "You are utterly impossible!" She ran away across the dance floor, her progress noted by curious glances.

Mr. Hawkins did not follow her.

For the next hour, Evelyn was careful not to be unattended so that Mr. Hawkins would not have an opportunity to pursue their abortive conversation. However, that gentleman did not seem the least inclined to do so. Instead, Mr. Hawkins led out several ladies, both young and old, and to all appearances enjoyed himself. Evelyn was by turns infuriated or felt herself driven perilously close to tears by Mr. Hawkins's seeming indifference toward her. She did not know whether she was glad or unhappy when he finally took his leave, but she put on a bright smile to show him how utterly inconsequential his leave-taking was to her.

Soon after Mr. Hawkins's departure, other guests also began to make their excuses. Evelyn was astonished that the hours were so swift to depart, but she was not altogether regretting that it was so. She had never been in such a whirl and the unaccustomed excitement inevitably took its toll of her.

By the end of the evening, Mrs. Dower was flushed with the success of the dinner party. "You are well and truly launched, Evelyn! I do not think that I ever saw you without at least one gentleman in attendance. And the kind words and the invitations that I received on your behalf! Why, we shall be quite run off our feet with all the treats in store, I promise you."

"I am happy to hear it, Mama," said Evelyn, covering a wide yawn. "But truthfully, it matters little to me at the moment."

"You are exhausted, poor dear, and no wonder," said Mrs. Dower sympathetically. "Go up to your bed now and catch as much sleep as you possibly can, for tomorrow we shall receive innumerable callers."

"Do you truly think so?"

"Depend upon it, dearest. You have made an impression on our little society. I dare say we shall not have a moment to ourselves, nor shall we be able to set foot outside to make our own visits," said Mrs. Dower in a surprisingly dry tone.

"But what of you, Mama? Are you not taking tea with Lady Pomerancy tomorrow?" asked Evelyn.

Mrs. Dower was dismayed. "Oh dear, I had quite forgotten!" Deep gloom settled onto her countenance as she contemplated her fate. Suddenly her expression lightened and an artless laugh escaped her. "I fear that I shall be forced to send my excuses to her ladyship, Evelyn. Certainly I cannot neglect my duty and leave my daughter unchaperoned whilst she receives gentlemen callers."

"You are a complete hand, Mama," said Evelyn, marveling at that lady's ingenuity.

Chapter Thirteen

Evelyn's come-out was marked by singular success. There followed a delightful round of parties, teas, soirees, and picnics. Evelyn knew herself to be a social success and it was a heady feeling. Gentlemen came to call or sent sweet nosegays. They flocked flatteringly about her at routs and assemblies. Several gentlemen even professed themselves to be at her feet, including two or three whose declarations truly astonished her.

One of these was Miss Woodthorpe's young brother, John.

The Woodthorpes had come to call, bearing a gift from the manor. Mrs. Dower could scarce wait to give to her gardener the rose slips sent by the squire's wife. When Miss Woodthorpe and their elder brother accompanied Mrs. Dower out into the garden, John seized the opportunity offered him by fate and declared himself to Evelyn.

Evelyn was stunned when John grabbed her hands, flung himself on his knees before her, and launched an impassioned accolade to her eyes. "John!" she spluttered, laughing.

John looked up at her, considerably annoyed. "Is that any way to treat a fellow who is pouring out his heart to you?"

"You haven't the least feeling for me and I know it," retorted Evelyn. She pulled her hands free and begged, "Do be sensible, John. We've known one another simply forever."

He got up, somewhat sheepishly. "I've little taste for making a cake of myself, but dash it, you've become the high kick of fashion, Evelyn, so what else is a fellow to do?"

"Have I really?" Evelyn asked, a smile teasing at her lips.

John Woodthorpe flashed a wide, knowing grin. "As if you don't already know it! Why, you are the envy of all the other females of my acquaintance, including my own mother, because you've attached these three fine London gentlemen to your skirts as well."

Evelyn hastened to disabuse him of the mistaken notion that she had done any such thing. "Oh, but Mr. Hawkins is too utterly polite *not* to ply his gallantries, while Lord Waithe and I are only the very best of friends."

John looked askance at her, totally disbelieving. His voice heavy with sarcasm, he said, "And I suppose that very cool customer Sir Charles is to be relegated to the same category as that importune artist I discovered here last week mooning over how the light fell 'so pleasurably across your alabaster brow'!"

Evelyn laughed at his disgusted tone, even as faint color rose in her face. She shook her head. "Hardly that, no." She would not say so to John Woodthorpe, even though he was one of her oldest boon companions, but in the last few weeks she had become altogether too aware of the gentleman in question.

Her companion's brows rose at her reticence. "Well, I see that I shall get nothing more out of you on that score," he said.

"No, you shan't," said Evelyn coolly, even as her thoughts turned. She had heard much about Sir Charles from Viscount Waithe and others, and she had found all of it to be fascinating.

Sir Charles Reginald was an Exquisite, every inch the Tulip, a Pink of the *Ton*. His fastidiousness in dress and fashion was known to be considerable, and his way of tying a neckcloth was closely scrutinized by those who aspired to dandyism. He was said to be deadly with a pistol, and even though he disliked the sweat and exertion required by the sport of fencing, he was a match for any of the half-dozen known masters of the blade.

His greatest claim to admiration and envy, however, was his uncanny ability with horses. Even amongst those of his peers who also indulged a passion for excellent horseflesh and equipages, Sir Charles was something of a legend. He was a member in good standing of the Four-Horse Club, and his yellow-bodied phaeton and team of bays were said to be among the most expensive, and quite the fastest, in all England. There was no one now who cared to challenge him to a race, for he got more out of his team then could any other driver. In short, Sir Charles Reginald was a consummate whip.

All this and more Evelyn had heard, but little of it had made as great an impression upon her as had the gentleman's personality. Upon first making Sir Charles's acquaintance, she had been thrown off balance by him. All that she consequently heard only confirmed her startled conviction that Sir Charles Reginald was destined to be important to her life.

She had learned for herself of Sir Charles's perfect turn of phrase and his exquisite compliments, for he quickly made her the prime object of his gallantry.

While Viscount Waithe was soulful in countenance and anxious to please in his attentions, his compliments seemed clumsy in comparison to Sir Charles's urbanity. Sir Charles with his dry, quick wit, his lingering eyes, and his double entendres had the power to set her pulses to tumbling in confusion.

On the very heel of Evelyn's thoughts, the viscount and Sir Charles were announced and her heart leaped. She hardly heard John Woodthorpe's resigned mutter as she rose to greet the two London gentlemen. "My lord, Sir Charles! This is a pleasant surprise indeed."

Viscount Waithe saluted her hand in a lingering fashion. "You are in exquisite looks today, Miss Dower."

Evelyn laughed gaily. "I shall not take you so fully to task for exaggeration as I should, my lord. I shall only say that you are a great deal too kind."

"One can never exaggerate your beauty, Miss Dower," said Viscount Waithe fervently.

Evelyn laughed again. She had remained flattered by Viscount Waithe's admiration and she genuinely enjoyed his company. However, she preferred to think of him with all the fondness of a younger sister, much as she had always regarded John Woodthorpe.

Though she suspected that Viscount Waithe was enamored of her, she had never been tempted to think of his lordship in those same terms, and because his lordship did not press the issue she could persuade herself the majority of the time that the viscount was simply being terribly kind in playing the part of a devoted admirer. At least, she preferred to believe it was so.

Evelyn turned then to offer her hand to Sir Charles, appreciation in her eyes for the picture that he presented to the world. His dark hair was carefully curled, the height of his stiffly starched shirtpoints were fashionably exaggerated, his silk waistcoat was palest yellow, and his well-cut coat spanned a generous breadth of shoulder. If his unusual height or the thinness of his long shanks did not perfectly conform to the epitome of fashion's taste, it was generally agreed that his polite manners, his quick wit, and courtly flirtations more than made up for these deficiencies.

She smiled up at him. "Sir Charles, welcome."

"The warmth of your greeting is all one could ever require, Miss Dower," he said. He bowed over her hand, his lips deliberately brushing her fingers.

The color rose in her face and Evelyn thought propriety would be best served if she should retrieve her hand. As she did so, the gentleman smiled at her. Evelyn had the uncomfortable feeling that he was well aware of how he always managed to overset her, and she felt a prick of annoyance.

"Pray be seated, gentlemen. My mother stepped out into the garden for a few moments, but she will be back directly and will be most pleased to discover that you have come to call."

The gentlemen expressed themselves happy to wait on Mrs. Dower's return and acknowledged John Woodthorpe's greeting. The conversation settled into general talk of the weather and other mundane topics, and even as Evelyn did her part as hostess, smiling and adding a few words when warranted, her thoughts were otherwise occupied.

Sir Charles Reginald, with his lazy sardonic smile and his enigmatic gaze, most nearly fit her ideal of the romantic hero.

Evelyn had begun to weave little fantasies about Sir Charles, casting him into whatever contretemps her fertile imagination and the ample inspiration provided by her reading of romances could provide. Always Sir Charles won through all obstacles in his heroic exertions to rescue the fair maiden, whose role was naturally that of her own.

Sir Charles took the opening given him by a short discourse between the viscount and John Woodthorpe to hand her a slender roll of parchment bound by a thin satin ribbon. "A small offering of my eternal devotion," he said softly.

Evelyn accepted it and slid it into her pocket for later perusal. "Thank you, sir. You must know that I always appreciate your verses," she said equally quietly.

The enigmatic look in his eyes momentarily shortened her breath, and she looked away hastily. Evelyn felt some relief when her mother and the Woodthorpes returned at that moment, for as always Sir Charles had put her out of countenance.

Evelyn treasured the sonnets and verses that Sir Charles presented to her. If she had known with what carelessness he dashed them off, or that his past masterpieces were generously scattered among several of the ladies of London, she might have been less awestruck at receiving them. But she did not know, and so she attributed Sir Charles's offerings with a uniqueness that was quite wide of the mark.

Mr. Peter Hawkins might still embody her romantic ideal in physical appearance. Even at the height of her gudgeon, she had never found fault with his tall, athletic build, his handsome face, or the charm of his smile. His vivid blue eyes were perhaps, at times, more knowing than she liked, but nevertheless the expression in his glance always warmed her. Oh, indeed, Mr. Hawkins was still very much the picture of romance.

However, Sir Charles had breathed the very essence of life into it.

Through the past weeks, she had gained a greater understanding into Peter Hawkin's character, and she admired and respected him. She knew now that she had gravely underestimated his interest in her. Upon reflection of their conversation at her come-out, she had come to understand that it had not been at Lady Pomerancy's urging that he had offered for her. Her mother had simply misstated the matter to her. Evelyn faced the unmistakable. It had been her stung pride that had prevented her from divining the truth. If she had not been so blinded, she would certainly have questioned her mother more closely, for she knew that lady's disorganized communication style too well.

However, that was all long past and done. The mistake could not be recalled. She had only her own remembered embarrassment to remind her how idiotic she had acted toward Mr. Hawkins, for he had not once alluded to her behavior.

Nor had he renewed his offer for her hand, said a tiny voice in her head.

Evelyn ignored it, as she reflected upon the other thing that had so turned around her opinion of Mr. Hawkins. She had learned from Viscount Waithe that Mr. Hawkins had once contemplated taking orders. When he had told it to her, Evelyn had stared at his lordship in such astonishment that he had sworn it was true.

"My cousin is a very good sort, you know. I've never known a truer gentleman," said Viscount Waithe.

"But why—?"

The viscount had smiled, a little lopsidedly. "Why did he not after all? Peter deemed himself to be too deficient in character for service in the Church. My cousin understands himself and his failings better than any other gentleman I can name, which, as I told him, is a genuine treasure for a man of the cloth. But he would have none of it and laughed and said he would have made a mull of it all."

Certainly such an honorable man would never offer her less than an honorable proposal. Evelyn felt an odd regret that she had not understood Mr. Hawkins better then. Perhaps if she had, she would now have been planning for her wedding.

She shook off the faint desolation that rose in her at the thought.

Mr. Peter Hawkins was undoubtedly the type of gentleman that any lady would be very honored to accept as a suitor. But Evelyn knew that he would never whisper sweet, exciting words into her ear, nor would he ever pour out his soul onto paper for her breathless perusal; whereas Sir Charles was quite ready to do both.

Evelyn thought herself to be falling in love with Sir Charles, and she was happy to have it so.

For his part, Mr. Hawkins knew that Sir Charles had made a strong impression on Miss Dower. However, he assured himself that she was not like the London ladies. She was more levelheaded and perceptive of people than most other women of his acquaintance. Despite her inexperience, surely Miss Dower was too sensible not to see through Sir Charles's fulsome compliments and exquisite lovemaking.

That afternoon when he entered the drawing room in his turn, however, it was unpleasantly borne in on him that Miss Dower was not as insusceptible as he had assumed her to be. As he was ushered in, he saw that Mrs. Dower was conversing with Viscount Waithe, Miss Woodthorpe, John Woodthorpe, and another gentleman, who was vaguely familiar to him, while Miss Dower and Sir Charles were seated on a settee a little apart.

In one swift glance, Mr. Hawkins took in the tableau. Viscount Waithe was holding up his end in a conversation that he had no interest in whatsoever, though his upbringing would never allow him to show by word or expression that it was so. Mr. Hawkins, knowing his cousin so well, read through the polite veneer and saw how the viscount's head was canted just slightly so that he could keep Miss Dower and Sir Charles in the corner of his vision.

"Oh, Mr. Hawkins! How delightful of you to join us," said Mrs. Dower. "I believe you must know everyone here?"

Mr. Hawkins nodded to the company, introducing himself to the gentleman seated with Miss Woodthorpe. There was a remarkable similarity in their features, and he shrewdly guessed that the gentleman must be another of Miss Woodthorpe's brothers. Nor was he mistaken.

Mr. Woodthorpe expressed himself pleased to make the gentleman's acquaintance. Mr. Hawkins recognized him to be of a more pompous spirit than either Miss Woodthorpe or the irrepressible John.

Sir Charles nodded upon Mr. Hawkins's entrance, while Evelyn acknowledged his presence with an inquiry into Lady Pomerancy's health.

"Her ladyship is very well, thank you, ma'am," said Mr. Hawkins, regarding the couple thoughtfully.

Mr. Hawkins was aware that Sir Charles Reginald was a ready hand with the ladies. In London, Sir Charles's flirtation had afforded him amusement. However, he did not find his friend's activities quite so amusing as he once had. At first he had been disconcerted that Sir Charles would mark Miss Dower as a pleasant flirt. Then he had realized that anything else would have been even more surprising. Sir Charles Reginald was notorious for his keen eye for a good horse or an alluring woman, and certainly Miss Dower was a beautiful young lady.

As for Miss Dower, an unmistakable rose had mounted in her cheeks, and her eyes sparkled as she laughed at something that Sir Charles said, even as she gently and with obvious reluctance freed her hand from his.

Mr. Hawkins saw how Miss Dower's eyes shone when she gazed up at Sir Charles before her lashes had swept down in modest confusion.

Alarm bells went off in his head. Even as he conversed with Mrs. Dower and the others, his mind worried at the problem at hand. He now knew Sir Charles to be a formidable rival for Miss Dower's affections, and how he was to derail that gentleman's attentions was a tricky question, indeed.

His gaze fell on Mr. Woodthorpe. Mr. Hawkins smiled as he noticed the whip points thrust through the young gentleman's lapel.

Chapter Fourteen

He gestured at the whip points and deliberately pitched his voice to carry. "Are you a driver, Mr. Woodthorpe?"

Mr. Woodthorpe threw out his chest. "Indeed I am, sir. I daresay I have the sweetest goers in the county."

Mr. Hawkins did not need to look around to know that Sir Charles had heard. He could actually feel that gentleman's sudden alert attention. He raised his brows in a show of polite inquiry. "You must tell me about them, Mr. Woodthorpe. I count myself to be but a modest whip. Nonetheless I appreciate a decent team of horseflesh. I shall confess to you, however, that I have yet to see a team that can rival that of my friend, Sir Charles."

Mr. Woodthorpe frowned, quick to catch an implied slight. "I fancy my cattle are the equal of any, Mr. Hawkins. I'd stake them against any comers."

Miss Woodthorpe had been listening curiously, her intelligent gaze all the while fixed on Mr. Hawkins. As she noticed that Sir Charles had openly turned to listen to the conversation, a slight smile touched her lips. She said casually, "I have seen Sir Charles's bays in action, Ned. I do not think that yours could hold a candle to them."

Mr. Woodthorpe glanced quickly at his sister. He was impressed despite himself by her opinion, for he knew her to be an expert judge of horseflesh. Yet he had great pride in his own team, as well as confidence in his own abilities as a driver. It rankled to hear that another man's horses were considered to be the better. "Indeed! Then I should very much like to see the gentleman's team."

As Mr. Hawkins had anticipated, Sir Charles could not resist coming over to join in the conversation.

"What is this, Peter? Have you found a race for me?"

asked Sir Charles. There was a competitive gleam in his eyes. Miss Dower trailed behind, a somewhat puzzled expression in her eyes.

Mr. Hawkins laughed, well satisfied that his ploy had successfully broken up the tête à tête between Miss Dower and Sir Charles. "No, no! Mr. Woodthorpe, who is himself something of a whip and the proud owner of an excellent team, has merely requested the favor of watching your team in action. No one has said anything of a race."

Mr. Woodthorpe possessed strong sporting instincts, and he immediately protested. "Here, now! If it is a question of a race, I am game enough for it." He turned to Sir Charles. "Sir, I would count it an honor to race you."

"You have a race, sir," said Sir Charles instantly.

The gentlemen shook on it, both vastly pleased with the way things had turned out.

"I fear that I must bet against you, Ned," said Miss Woodthorpe.

Her brother threw a startled glance at her. "Pol! I thought you would back my chances in this."

"Yes, and so did I," said John Woodthorpe indignantly. He clapped a hand to his brother's shoulder. "I shall back you, Ned, never fear!"

Miss Woodthorpe gave her deep-throated laugh. She patted her elder brother's arm in a conciliatory fashion "Despite my loyalty as a sister and my solid faith in your skill, I *have* seen Sir Charles's team on the road, and I must tell you that it will be all uphill for you."

"So much the better," said Ned staunchly. "There is nothing I prefer more than a good challenge."

"Well said, sir! Though I must admit to a certain prejudice which forces me to agree with Miss Woodthorpe's assessment of my chances"—Sir Charles made the lady a sweeping bow—"I shall endeavor to make the occasion a memorable one. Perhaps a small wager of twenty pounds would be acceptable to you?"

"Done, Sir Charles!" exclaimed Mr. Woodthorpe, shaking the gentleman's hand with enthusiasm.

"I should like to add to the sporting nature of the occasion, if I may," said Viscount Waithe, having listened to the proceedings with great interest. "I would normally back Sir

Charles against all comers, but in the interest of supporting the local champion, I shall put twenty pounds on Mr. Woodthorpe."

"A mistake, Percy," said Sir Charles, shaking his head.

"Perhaps, but then again it is Mr. Woodthorpe's home turf," said Viscount Waithe with the flash of his boyish grin. He turned to the only gentleman who had not yet made known his preference. "Whom shall it be for you, Peter?"

Mr. Hawkins shrugged his shoulders and with a smile said, "My apologies, Mr. Woodthorpe, but I feel compelled to defend my previous observation regarding Sir Charles's team."

"Not at all, sir. Of course it is understood. A matter of honor and all that," said Mr. Woodthorpe.

Evelyn had listened to the spiraling talk with disbelief. Not moments before, she had been entertaining deliciously outrageous compliments from Sir Charles. Now she stood virtually forgotten by that fascinating gentleman and quite neglected by every other gentleman in the room, including even Viscount Waithe, who could previously have been counted upon to leap forward whenever the opportunity had offered.

Evelyn caught her soft underlip between her teeth in vexation as the gentlemen entered into a discussion to determine when and where the impromptu race was to be held. A quiet suggestion made by Miss Woodthorpe was taken up with enthusiasm, earning her a compliment from Mr. Hawkins for her speedy rendering of a proper solution.

"How prodigiously exciting it all is!" Mrs. Dower exclaimed in Evelyn's ear. "I vow I never thought to hear anything so stimulating discussed at tea. I know young Ned Woodthorpe to be a very skillful driver. Why, he could be naught else coming from that family! Yet Sir Charles for all his dapper ways gives one the impression of complete confidence in his own abilities. I am sure I do not know how to choose between them."

"Nor I, Mama. I wonder that we should bother our heads about it at all," said Evelyn.

Mrs. Dower regarded Evelyn with slight surprise. Her expression altered almost instantly to one of sympathy as understanding came to her. "I *am* sorry, dear! But when gentlemen begin to talk about racing and horses and such, one cannot really expect them to notice one in just the same way as before."

Evelyn felt telltale heat rise in her face. "Really, Mama, you speak as though you suspected me to be in a state of pique. I care not one whit, I assure you," she declared.

Mrs. Dower patted her daughter's slender arm. "Never mind, Evelyn. I am certain that they must recall your existence when they have exhausted this talk of the race. Silly creatures that they are. I wonder—shall I ring for sandwiches? Gentlemen do seem to cultivate an appetite simply from talking over sporting matters."

It was on the tip of Evelyn's tongue to make an acid rejoinder, but she managed to resist it. She sighed instead. "Yes, Mama, perhaps that would be a good notion."

There were two more callers while tea was being served, both of them gentlemen, and when they learned of the proposed race, the conversation inevitably rounded back over familiar ground. The latecomers staunchly defended their local whip against the unknown challenger, and the stakes placed on the outcome of the race rose.

By the time tea finally ended, Evelyn thought she would fly into hysterics if she heard one more word about the race. She smiled and said polite good-byes to her so-called admirers. None of the gentlemen had given her any real notice at all once they became aware of the upcoming race. The occasion had been both disillusioning and illuminating. Gentlemen were fickle in the extreme, and Evelyn was heartily glad to be done with the lot.

Evelyn's leave-taking with Miss Woodthorpe was a shade cooler than usual, for she had not been behind in observing that her friend had been perfectly comfortable with participating in the masculine conversation. She knew that it should not have mattered, especially when she was aware that Miss Woodthorpe was a great horsewoman and talented driver in her own right, but nevertheless it bothered Evelyn that Miss Woodthorpe had become the recipient of attention that by rights should have been paid to the daughter of the house.

Viscount Waithe's admiration for Miss Woodthorpe's

knowledgeable observations, in particular, had been most patent. Though Evelyn had never actually considered the viscount in the light of a serious admirer, nevertheless his defection rankled even as it astonished her.

At one point, his lordship had exclaimed, "By Jove, ma'am! I had no notion a gentlewoman like yourself could take such interest in these things."

"Pol has a better eye for horseflesh than most gentlemen I know," John had declared proudly.

Viscount Waithe had looked at Miss Woodthorpe as though seeing her for the first time, and his regard had been so pointed that it had caused a faint blush to come to the lady's cheeks.

Evelyn assured herself that it was not that she was jealous of her friend. It was simply that she had grown accustomed to being the focus of the pretty speeches and elaborate compliments. It was humiliating, indeed, to be superseded by all this interest in an idiotic horse race, and it was made especially so when Miss Woodthorpe had not suffered the same neglect.

Mr. Hawkins was the last to take leave of Evelyn, having lingered behind the others to speak quietly with Mrs. Dower. When he took the hand that Evelyn offered to him, he smiled into her eyes. There was a pronounced twinkle of amusement lurking in his own. "Until we meet again, Miss Dower. I hope to be granted a few more minutes with you than I managed to snatch this afternoon."

Evelyn cast him a suspicious glance. Mr. Hawkins had been as unattentive toward her as the rest, and so his statement was decidedly odd. He did not say so, but Evelyn gathered the impression from the humor in his eyes that he knew very well of the dissatisfaction that she was feeling and the reasons for it. She stiffened therefore and injected a haughtiness into her tone. "Indeed, Mr. Hawkins?"

Mr. Hawkins laughed as though she had uttered a cordial witticism and took himself off, promising to call again quite soon. "Perhaps I may even persuade you to watch the race with me," he said.

Evelyn smiled, but daggers flew from her eyes. "Good day, Mr. Hawkins."

When the door closed behind him, Evelyn stamped her

foot. Really, Mr. Peter Hawkins was the most infuriating, the most insensitive gentleman of her acquaintance. If he were not always so very proper, she could suspect him of having purposefully needled her. As it was, he had managed once more to put himself into her ill graces, and that, she could have informed him, was not the way to win her heart.

But, said that tiny voice, did he really wish to any longer?

"My dear! Whatever can the matter be? I rather thought tea went very well," Mrs. Dower said, startled.

"Oh! You are utterly impossible, Mama!" Evelyn whirled and exited the drawing room, unable to endure more.

Chapter Fifteen

An unseasonal rainstorm swept the street and tossed the trees as a coach drove up to the steps of a certain town house in Lansdown Crescent. A servant climbed down from the coach and ran up the steps to the town house door to bang hard the knocker.

Thus was the household alerted of the advent of an unexpected visitor.

Lady Pomerancy received the gentleman in her private salon. As he entered the room, she raked him with piercing eyes. A gentleman in his late fifties, he was still handsome even though his eyes were world-weary, and a permanent cynicism seemed to have settled onto his countenance. He was dressed fashionably with an obvious taste for magnificently embroidered waistcoats and rich living.

"You have begun to go corpulent, Horace," she said.

There was little in her expression or her voice to suggest welcome, but Lord Horace Hughes, Viscount Perigree, merely laughed as he advanced to take the hand that she held out to him. "As brittle as ever, I see. I am glad that you, at least, have not changed, dear Sister."

His glance passed over her with seeming indifference, but those acquainted well with the gentleman would have noticed a shadow of shock in his eyes. Lady Pomerancy was the elder by fifteen years, and from his earliest memories she had always appeared a commanding figure. He had not expected to find his indomitable sister confined to a wheelchair.

"Are you indeed!" Lady Pomerancy smiled satirically. "Pray save your charm for those who are gullible enough to swallow it. Sit down. You will take wine with me, of course." She raised her hand in command. The footman in attendance stepped forward with a decanter tray and placed it on the small table beside her chair.

Lord Hughes settled himself into a wingback chair. "Of course I shall," he agreed with a rakish grin. He took the glass offered him and sniffed at the wine before he took a small amount. After a moment of rolling it on his tongue, he nodded to Lady Pomerancy, swallowed, and said, "A superior vintage, my lady. I am impressed that you possess such an excellent cellar."

"I may not reside in London, but that does not mean I am become a rustic," said Lady Pomerancy. She set aside her own barely tasted wine and settled back in her chair, her arthritic hands folded in her lap. "Now, to what do I owe this totally unprecedented visit?"

"You were always such an abrupt creature," Lord Hughes complained. He flicked a glance in the direction of the footman, as well as to the maid that stood in attendance behind Lady Pomerancy's chair. "Might I not take it into my head to visit my only sister out of family feeling? You wound me to the heart, I assure you."

Lady Pomerancy snorted, not at all taken in. That her brother wished to speak privately with her was evident, and his uncharacteristic desire for discretion was such that her curiosity was engaged. Quietly she requested that she be left alone with her visitor. When the footman and maid had left the room, Lady Pomerancy turned her glance back to her brother to regard him with narrowed eyes.

Lord Hughes had calmly and appreciatively sipped at his wine while the servants exited. When he noticed that he had come under close scrutiny, he gave a broad smile. "Are my motives so suspect, then, Agatha?"

When she said nothing, merely by the lift of her brows indicating her opinion, he sighed and crossed his elegantly shod ankles. "Very well then. Mea culpa and all the rest. I am here for purely selfish reasons."

"I did not doubt it for a moment," Lady Pomerancy dryly assured him.

Lord Hughes laughed. He cast her a fond glance. "Ever up to all the rigs. You were the only one whom I could never fleece, in one way or another. I have often wondered, if we had been born closer in age and temperament, whether our relationship might not have been somewhat different."

"If I take your meaning correctly, you harbor regrets about not being able to use me as you have anyone else who was unfortunate enough to come into your sphere," said Lady Pomerancy mendaciously.

A flash of temper crossed Lord Hughes's face, but it was as quickly gone with his returned smile. "That is it exactly. You have not lost the touch of annoying me, Agatha, but pray do not take that admission as a compliment."

Lady Pomerancy laughed. "No, I shall not." There was actually a twinkle in her eyes. "You are a rake and a rogue, but a likable fellow for all that."

Lord Hughes pressed a wide hand vaguely over the region of his heart. "I am touched, dear Sister. I never thought to hear such accolades of my poor self pass your prim lips."

"I have always given you that much, Horace. As for the rest, I prefer never to think on it," said Lady Pomerancy.

"On the contrary. You have thought on it often and often."

Lord Hughes's voice was stripped of its former jocularity. He regarded his sister with shrewdness. "It is why you refused to allow me to take poor Lionel's brat. It is also why not I, nor any of the rest, were given the opportunity to have any hand at all in the boy's raising or education. Imagine my astonishment when a handsome young buck approached me at a function a few years back and announced that he was my grandnephew. I was never more taken aback in my life when Peter Hawkins claimed kinship with me."

"I would not have expected less of my grandson," said Lady Pomerancy composedly. "He is a gentleman born."

"He is a gentleman made," Lord Hughes corrected. He swirled the wine left in his glass. "It is on Peter's account that I have come."

He looked up and saw that he had succeeded in startling her at last. He smiled, rather wearily. "I have no designs of corruption in mind, my lady. Those days are past, would you not agree? He is too much settled in his ways to be swayed by anything that I might throw in his way."

"I must give thanks for that in my evening prayers tonight," said Lady Pomerancy sharply. "Why *have* you come, Horace? You said before that it was purely for selfish motives, and now you say it is on Peter's account. Which is it, then?"

"It is one and the same."

Lord Hughes chuckled at her stiffening expression. "No, I do not mock you. The honest truth of the matter is that I am beginning to feel my own mortality. I am not as impervious to the effects of riotous living as I once was. Your grandson is my only heir and—"

"What, have you no byblows to show for the excessive sowing of your wild seed?" Lady Pomerancy asked sarcastically.

There was a moment's silence. Lady Pomerancy was surprised by the pained expression that fleeted across her brother's face.

"None that have survived," said Lord Hughes evenly. "The last died this two months past."

Lady Pomerancy was silenced. She turned her head so that she was looking into the fire, her expression shuttered.

Lord Hughes set down his wineglass with exaggerated care. "As I was saying, Peter Hawkins is my only heir. He will inherit the title. I wish to be assured that there will be another after him, and that is why I have come to Bath. I intend to see the boy wed."

Lady Pomerancy stared at her brother. "You must be mad."

Wrath kindled in her eyes. "How dare you come here and state your *intention,* as though your wish is all that matters. I take leave to tell you that I find it both insulting and ludicrous that you have taken it upon yourself to attempt such an ordering of my grandson's life."

"Why not?" The viscount shrugged. "You have had a free hand in ordering it for more years than I care to count. Now the time has come for someone else to speak up."

"Your concern is unnecessary and unwarranted, Horace. Peter and I go along very nicely as we are," said Lady Pomerancy, ruffled.

"Perhaps I have Peter's future interests closer to heart than yourself, dear Sister. I do not hold him still tied to my apron strings." Lord Hughes spoke with his habitual smile, yet there was a hard look about his eyes and mouth.

Lady Pomerancy shook with reaction. Her hands clawed at the arms of her chair. "I shall not sit still for this tripe! I have done all in my power to give that boy the best of everything. Everything! I will not have you—*you*!—cast aspersions upon—" She struggled to rise, and in her clumsy fury she knocked over the decanter table beside her chair.

Lord Hughes scrambled up out of his chair, alarmed by the extent of her rage as well as her helplessness. Nothing could have driven aside his own self-centered interests so effectively. "Agatha! Have a care!"

She would have fallen except that he caught her in his arms.

The commotion brought in the servants. The footman stopped short, but the maid rushed forward. "My lady!"

Lord Hughes looked around as he gently helped Lady Pomerancy back into her chair. The maid clucked with distress and hurried to replace the rug over her ladyship's knees. "Her ladyship misjudged her strength. But I do not think that she took hurt. Am I mistaken, my lady?"

The footman stared hard at the gentleman, then looked at his mistress. "My lady, are you quite all right?"

"Of course I am. Why shouldn't I be?" Lady Pomerancy flashed. "Get out, the both of you. Oh, do stop fluttering over me, woman. I shall ring when I wish for anything. You may clean up this mess later."

The footman had righted the table and had gone down on one knee to begin collecting the tray and pieces of glass from the broken decanter. He looked up. "The stain, my lady—"

"The carpet is undoubtedly already stained so that it can scarcely matter if it is done now or later. Get out, I say."

The servants left with obvious reluctance. The footman sent a last meaningful glance in Lord Hughes's direction before closing the door.

Lord Hughes was not amused by the manservant's obvious mistrust, but he merely commented, "A good man, that. I never could command that sort of loyalty."

Lady Pomerancy sighed. After ordering out her servants, she had shaded her face with her fingers. But now she dropped her hand. "I apologize, Horace. It is unlike me to flare up in such a fashion."

"On the contrary. Whenever we have chanced to meet through the years, we have come to cuffs within minutes. You usually end by telling me to go to the devil," said Lord Hughes.

Lady Pomerancy chuckled faintly. "I had forgotten. Very well, Horace, you have my continued leave to go to the devil." Her expression turned thoughtful as she met and held his eyes. "Yours is a fickle, self-absorbed character, but on the rare occasion you have actually surprised me. In both instances, it has been in regard to Peter's future."

Lord Hughes stirred uncomfortably. "Pray do not make me out some sort of saint, Agatha. Nothing would irritate me more, you know. I told you, I merely wish to satisfy myself that the title will continue to be held by someone with whom I have a vague blood connection."

"I suppose that is not an unreasonable ambition," said Lady Pomerancy. "I, too, could wish that Peter would take a bride. He has grown increasingly restless since his return from the Continent. However, I have good reason to know that he has recognized for himself that it is time to be looking about him for a suitable party."

Lord Hughes recognized a tacit truce when it was offered him. He smiled. "Then you will have no objection to my broaching the subject to the boy?"

There came an odd smile into Lady Pomerancy's eyes. "None at all, Horace. Perhaps your advice may even be of some benefit. You may steer Peter clear of all sorts of ill-advised starts through your patent example."

"Thank you for that vote of confidence, dear Sister," said Lord Hughes with fine irony. He levered himself out of the chair. "If you have no objection, I should like to discover which room my possessions have been put into so that I may begin changing for dinner. I assume that you do keep country hours in Bath?"

"We are not so provincial as that, Horace. However, if you should wish it, I shall ask that a tray be carried up to your room so that you may dine early," said Lady Pomerancy generously.

Lord Hughes laughed. "No, no. I would not think of

putting the kitchen out on my account. I shall see you and my grandnephew below at the usual hour."

"It will be my company only tonight. Peter dines out this evening," said Lady Pomerancy. She lifted her brows at her brother's surprised expression. "Surely you did not think that he was kept quite so close by my apron strings as all that, my lord?"

Lord Hughes lifted her hand to his lips. "You are magnificent as always, my lady. And as usual, you have left me with nothing to say."

"I do not believe it, but courtesy forbids me to put it to the test," said Lady Pomerancy.

Lord Hughes laughed again. He made a flourishing bow to her before he left the salon.

Lady Pomerancy sat before the fire, reflecting for several moments. Then she rang the bell that she always kept in her possession. Immediately the door opened to admit her maid and the footman. "I wish to go up to my rooms. When my nephew comes in, pray send him up to me whatever the hour."

"Very good, my lady."

The hour was well advanced when Mr. Hawkins returned. As he handed over his drenched overcoat to the butler, his brow was creased in a frown. His somber expression deepened upon being informed of his grandmother's summons, but without comment he went upstairs and along to Lady Pomerancy's private salon.

Lady Pomerancy greeted him civilly and bade him sit down. He declined, preferring instead to stand at the mantel with one arm laid along its length. With an encompassing glance, she said, "I appreciate that you humor me at such a late hour, Peter."

He smiled at her, somewhat tiredly. "Well do I know that if I did not, I would gravely offend your sensibilities, ma'am."

"Quite true," said Lady Pomerancy equitably. She gestured for the maid to leave them, and when the woman had done so, closing the door softly behind her, she said, "I would not ordinarily have left so insistent a message, as you know, but I wished to forewarn you before you went down to breakfast."

Mr. Hawkins raised a brow. "My attention is thoroughly engaged, my lady. What calamity is to befall me in the morning? Am I to be hauled away for some crime that quite escapes my memory at the moment?"

"Nothing so dire, dear boy, though I suspect that you might wish it to be so simple a matter before all is done and said. Your uncle arrived this afternoon while you were out and expressed to me his intention to see you properly wedlocked. He will undoubtedly importune you at first opportunity," said Lady Pomerancy.

"Oh Lord," said Mr. Hawkins ruefully. He passed a hand over his thick hair. "It needed only that."

Lady Pomerancy regarded her grandson with shrewd eyes. "Am I mistaken in concluding that the advent of Lord Hughes is but an additional annoyance?"

Mr. Hawkins laughed a shade grimly. "That is mildly put, ma'am. I have come away from a solemn half hour with Percy, in which he confided to me his intention to offer for a certain young lady."

Lady Pomerancy stared up at him. "Surely *not* Miss Dower!"

He laughed at her ladyship's appalled comprehension, then shrugged. "I fear so. I wish now that I were not so insistent that my cousin unburden himself. Percy was moody all the evening so that even Sir Charles commented upon it. He recommended that I take Percy off after dinner and talk to him. The upshot of it is as I have told you."

"Will the dratted girl have him?"

Mr. Hawkins frowned. He toed a burning faggot further into the fire. "I would not have thought so, for Miss Dower accords Percy all the friendliness of a sister. I have never detected anything else in her manner toward him. But Percy seems to think that she feels quite otherwise."

"Percy is a nodcock," said Lady Pomerancy succinctly. "I have spoken enough with Miss Dower to have gained some insight into her intelligence. Though she had the incomprehensible bad judgment to turn down your offer, she is needlewitted enough to realize that she and Percy would never suit. If what you say is true, I do not think that you need be anxious over Percy's offer for her."

"Where Miss Dower is concerned, however, I find that I do not care to wait upon fate to decide the outcome," said Mr. Hawkins quietly, still staring into the fire.

"Then what will you do?"

Mr. Hawkins looked around. There was a glimmer of a smile in his eyes. "Perhaps Percy himself will provide the answer," he said.

Lady Pomerancy saw that there was no more to be got out of him, and so she recommended that he go to his bed. She rang her bell. As the maid returned, she said, "You will need your rest to fortify you for your confrontation with your uncle."

Mr. Hawkins laughed and agreed. He dropped an affectionate kiss upon her head and left her to the ministrations of her maid.

Chapter Sixteen

Lord Hughes rose and went down for a late breakfast, as was his usual custom. As he entered the breakfast room, he was unsurprised to be informed by the butler that his grandnephew had already gone out. "I shall catch him later, I expect," he said, at once helping himself to a generous portion of steak and kippers.

"Indeed, my lord. Mr. Hawkins asked me to convey his apologies as well as his intention to return in time to take luncheon with you," said the butler, pouring his lordship's coffee.

Lord Hughes paused in the act of raising the loaded fork to his lips. "Said that, did he?" A ruminative look entered his eyes as he stared at the steak on his fork. Then he shrugged and set to doing justice to his plate.

The butler quietly exited, certain that his lordship was not inclined to address him further.

Upon hearing that Mr. Hawkins had left him a message, Lord Hughes had instantly and correctly concluded that Lady Pomerancy had already apprised his grandnephew of his sudden visit. It remained to be seen whether her ladyship had also enlightened Mr. Hawkins of the reason behind it, but knowing Lady Pomerancy as he undoubtedly did, Lord Hughes thought he could depend upon her ladyship for doing him that kindness. He snorted in amusement. Of course she had, if for no other reason than to annoy him.

Lord Hughes sat back from the table, feeling all the benevolence of a gentleman comfortably sated, and plied his linen napkin to his mouth. "But I am one move ahead of you, dear Agatha," he murmured to himself, and laughed.

It actually suited him very well that his grandnephew had been warned off him, for it saved him the trouble of finding a tolerably polite way of broaching the topic. Now he considered himself to be free to plunge right into the matter without any delicate manuevering. He'd look over the offerings of Bath, and coupled with a few eligible prospects that he had decided upon before leaving Town, he would have his grandnephew affianced before Peter could blink twice. With any luck, he would be able to return to London and its amusements within a solitary month.

Lord Hughes rose from the breakfast room feeling himself to be in charity with the world. After inquiring after Lady Pomerancy, only to be informed that her ladyship had not yet risen, and not being one to wait patiently about, Lord Hughes decided to leave the town house.

A half hour later he descended the front steps of the town house. He had refused the footman's offer to order around a carriage and set out at a leisurely pace, jauntily swinging his brass-headed cane.

Lord Hughes actually enjoyed to walk, a surprising idiosyncrasy in one whose reputation for self-indulgence and pleasure-seeking was a byword. However, his had been an active childhood spent in the country, and though his lordship had long since abandoned the energetic pursuits of his youth, he had retained his early habit of seeking the outdoor air in this gentler fashion.

Lord Hughes's perambulations carried him in the direction of Queen Square. The fall of rain during the night and the subsequent passing of carriages had churned the streets around the square to mud, but the pavement walks were relatively dry, and a number of ladies were also taking the air. His lordship's eyes rested appreciatively on several tolerable female figures. Belatedly he bethought himself of his purpose in coming to Bath, and he began glancing at faces, as well, rationalizing that he must be able to point out to his grandnephew that there were eligible ladies to choose from of suitable attractiveness and age.

It was with this thought in mind that he courteously stepped aside to give a pair of ladies right-of-way, when his glance fell on the face of the elder of the two. His mind suffered a shock. "Amanda Dower?"

The lady glanced around at him, smiling in polite in-

quiry. Her eyes widened in startled recognition. "Dear
Lord! It surely cannot be you. Is it indeed you, my lord?"

Lord Hughes burst out laughing and approached her with
his hands held out. "My dear lady, you have not changed in
the least," he said in an affectionate tone.

The lady blushed, taking his hands in her own for a brief
moment. With a pretty air of confusion, she said, "My lord,
pray allow me to make you known to my daughter. Evelyn,
this gentleman is Lord Hughes, Viscount Perigree. He—he
is an old friend."

Evelyn stared at her mother in astonishment. She had
never seen that lady so obviously out of countenance.

"Ah, little Evelyn. I remember you, of course." Lord
Hughes shook her hand, then held it between both of his
palms. He swept a glance over her. "But you are a young
lady!" Lord Hughes gave a regretful sigh, shaking his head.
"Alas, one does not realize the passing of the years. She is a
lovely gem, Amanda."

Evelyn murmured something polite. She hardly knew
what she said as she continued to absorb the strange effect
that the gentleman was having upon her mother. However,
she suspected that it did not actually matter, for Lord
Hughes seemed to be as equally engrossed with Mrs.
Dower as that lady was with him. He had scarcely glanced
at her before his eyes had returned to Mrs. Dower.

"I cannot contain my curiosity a second longer, my lord.
How came you to be here—in Bath! And after so many
years!" exclaimed Mrs. Dower.

"I wish that I might say that I came to renew my delightful acquaintance with you, Amanda, but in all truth I had no
notion that you had made Bath your home," said Lord
Hughes. His voice held almost a caressing note. "If I had
known, I might have come down from Town before this to
try the waters."

Mrs. Dower blushed again. "Really, my lord!"

"We were once such good friends that you addressed me
by my Christian name. It would please me greatly if you
did so again. Dare I hope that you recall it?" said Lord
Hughes softly.

Mrs. Dower's blush deepened. "Of course I do—Horace.

I—I cannot believe that *you* have come for the waters. Why, you were used never to be ill a day of your life."

"Of course I have not," agreed Lord Hughes, smiling widely. "No, I have come to pay a long past due visit to my sister and grandnephew. Perhaps you are acquainted with Lady Pomerancy and Mr. Peter Hawkins?"

"Why, I had forgotten that Lady Pomerancy and you—. It has been so very many years, you see, and the connection had quite faded from my memory," said Mrs. Dower apologetically. "But of course we are acquainted with her ladyship and Mr. Hawkins. In point of face, Evelyn—"

"Mr. Hawkins and I have developed something of a friendship," Evelyn interposed, fearing what her mother's indiscreet tongue might inadvertently reveal to this urbane, worldly gentleman. She sent a quelling glance in her mother's direction.

"I see." Lord Hughes's lazy, half-amused glance rested briefly on Evelyn's face. He had not been behind in catching the warning light in the young lady's swift look, and his curiosity was stirred. "This is a happy coincidence, indeed. I am presently staying with Lady Pomerancy and my grandnephew in Lansdown Crescent. Perhaps you will do us the honor of joining us at luncheon? I should like very much to renew my treasured acquaintance with you, Amanda, and I am certain that Miss Dower and Peter will have any number of friendly topics to relate to one another."

"I am sorry, my lord, but—" Evelyn began.

"I will be delighted to accept your invitation to us, Horace. I have been behind in paying my respects to Lady Pomerancy, in any event. She asked me to tea not long ago and I begged off," said Mrs. Dower.

Lord Hughes smiled at her. "She scares you to flinders, does she?"

Mrs. Dower laughed somewhat shamefacedly, casting an appealing look up at Lord Hughes. "It is bad of me, I know. But I have always been such a coward."

"Never mind, my dear. I shall be present, and I shall guard you against the gorgon," said Lord Hughes expansively. "Are you shopping this morning? I should be very happy to accompany you if you had no objection to it."

"Oh, none whatsoever," Mrs. Dower assured with a soft smile.

"We are just returning from the Pump Room, my lord, and had not intended to visit the shops this morning. Perhaps another time," said Evelyn politely.

Lord Hughes's lazy glance again touched her. Evelyn had the distinct and unpleasant conviction that he had looked straight through her. She bit her lip, disliking that he had so easily discerned her suspicion of him even though she had spoken with perfect propriety.

Lord Hughes took Mrs. Dower's hand and slipped it comfortably into the crook of his arm. Smiling down at her, he said, "I shall accompany you home, then. And your lovely daughter, of course. Perhaps later you will allow me to provide escort to Lansdown Crescent."

"That will be perfectly agreeable, Horace," said Mrs. Dower, the brightness of her eyes but a foil for the brilliance of her smile.

Evelyn had no choice but to follow her mother and Lord Hughes in their slow progression to the town house. The couple ahead indulged in much laughter and shared reminiscences. It was gradually borne in on Evelyn that Lord Hughes had once been a great admirer of her mother's and that the lady had not been entirely indifferent to the gentleman.

The amiable memories continued to flow over refreshments, while Evelyn listened in growing amazement. She could see how affected both Lord Hughes and her mother were becoming by the reminiscing, Mrs. Dower even wiping aside a sentimental tear for the wonderful days long since past. They would soon be reduced to maudlin weeping at this pace, Evelyn thought, appalled. She lifted the comfit tray and offered it to Lord Hughes. "Perhaps another, my lord? They are from my mother's own recipe."

Lord Hughes was sufficiently distracted. He cast a benevolent glance at Mrs. Dower as he accepted the treat. "I suspected that it was so, for these delicacies could only have come from the hands of an angel."

While Mrs. Dower blushingly disclaimed such high station, Evelyn smiled to herself, reflecting that Cook would be astonished to have heard such an accolade rendered to her strong broad hands.

Evelyn was relieved when the conversation thereafter remained in the flattering vein that she was accustomed to hearing from her mother's admirers. It made it so much more comfortable when she was not put into the position of politely smiling at anecdotes about personages that she had never known or of witnessing what she had labeled astonishingly mawkish behavior.

Lord Hughes remained until it was time for the ladies to change for luncheon. When they had returned downstairs, having put on attractive straw bonnets and fashionably cut carriage dresses, he professed himself honored to be escorting two such lovely ladies. He bowed gallantly over both their gloved hands. However, Evelyn took note that he pressed a light kiss onto her mother's fingers before releasing them, an action that brought the high color into her mother's face.

Evelyn had much to reflect upon during the short drive to Lansdown Crescent. She could not recall a time when her mother did not have admirers, some of whom, she knew, would have pressed their suits if they had been given the least encouragement. However, Mrs. Dower had never favored any of her admirers over the others, and Evelyn had taken for granted that though her mother enjoyed male admiration, that lady was also disinterested in changing her widow's status.

Then Lord Hughes had appeared, out of the blue and out of the past, and suddenly her mother had metamorphized into a blushing and obviously smitten lady.

Evelyn was not certain what her opinion should be on the matter. She felt dismay and disapproval on the one hand because it had happened so very swiftly. It was shocking at the very least to discover that her mother had once held a *tendre* for anyone else but her own father. Evelyn had difficulty adjusting to that. Even the romantic bent of her own nature could not entirely accept it, at least not all at once.

Yet, when she looked at her mother's happy face and saw the singular attentions that Lord Hughes paid to her mother, she felt like an old jealous cat.

Surely it would not be such a bad thing if her mother remarried. After all, Mrs. Dower was of an age where such opportunities did not come round as often as they might once have done, and certainly her mother would need someone to look after her when she herself had wed. Evelyn knew that Mrs. Dower would not easily countenance living with a son-in-law, if for no other reason than that she preferred her own freedoms and amusements.

Evelyn thoughtfully regarded Lord Hughes, trying to quell the wary antagonism that she felt toward the gentleman. Lord Hughes was well dressed, though perhaps his shocking pink silk waistcoat was a bit flamboyant and his collection of beribboned fobs an obvious affection. However, there was nothing about his stocky person nor in his manner to suggest he was other than the worldly, idle gentleman that he appeared.

His lordship was obviously a mature gentleman of some means so that Mrs. Dower would not go wanting for any little thing. In that light, it was absurd to feel anything but the most charitable of emotions toward a gentleman who could provide both companionship and material comforts for her mother.

Of course, Evelyn thought with a small frown, she was making assumptions. Lord Hughes might merely be indulging himself in a light flirtation with a lady he had once admired in order to relieve the tedium of a familial visit. In that case, Evelyn was categorically against any sort of acquaintanceship with Lord Hughes, for she did not wish her well-meaning but sometimes foolish mother to be hurt. There was nothing she could say at this early date, however, for to be fair to Lord Hughes and her mother, she must give his lordship a chance to prove his intentions.

Such were Evelyn's tumbling thoughts when the carriage arrived in Lansdown Crescent, and they descended from it to go inside. Lord Hughes had had the presence of mind to send a message round earlier that he would be bringing two guests for luncheon so that the ladies would not be unexpected. Informed that Lady Pomerancy awaited them, Lord Hughes and his guests were ushered into the drawing room.

Chapter Seventeen

Lady Pomerancy sat with regal posture in her wheelchair. She looked round as the trio entered, a thin smile on her lips. Her brows lifted in the slightest arch. "Ah, Mrs. Dower. I am honored indeed that you chose to join me for luncheon."

Mrs. Dower was at once thrown into apprehension, her sensitive ear having detected a sarcastic undercurrent in her ladyship's polite greeting. "It has been such an age since I last saw you, my lady. I—I trust that you are well?"

Lord Hughes placed his hand under Mrs. Dower's elbow and guided her to a comfortable chair. "Her ladyship is always well," he said easily. He was rewarded by a grateful look from Mrs. Dower and an obelisk stare from Lady Pomerancy.

Mr. Hawkins and Lord Waithe were also present, and they had at once risen at the ladies' entrance. Mr. Hawkins greeted the Dowers with every appearance of pleasure, though his attentions toward the ladies were not as marked as those of the viscount.

Lord Waithe made his polite bow to Mrs. Dower, then eagerly turned, smiling, to Evelyn. He said quietly, "I had no notion until a moment ago that you and your mother would be taking luncheon here as well. The occasion has become quite special in light of your appearance."

Evelyn smiled up into his admiring eyes as she gently withdrew her fingers from his warm clasp. "You will spoil me with compliments, my lord."

"That I could never do," Lord Waithe assured her. "I am constantly aware of how little justice I have done you. It would take a lifetime to express myself adequately."

Evelyn realized that the viscount's singular attention had

caused them to become the center of attention. Her mother's eyes were as large as saucers; she hoped that lady would not leap in with an embarrassing observation. Lord Hughes gave the appearance of condescending amusement, while Lady Pomerancy's expression could only be described as cross. Evelyn dared a fleeting glance at Mr. Hawkins, but she could not read anything in that gentleman's polite visage.

Evelyn could not imagine what could have gotten into Lord Waithe to behave with such little propriety. She had to stem his ardency, which bordered perilously close to a declaration, before they were both overcome with humiliation. "Lord Waithe, pray—"

She had thrown out her hand as if to hold him away, but the viscount apparently misinterpreted her gesture, for he caught up her hand. He pressed her fingers. "Miss Dower, I—"

As Lord Waithe began to speak, Mr. Hawkins made an abrupt move, then stilled. His wide shoulders were tense, his face seemingly carved from stone. He did not notice that he came under the inscrutable eyes of his great-uncle.

"Pray do leave off, Percy. One should never indulge in a diet of sweets. It utterly destroys appreciation for decent fare. My appetite is quite off as it is," said Lady Pomerancy in a testy voice.

Abashed, Lord Waithe dropped Evelyn's hand, much to her relief. He turned to bow apology to her ladyship. With a charming smile, he said, "My pardon, ma'am. I forgot myself for a moment. I shall be bound by your wishes, of course."

Lady Pomerancy snorted and waved at him. "Yes, and butter would not melt in your mouth, either, I suppose. You were always a honey-tongued rogue. Peter, I think that we may go in to luncheon now."

Mr. Hawkins gestured to the footman waiting beside the open door. The servant nodded and came forward to push Lady Pomerancy's chair. Lady Pomerancy ran a swift eye over the company. "Fortunately enough, our numbers are even. We shall not have any awkward juggling of places. One could not have planned it any better."

Evelyn warily accepted Lord Waithe's escort, casting up

a glance at his countenance to see whether he was going to continue in his fulsome manner. Lord Waithe merely smiled at her, and she was reassured that his lordship meant to keep close to his word to Lady Pomerancy. Evelyn could not but be grateful for it, especially when she had the oddest feeling that Mr. Hawkins was closely observing them.

"Oh, is Sir Charles not going to join us?" asked Mrs. Dower, accepting the hand that Lord Hughes offered. She looked about in a vaguely hopeful fashion, as though to catch that gentleman suddenly materializing.

At her mother's words, Evelyn looked around quickly. She had been wondering at Sir Charles's absence but had not wanted to draw further attention to herself by asking after him. She was for once glad of her mother's own lamentable lack of social inhibition.

"Sir Charles had a previous engagement, I believe," said Mr. Hawkins. He was looking at Miss Dower as he spoke, or otherwise he would not have seen the flicker of disappointment in her eyes. He felt a surprising flash of irritation, which he kept well hidden.

He was fairly certain that no one else had noticed anything, for Miss Dower's expression did not betray anything more than polite interest. For himself, however, what he had seen was but one more warning that he must somehow turn Miss Dower's interest. If she never perceived him in any other light than that of the spurned suitor, but continued to treat him with the same degree of cool friendliness, he thought that he could very well lose her to someone else.

It had been a near-run thing but a moment ago, he thought grimly. If it had not been for his grandmother's irascible interruption he believed that Lord Waithe might have actually declared himself before them all. Whatever Miss Dower's reaction might have been, it would have created immense difficulty for himself.

He could not afford to wait any longer on patience and hope.

But Miss Dower still did not regard him as he most fervently desired to be seen.

His dilemma demanded action. Though he had no notion as yet how he was to take Sir Charles's place in Miss Dower's affections, he thought he knew how to make a dent in the ranks of her other admirers. For an instant, Mr. Hawkins's glance rested almost regretfully upon his cousin, Lord Waithe. He knew the viscount so well, both his admirable qualities and his weaknesses. What had occurred to Mr. Hawkins the previous evening to do was simple, almost laughably so, but with any luck at all it would be most effective. He needed only to choose the proper moment, he thought.

The party passed out of the drawing room to the luncheon room. Lady Pomerancy was wheeled to the bottom of the table, while Mr. Hawkins claimed the head, and the rest found their preferred places.

"It is so odd that Sir Charles is not here. I am so used to seeing the three gentlemen together that it throws me quite off balance when one is missing," remarked Mrs. Dower as she was seated by Lord Hughes.

Lady Pomerancy snorted again. "You are of delicate sensibilities, Mrs. Dower."

Lord Hughes's smile was even. His eyes were very hard as he looked over at his sister. "Mrs. Dower is indeed a lady of sensibility, Agatha. I, however, as I am certain you are particularly aware, possess not the least measure of that virtue. Quite the contrary. I have been known to issue quite cutting remarks."

Lady Pomerancy's brows arched, a telltale indication of her astonishment. Her glance passed from her brother to the lady that he had chosen to seat himself beside. "I am certain that you malign yourself, Horace," she said softly. She uttered nothing of her thoughts as she continued to regard Mrs. Dower, though there could be seen ripe speculation in her eyes.

Luncheon was served, and for several moments thereafter conversation was taken up with appreciation for the excellence of the repast.

Mr. Hawkins finally introduced the topic that he hoped would be the catalyst in weaning his cousin of his infatuation with Miss Dowers. "I suppose that you, like the rest of us, must be awaiting the race between Sir Charles and Ned Woodthorpe with great anticipation, Miss Dower."

Evelyn looked over at him coolly, instantly aware that he was baiting her. However, she could not conceive of his motive for doing so, and the blandness of his expression did not present a clue.

It hardly seemed credible that the correct Mr. Hawkins would deliberately set about putting a lady to the blush. He had made it so patent that he had known how piqued she had been over the origination of that race, so that she was now in the position of having to pass off a polite fib or admit to her true feelings. Either choice must cause discomfort for her; if she said everything that was polite, he, at least, would know that she had told less than the truth; but if she revealed her disaffection with the race, she could inadvertently touch match to just the sort of sporting discussion that she had discovered she most detested.

Evelyn set her chin, determined that Mr. Hawkins would be disappointed in his ploy. He expected her to swallow, or, at the least, water down, her opinion. However, she would prove that she had the backbone of her convictions. *She* was not to be so easily put out of countenance. In a repressive voice, she said, "You know well that I am not, sir. I think it a boring matter in the extreme."

Lord Waithe's hand and fork stopped in midair and abruptly dropped to his plate as he exclaimed, "I say! Surely you jest, Miss Dower. Why, it is to be a splendid contest!"

Evelyn shook her head, her icy expression easing into a laugh as she turned her warming glance on the viscount. "I fear not to me, my lord. I have never cared overmuch for such sporting events, nor even very much for horses. It is odd in me, I know, but there it is."

Lord Waithe's mouth opened and closed. He gaped at Miss Dower with an expression of utmost astonishment. "You do not care for horses?"

"Evelyn is frightened of the beasts, you see, which is perfectly understandable when one considers how close she came to being killed by that awful toss she took last year," said Mrs. Dower. She shuddered. "I do not particularly like horses myself now."

"Oh! Well, I do see. Of course I do. Perfectly understandable," said Lord Waithe, awash but manfully attempting to uphold civility despite his shock that anyone could lay claim to such an unnatural attitude. He had taken more

falls than he cared to remember, and some devilishly serious to boot, but none had ever served to turn him from his
beloved horses.

Lord Waithe was hideously surprised that Miss Dower
could harbor such an opinion about sporting events and,
most particularly, about horses. He was himself an enthusi-
ast regarding anything having to do with equines and in fact
his close-held ambition was to one day retire to his father's
expansive country estate and breed steeplechasers. One did
not wish for the old gentleman's demise, of course, especially when his lordship was still a hale fellow at three-
score; but it could not be denied that his own place would
not support the bloodline that he had always envisioned
building up.

In recent months, there had been a vague feminine image
accompanying him in his imaginings, that of his chosen
lady who would encourage and aid him in attaining his
goal. Since meeting Miss Dower, the viscount's vision of
what he thought of as his lady had taken on her face and
figure.

Now as Lord Waithe glanced at Miss Dower with trou-
bled eyes, he saw her for the first time without the gilding
of his assumptions. She was still one of the loveliest ladies
and possibly one of the kindest that he had ever known, yet
he felt the hopes of his heart crumbling slowly into disillu-
sion. He had taken for granted that Miss Dower would be
everything that he had envisioned and that she would enter
wholeheartedly into his ambitions. It was distressing to discover that the lady one had intended to offer for was not at
all as perfect as one had thought.

At that instant, Lord Waithe realized that he no longer
meant to press his suit with Miss Dower. He had fallen out
of love in scarce than a heartbeat. "A singularly lowering
reflection," he murmured under his breath, disliking his
own flits of affection. His wayward nature had caused him
pain in the past and he was grown rather weary of the tem-
porariness of his own emotions.

Evelyn realized that her declaration had for some reason
proven upsetting to Lord Waithe. She smiled apologetically
at him. "I do hope I have not given you a disgust in me, my

lord, for I know that you are quite smitten by our four-legged friends. They are very beautiful, of course."

"Yes, yes, they are," said Lord Waithe, at once feeling the inanity of his reply. He managed to summon up his usual smile, though there was a shadow in the depths of his eyes. "I have suffered no disgust, as you put it, Miss Dower. It—it merely caught me by surprise. However, I shall manfully accept that one of my acquaintance does not share my own inordinate interest."

There was such a note of amazement in his voice that Evelyn laughed. Her eyes gleaming with a rueful light, she said, "I am quite pea-brained, in fact. Thank you, my lord, for that salutary set-down."

Lord Waithe was for once bereft of a polite word. He could not think how he had come to deliver a set-down, but that he had done so could not be denied in the face of the lady's amusement.

"A well-deserved one, I might add," said Mr. Hawkins, coming to his cousin's rescue. He said lightly, "I must inform you, Miss Dower, that your disinterest in this area of masculine obsession is quite, quite beyond the pale."

Evelyn eyed Mr. Hawkins a moment, wondering at his about-face, before she responded to his bantering tone. "I am cast down, then, indeed, Mr. Hawkins. However, it is my guarded opinion that I shall come about, for I am not one to fall easily into a decline."

"No, I am certain that you are not. Fortitude is an admirable quality," said Mr. Hawkins. He smiled slightly. "I suspect that you will be required to call upon your reserves many times over before this race becomes past history."

Evelyn laughed outright at that. "Indeed, sir! I fear that you are quite correct. In light of my coming trial, do, pray, take pity on me at least for today and introduce a decidedly different topic."

"Your wish is naturally my command," said Mr. Hawkins.

For the remainder of luncheon, neither the race, and by extension, Sir Charles, was discussed. Mr. Hawkins endeavored to direct the conversation into channels best calculated to capture Mrs. Dower's interest and succeeded so well that Mrs. Dower forgot her nervous awareness of Lady Pomerancy and chatted away with all at the table.

When it came time for the Dower ladies to take their leave, Mrs. Dower was able to say to Lady Pomerancy with perfect truth that she had thoroughly enjoyed herself. Lady Pomerancy was apparently so gratified by this observation that she was made speechless and in the carriage Mrs. Dower remarked, "Her ladyship is not half as frightening when one comes to be better acquainted with her. Of course, Lord Hughes's presence made me feel at once at ease."

"I am glad, Mama," said Evelyn, laughing a little.

"I was quite certain that Lord Waithe meant to offer for you."

Evelyn glanced quickly at her parent. "But he did not, nor do I wish him to do so."

Mrs. Dower shook her head, her expression regretful. "A pity. He is such a nice young gentleman. However, I shall not press the point, for there is still Mr. Hawkins."

"Oh really, Mama!" Evelyn laughed, shrugging her shoulders. "Mr. Hawkins is quite content with the way things stand between us. We are mere acquaintances, and likely to remain so."

"I do know a few things, Evelyn, however flighty I may appear. Mr. Hawkins will call again, and his intent is quite other than friendship," said Mrs. Dower complacently.

Evelyn knew that it was of no use at all to attempt to disabuse her mother of the absurd notion, so she sat back with a sigh. Time would prove her mother wrong, of that she was certain. For some unfathomable reason, the reflection was not particularly contenting.

Chapter Eighteen

On the afternoon of the race, Mr. Hawkins appeared at the town house to request the pleasure of Evelyn's company in watching it. Evelyn, who was unreasonably annoyed that he had chosen not to call in the two days since the luncheon in Lansdown Crescent, hesitated in giving her answer.

She wanted to let the gentleman know that she had noticed his neglect, when actually she had nothing whatsoever of which to complain. Mr. Hawkins was merely an amusing companion, after all. Certainly she should not care whether he extended an invitation to her for the race or to some other lady. It was the thought of that other unknown lady that Mr. Hawkins could well take up in her stead that unexpectedly made Evelyn hesitate in spurning his offer outright.

"Oh, do go with Mr. Hawkins, dearest. You know that you do not wish to be sitting here at home when all the rest of the world is going," said Mrs. Dower.

Evelyn directed at her mother a reproachful glance. She knew that her mother had accepted a similar such invitation from Lord Hughes, and though that gentleman had politely extended it to include her as well, it had been obvious to her that his lordship would prefer to have Mrs. Dower to himself. She had consequently declined, citing as her excuse a stack of correspondence that required her attention. Lord Hughes had not urged her to change her mind, but had said merely that he would not press her against her inclinations.

Evelyn had half expected that her mother would attempt to persuade her to join the party, but Mrs. Dower had surprised her by doing no such thing. That lady had uncharacteristically held her tongue until after Lord Hughes had taken his leave, and then her argument was so tepid that Evelyn had had no difficulty in discerning where her mother's heart really lay.

"Mama, you know quite well that Lord Hughes would much rather have you to himself, and I suspect that perfectly suits your own inclinations," Evelyn said dryly.

Mrs. Dower had colored, confirming her daughter's observation. "I am quite . . . *fond* of Lord Hughes's company." She gave Evelyn an anxious look. "You do not mind so very, very much, do you, Evelyn?"

Evelyn laughed, shaking her head. She went over and hugged her mother lightly. "You silly goose. Of course I do not. I wish only for you to be happy. I would never cut up stiff over one of your flirtations unless I saw that the gentleman was completely unworthy of you."

"Oh, my dear!" Mrs. Dower smiled tremulously up at Evelyn, not having heard the underlying seriousness in her daughter's voice. "I am happy, I assure you. Happier than I have been in many years."

"Then that is all there is to be said," Evelyn said gaily. "I shall write my letters, and you shall go off to the race with Lord Hughes."

That had been the end of the subject until Mr. Hawkins had come to make his own invitation. Suddenly Mrs. Dower was absolutely set against Evelyn missing such an unusual treat. She smiled brilliantly at Mr. Hawkins and her daughter.

"It is so very pretty out of doors, dearest, and you have been looking wan this age. It will do you good to be out in the fresh air, and I trust completely to Mr. Hawkins to be all that is solicitous. There can be no question of impropriety, you know, for you may take your maid with you," she said.

Evelyn was caught on the horns of a dilemma. She knew that Mr. Hawkins had rightly divined her pique at being oversighted by the gentlemen when the race had originally been discussed, and her pride urged her to prove to him that she cared not one wit for such an idiotic event. In addition, she wished very much to prove the nonchalance of their relationship by giving him the go-by. But the dull program she had set for herself that afternoon held little appeal when the sunshine streamed in the window and she knew that most of her acquaintances would be attending the race.

Despite her reluctance to give any notice to an event whose planning had so discommoded her, Evelyn was forced to acknowledge to herself her own rampant curiosity. Everywhere she had gone there had been talk of little else but the race, until even she was beginning to catch the spirit of the thing. In the end, she yielded to the temptation.

Mr. Hawkins was not to take it for granted that she was excited at the possibility of witnessing the race, however, so she accepted his invitation with a small sniff. "Oh, very well, Mr. Hawkins. I shall accompany you for the occasion," she said with a singular lack of enthusiasm.

"I am gratified by your gracious assent, ma'am," said Mr. Hawkins. He saw her out of the drawing room, his eyes resting on her profile. Evelyn refused to turn her head and meet his glance, suspecting that if she did so she would discover a disaccomodating twinkle of amusement in their depths.

Evelyn went upstairs to fetch her bonnet and informed her maid of the treat in store.

"Are we actually, miss? Well, isn't it grand!" exclaimed the maid, pleased.

"I suppose," said Evelyn, covering a false yawn. However, when she met the maid's knowing eyes in the mirror, she could not help laughing. "Oh, very well! Have it your own way. It is grand, indeed."

When Evelyn returned downstairs to the drawing room, it was to find only Mr. Hawkins, Lord Hughes having already called for her mother. Evelyn was at once aware of the gentleman's proximity and that they were alone, for she had naturally left her maid to wait in the entry hall. Her sudden nervousness was not aided when Mr. Hawkins gave her a slow approving glance.

"That is a very fetching bonnet," he said softly.

Her pulse fluttered at the unexpected intimacy of his voice. She hid her reaction beneath a very correct exterior. "Shall we go, Mr. Hawkins?"

"Of course, Miss Dower." He held open the drawing room door so that she could precede him and then accompanied her to the front door. The maid trailed them.

When Evelyn stepped outside, she was unsurprised to see that Mr. Hawkins had brought a cabriolet. He had not turned a hair when her mother had suggested that the maid accompany them, which, if he had been driving a gig, would have meant squeezing three persons on a seat meant for two. But of course Mr. Hawkins had anticipated that there would be a chaperon and had provided for their comfort accordingly.

Mr. Hawkins flashed what Evelyn had come to think of as his infuriating smile, but she managed to ignore his obvious satisfaction as he handed her up onto the carriage seat. Her maid sat on the seat behind.

As he joined her on the narrow seat, his broad shoulder brushed hers, startling her.

He glanced down. "My apologies. I trust that you are comfortable, Miss Dower?"

Evelyn nodded as though it were the most mundane occurrence. "Of course, Mr. Hawkins."

Evelyn forgot her studied indifference as Mr. Hawkins drove them in the direction of the scheduled event. Carriages of all sorts as well as those on horseback had created a stream of the curious. There was such an exchange of lighthearted banter and speculation called between the various racegoers that Evelyn could not ignore, or be unaffected, by the general atmosphere of excitement.

What had begun as a private wager between Sir Charles Reginald and Mr. Ned Woodthorpe had quickly become a major public event. It was said that a small fortune had been wagered, the odds running heavily in favor of the local favorite. But Sir Charles had his supporters, as well. Those who were already familiar with his reputation and those who had thoughtfully and knowledgeably inspected his team contended vocally that their man must win. Ned Woodthorpe's backers just as vociferously defended their own champion, and so at the hour of the race the designated course was lined with spectators.

Mr. Hawkins had wisely marked out a spot above the course and the jostling crowd on a small hill. As the cabriolet emerged out from under the lace-leafed trees, Evelyn was delighted at once by their splendid view.

She became filled with amazement as she looked down

over the innumerable filled carriages and riders that lined the road below. "I had no notion that a simple race would garner such attention."

"It bids fair to be a satisfying entertainment," said Mr. Hawkins, maneuvering his carriage so that it faced the edge of the small promontory overlooking the course of the race. "I have had an opportunity to see Mr. Woodthorpe's horses since the race was first proposed, and I must admit that they are some of the best I have ever seen."

"Better than Sir Charles's team?" asked Evelyn, glancing at him curiously.

"I think it more accurate to say their equal. It will not be the teams so much as the skill of the drivers that will make the winning difference," said Mr. Hawkins.

"Ned knows the roads," said Evelyn thoughtfully.

"Yes," Mr. Hawkins agreed. Suddenly he flung out his arm, pointing. "There! They have begun."

Evelyn craned her neck to see what was happening. The two carriages were made small by distance, but it was nevertheless easy to discern Sir Charles's yellow phaeton from the other.

Evelyn watched, fascinated. The teams surged up and down, the faint thunder of their hooves a counterpoint to the dust that boiled up from behind the streaking carriages.

"Oh! Ned has taken the lead!" she exclaimed.

After a long, tense moment, she threw a glance at the gentleman seated beside her. "I am let down, indeed! I thought it would be a spirited contest, but it is obvious that Ned has it in his pocket."

"I would not be so certain of that, Miss Dower," said Mr. Hawkins, not removing his gaze from the race below.

Evelyn looked down quickly, and drew in her breath on a gasp.

Sir Charles had pulled out to one side, his obvious intention to pass on the impossibly narrow road. His team began to move up on Mr. Woodthorpe's off-wheel. But Mr. Woodthorpe seemed to anticipate his opponent's intent and he quickly flung his carriage into the gap. Sir Charles was obliged to fall back behind to his former position.

"There! You see! Ned has it well in hand," she exclaimed, turning to Mr. Hawkins. Her tawny eyes sparkled and her face was brightened by excitement.

"Mr. Woodthorpe is indeed a credible whip. I shall give him that," said Mr. Hawkins.

Evelyn turned full-face to her companion. "But you do not believe that he will win?"

Mr. Hawkins smiled. In an apologetic tone, he said, "I know Sir Charles so very well, you see."

Evelyn's eyes flashed. "A wager then, sir!"

Behind her, she heard her maid give a startled gasp. A faint flush rose in her face, but otherwise she paid no heed to the woman's horror. She set her chin challengingly. "What say you, Mr. Hawkins? Shall you back Sir Charles against my wager on Ned Woodthorpe?"

"That is highly unorthodox for a lady, surely?" asked Mr. Hawkins quietly.

Evelyn tossed her head, refusing to give in even to her own amazement at her impulsive challenge. "I do just as I please, sir. I have no need of anyone else's approval, as long as I am satisfied with my own conduct."

The maid squeaked in protest. "Miss!"

Evelyn's cheeks burned, but she had, however rashly, thrown down the gauntlet and she would not retreat. Instead she stared daringly at Mr. Hawkins. "What is it to be, Mr. Hawkins? I shall wager ten pounds on the outcome."

"Very well, Miss Dower. I accept your wager," said Mr. Hawkins. He smiled at her, the corner of his mouth quirking in that fascinating way it had.

Evelyn felt quite suddenly short of breath. Her eyes widened, caught by the degree of warmth in the vividness of his blue eyes. She turned quickly away, her heart pounding loud in her own ears.

She pretended to watch the remainder of the furiously contested race, but her attention was not entirely fixed on the duel below. She puzzled over the extraordinary effect that a singularly attractive smile had on her.

It simply made no sense at all when she was so completely interested in Sir Charles Reginald.

At the thought of that other gentleman, her attention abruptly snapped back to what was happening. Disbelievingly, she saw that the carriages were running neck to neck, in danger of either locking their wheels or of slewing off the road to disaster. The crowd lining the course fell back before the oncoming carriages, only to wave back into place after their furious passing.

Evelyn's heart thudded as the horses pounded toward the designated finish point. She held her breath, scarcely aware that she did so. She clenched her hands. Finally unable to contain herself, she exclaimed, "Oh, *do* come on, Ned!"

The impossible tableau held, wavered. Then Sir Charles's yellow phaeton swept cleanly past the other and away. His team plunged strongly, pulling him steadily ahead of the contending carriage.

Evelyn leaped up, scarcely aware that she had done so or that Mr. Hawkins threw out a hand to catch her elbow to steady her. "Ned! Ned! Do not let him get away from you!" She continued to shriek encouragement, even though it was quickly apparent which driver was to be the winner.

In a moment, all was well over and Evelyn could hear the far-off cheering of the spectators as their ranks broke and they surged after the two slowing carriages.

Evelyn sat down limply. "I have never seen anything half so exciting in my life," she said wonderingly. A half smile curled her lips. "It quite makes one want to attempt it oneself."

"Miss Evelyn! 'Tis bad enough that you wagered!" exclaimed the maid, who then guiltily clapped her hand over her mouth for daring to speak.

Evelyn cast a startled glance at her maid. Then her eyes flew to Mr. Hawkins's bland expression. Color rose in her face, but she said bravely, "It is true, I lost my wager. You did not say what you were wagering for, sir."

There was a long moment's silence while Mr. Hawkins turned the cabriolet. Once on the road, he finally glanced down at the lady seated beside him. He was smiling in an odd fashion. "No, I did not say, did I?"

That was all he said, but Evelyn understood immediately that while she stood in his debt he could demand whatever payment that he wished. Her well-exercised imagination raised one or two speculations, but as instantly she banished them. Mr. Hawkins was first and foremost a gentleman. He would certainly not demand payment in improper coinage. Her heart tumbled at the thought and she did not know whether to be glad or disappointed.

In any event, she discovered herself to be in a very uncomfortable position in her relationship with Mr. Hawkins.

After a short silence, she ventured an observation. "I have been very foolish, haven't I?"

The maid snorted, but neither of the protagonists noticed. Mr. Hawkins briefly met Evelyn's eyes. "Yes."

Evelyn stared for several moments at the road as it unwound and descended the hill toward Bath. "You are not going to divulge the form my debt is to take, are you?"

It was said in a carefully neutral voice which caused Mr. Hawkins's smile to widen. He threw a rueful glance down at the somewhat anxious expression raised to him. "Not just yet, no," he confessed.

"Oh very well. Pray *do* be so disobliging," said Evelyn cordinally.

Mr. Hawkins laughed and merely introduced a new topic. The remainder of the drive was quite pleasant, Evelyn realized, as she was let down in front of her door.

She said a brief good-bye to Mr. Hawkins and thanked him for the invitation.

Chapter Nineteen

As Mr. Hawkins drove away and Evelyn entered the town house, her maid hissed, "Now you've gone and done it, miss. An unknown wager! There is no telling what a gentleman might take into his head to demand in payment!"

Evelyn's own uncertainty was such that she felt inclined to agree with the maid's dour assessment. However, she clung hopefully to an indisputable fact. Loftily she said, "Mr. Hawkins has never shown himself to be improper in word or deed. He is too much the perfect gentleman to take an unfair advantage. I have nothing whatsoever to be anxious about."

With those brave words, Evelyn gave her bonnet, gloves, and reticule into the maid's care before sending the scowling woman upstairs, while she went in search of her mother. She thought it was odd that there was no servant in the entry to whom she could make inquiry whether Mrs. Dower had already preceded her.

Evelyn discovered that Mrs. Dower had indeed returned. She found that lady in the sitting room, but she hesitated in the doorway at the sight that greeted her eyes. Standing in the midst of disarrayed furniture, Mrs. Dower was holding forth with much animation and gesticulation to the housekeeper and two footmen. "Why, whatever is toward?" asked Evelyn in astonishment.

"Evelyn, dear!"

Mrs. Dower swept about and quickly went over to take her daughter's hand in order to draw her into the room. "It is all quite taken care of so you need no longer feel the least bit of concern."

"What, Mama? What shouldn't concern me?"

"Why, Lady Pomerancy's chair, of course! Lord Hughes

had confided in me that her ladyship is doing somewhat poorly since that prodigious rain, and naturally if we are to have Lord Hughes and Mr. Hawkins to our soiree at the end of the week, we cannot expect Lady Pomerancy to remain at home," said Mrs. Dower.

"Mama, whatever are you talking about?"

"Evelyn, were you not attending to me this morning at breakfast when I said that I had got it at last?" Mrs. Dower frowned at her daughter. "Really, child, I expected better of you."

Evelyn vaguely recalled something to have been said about Lady Pomerancy over the bread and marmalade, but she had scarce attended as she had dwelled in a happy daze on Sir Charles's latest sonnet to her. "I am sorry, Mama," she said meekly. "What did you get this morning?"

"My splendid notion, of course. There you are woolgathering again. Perhaps I should box your ears, young lady. In any event, I think it will work very well. Do not you, my dear?" Mrs. Dower contemplated the confused state of the sitting room with a complacent smile.

Evelyn sighed. Sympathetic glances were bestowed upon her by the staff. "Yes, Mama. I completely trust your judgment of the matter."

Mrs. Dower looked around at her daughter with an expression of pleased astonishment. "How nice of you to say so, dear!"

"If I may say so, madam, I believe that clearing the downstairs drawing room and opening it up to the sitting room so that a buffet supper may be served adjoining the dancing was indeed quite brilliant," said the housekeeper.

"*Thank* you, Mrs. Howard. That is just what I wished to say. I could not have said it any better myself," said Evelyn.

As the housekeeper acknowledged her grateful glance with a small smile, Evelyn linked her arm with her mother's. She drew her parent over to a displaced settee that had been pushed flush against the delicately papered wall. "I see that you have been hard at work since your return, Mama. Perhaps a pot of tea would refresh us both, for I am positively parched. I fear that I was very unladylike in my expressions of encouragement for Ned."

While the ladies were seating themselves, Mrs. Dower exclaimed, "The race! I had completely forgotten, silly goose that I am. It was vastly exciting, was it not? Yes, indeed, tea would be splendid. Mrs. Howard, if you please?"

The housekeeper nodded and quietly exited, the footmen following.

"Do tell me, Evelyn! Who was the fortunate winner? Lord Hughes and I were quite unable to see the finish for the crowd. Such a press! I was almost overcome with the dust before Lord Hughes took pity on me and forced our carriage out of the way. But you have not told me yet! Who took the honor of the day?"

"Sir Charles, I fear," said Evelyn, her thoughts inevitably turning to the impetuous wager that she had embarked upon. It did not occur to her to wonder why that should be more consuming to her than the natural pleasure she must feel that the gentleman whom she favored over her other admirers had won.

"Oh, quite so. One can but feel for one of our own. Poor young Woodthorpe! I suppose that he was very disappointed. But that is the way of these sorts of larks. One really cannot take them too much to heart," said Mrs. Dower.

"No, Mama," Evelyn agreed, thinking once again of her own ill-judged challenge to Mr. Hawkins. She sighed slightly.

"Evelyn, are you quite all right?"

Evelyn looked round, startled, to meet an unexpectedly penetrating glance from her mother. She colored guiltily. "Of course I am, Mama. Why shouldn't I be?"

"I thought you might have a fever. Your color is rather high just now. And you have been so extraordinarily agreeable since you returned from your drive with Mr. Hawkins. Usually after you have been in his company, you are quite put out," said Mrs. Dower. There came a speculative look into her eyes. "My dear, did he perhaps—"

Evelyn hastened into speech to forestall whatever outrageous inquiry her mother might make. Any questions would lead uncomfortably close to uncovering her own folly. "Am I usually such a disagreeable old cat, then, Mama? I do beg your pardon! I shall promise to do better. Oh, here is our tea. Thank you, Mrs. Howard. I shall pour."

While she poured, Evelyn kept up a lively discourse on the fine points of the race. "It was all vastly exciting, and quite made me wish that I could drive in just such a dashing fashion."

Mrs. Dower set her cup into the saucer with a clatter. Anxiously, she said, "Evelyn, surely you cannot be serious? Why, you might be killed! Quite, quite suddenly like your dear papa."

Evelyn hastened to reassure her mother. "I was not thinking of racing, Mama. I am not quite that mad. However, I do think I should like to learn to drive. I—I do not care to ride, as you will recall, but I thought if I could drive then I would not be thought to be a complete coward."

"My dear! Who would dare say such a horrid, untrue thing about you? Even though there *are* so few of us who actually dislike horses—but that is nothing, I do assure you. Apollonia does not think the worse of you, and she is known to be a positively *bruising* rider," said Mrs. Dower.

Evelyn laughed. She was touched by her mother's defense of her fears. "No, but Pol thinks I should get back up on one of the brutes."

"Under no circumstances are you to do so, Evelyn. I do not mean to order you about, for you are such a strong-minded person that—However, I had such a fright when they summoned me up to the manor. There you lay, just coming to your senses—though one could scarcely tell it from the rattled way that you spoke! No, I would *much* prefer you to be up behind those great horrid creatures and handling the ribbons," said Mrs. Dower.

"Then have I your permission to learn to drive, Mama?"

"I cannot quite like it, but if it is to be that or riding, certainly you may do so." Mrs. Dower regarded her daughter anxiously. "You will promise me not to do as Apollonia suggests, won't you?"

"Of course I shall. I have as little wish to mount a horse as you have to see me attempt it," said Evelyn.

"Thank you, dear. You have relieved my mind of a most pressing worry," said Mrs. Dower.

The housekeeper returned, bearing a large bouquet of pale pink roses. She offered the fragrant flowers to Evelyn. "These have just been brought, miss. There is a card."

Evelyn took the bouquet and plucked free the card. "Oh, they must be from Sir Charles!" She broke the seal on the missive and opened it, to read, *"I have not forgotten—P. Hawkins."* Without Evelyn being conscious of it, her cheeks were swept with a tide of color. She knew instantly that Mr. Hawkins was reminding her of the lost wager.

She looked up to discover her mother and the lingering housekeeper both regarding her. "It—it is from Mr. Hawkins."

"I do not know why you should be so surprised, Evelyn. The gentleman positively dotes on you," said Mrs. Dower. "What does he say?"

Evelyn hesitated, then read the short message aloud.

"How very intriguing! What can the man possibly mean?" Mrs. Dower cocked her head as she regarded her daughter, whose expression appeared almost guilty. "One could almost say it was a mysterious sort of message."

"It is no great mystery, Mama. I—I promised Mr. Hawkins to go driving with him again," said Evelyn quickly.

"How very thoughtful of Mr. Hawkins! Though it does not surprise me in the least that he should extend such a courteous gesture. Not every gentleman would be so kind. I must say, Evelyn, that I shall not be in the least anxious if you are to learn to drive from Mr. Hawkins," said Mrs. Dower.

Evelyn felt herself sinking into the mire. Aware of the housekeeper's interested air, she said, "Mrs. Howard, I would be grateful if you could put these in water for me."

"Of course, miss." The housekeeper took the bouquet and silently withdrew, as Evelyn had hoped that she would.

Evelyn turned to her mother. "Mama, Mr. Hawkins has not offered to teach me to drive. I meant merely that he will take me up again." She squirmed inside, disliking the untruth even as she felt compelled to make use of it. "And—and we have not decided upon a day, so pray do not tease Mr. Hawkins over it. I—I should not wish to embarrass him if he should forget."

"Of course I would not tease the gentleman. What an odd notion you have of me, dearest," said Mrs. Dower. She reached out to give a reassuring pat to her daughter's hand.

"I do not anticipate that Mr. Hawkins will forget, my dear, for it is quite obvious that the gentleman positively dotes on you. Simply everyone has commented upon it to me. It is a pity, however, that Mr. Hawkins has not offered to teach you to drive. Perhaps I shall give him just a little hint."

"No! Pray do not, Mama." Evelyn drew in her breath at her mother's bewildered expression. "Mama, promise me that you will not mention driving at all to Mr. Hawkins."

"If that is what you wish, Evelyn. But I was quite certain that you told me that you desired to learn to drive, and it seems to me that—" Mrs. Dower saw the darkening expression in her daughter's eyes and said hurriedly, "I shall not say a word, I promise you."

"Thank you, Mama," Evelyn said on a sigh. She turned to the startling statement that her mother had made. "Whatever did you mean when you said everyone has commented upon Mr. Hawkins and myself?"

"Why, it is become quite common knowledge. I have been complimented several times on your good fortune in attaching Mr. Hawkins. The gentleman has always been scrupulously correct in our little society, no doubt out of regard for Lady Pomerancy's reputation. He has never before shown such partiality for a lady, and so his attentions have been particularly marked these last weeks," said Mrs. Dower. She regarded her daughter in surprise. "My dear, it is a vast compliment."

"*I* do not think so. Surely the gossip mill could find something other than my affairs to talk about," said Evelyn, her brows still formed in a frown.

"Well, if it were known that someone was actually having a lurid affair, naturally you would not figure at all. However, it has been a rather dull Season thus far, and you are enjoying a singular success, so really it is not at all surprising that you should find yourself talked about," said Mrs. Dower.

Despite her annoyance, Evelyn was forced to laugh at her mother's explanation. "I quite understand now, Mama. I suppose that I shall soon be the recipient of compliments regarding your own friendship with Lord Hughes. How lowering to reflect that the next *on-dit* will supplant us. What very dull personages we are, indeed!"

"I would not say that we are precisely *dull*, dearest," said Mrs. Dower. She frowned suddenly at their surroundings. "What color would you prefer for the silk awnings? I had conceived of draping the ceilings, just to add a touch of elegance, for it cannot be denied that these rooms are a trifle boring for an assembly."

Evelyn realized that her mother's thoughts had inevitably turned in a different direction. Relieved, she said airily, "Oh, burnished gold, of course. We are both of us well complimented by the shade."

Mrs. Dower regarded her with approval. "Quite, quite appropriate. I am so glad that you have taste and discretion, Evelyn. So many poor girls do not, and they fall into all manner of scrapes as a result."

"One indiscretion and I am in the basket with all the rest," Evelyn said, only half in jest as she was reminded of her wager. She slipped the gilt-edged card bearing Mr. Hawkins's strong script into her pocket, where it seemed to burn a hole through the fabric of her dress.

Evelyn knew very well the censor that would be hers if word of her idiotic wager was to come out. She could rely upon Mr. Hawkins's discretion, naturally, but she felt it would be wise to have a quiet word with her maid. Hopefully it was not too late to warn the woman against spilling what she knew in the servants' wing, for that was the surest way to see gossip spread throughout the town. It was bad enough that the housekeeper had been present as long as she had, for Evelyn suspected that Mrs. Howard would embellish the note with a romantic significance that was quite unwarranted. However, she would far rather have the staff believe that she was wheedling Mr. Hawkins for driving lessons than for them to know the lurid truth.

"Oh, I have far too much faith in you to be anxious on that head," said Mrs. Dower comfortably.

Evelyn started to laugh, struck by the irony. At her mother's bewildered look, she shook her head. "It is nothing that I can readily explain. A nonsensical thought, really. Quite, quite silly of me."

"I do believe you have had too much excitement, dear. Perhaps you should rest this afternoon before dressing for the ball at the manor," said Mrs. Dower. She got up from the settee to lay hold of the bellpull. "I should have the furniture put back where it belongs, do you not agree? It would look very odd to anyone coming to call."

Evelyn scarcely heard her mother's question. "Oh! I had quite forgot the Woodthorpe ball." Her amusement was abruptly cut short as she realized that she would see Mr. Hawkins again in a few short hours. Her heart thumped. She wondered with a flutter of dread if he would make known to her that evening the stipulations of the rash wager that she had lost to him. It was obvious from his note that he fully intended to have payment.

Her maid's opinion came back to haunt her, and she wondered whether she could indeed place her complete trust in Mr. Hawkins. He was a gentleman, albeit a finer one than most, but still a *gentleman*. Everything that she had ever observed and heard had long since led her to the conclusion that, for the most part, gentlemen took advantage of the fairer sex whenever they were given the opportunity.

It would really be too bad of Mr. Hawkins if he chose to take advantage of her. The possibility unaccountably cheered her, even as a frisson of nervousness went down her spine.

"Mama, I think that perhaps I will do as you suggest. I wish to speak to Millie, besides," said Evelyn, rising from the settee.

"Is there something wrong with your gown, dear?" asked Mrs. Dower, at once concerned.

"Oh no. I merely wished to be certain that she has everything well in hand," said Evelyn.

"I think that you may trust her on that score," said Mrs. Dower.

"I am certain that you are right, Mama," said Evelyn, again hoping that she was not already too late with her warning to the maid. She left the chaotic drawing room as the footmen entered it and were given directions from Mrs. Dower, and went upstairs.

Chapter Twenty

Evelyn had the private word with her maid that she intended. The woman was affronted that her mistress would suspect her of such disloyalty and let Evelyn know it by her wounded silence while dressing Evelyn for the ball.

Evelyn's temper was somewhat tried by her maid's martyred air, but when she tripped downstairs to join her mother her irritation vanished and was replaced by a growing anticipation for the delightful evening ahead.

The Dower ladies took their carriage to the Woodthorpe manor. After greeting the squire and Mrs. Woodthorpe, they joined the other guests already in the beautifully decorated ballroom.

The Woodthorpe ball was the most glittering affair of the Season. It appeared that everyone who had received an invitation had chosen to make an appearance. As she surveyed the crowd, Evelyn recognized virtually every personage. It was a good feeling and gave Evelyn confidence in her own social standing. She had always felt the faintest flutter of anxiety when first entering a crowded room, but now she was able to set it aside much more quickly because she was familiar with so many people.

Evelyn's dance card was filled almost at once, and she was able to completely relax without wondering whether she would suffer the ignobility of sitting out any of the sets. She noticed that her mother's card was also filled, and she said teasingly, "Mama, I did not know that matrons were in such high demand."

Mrs. Dower's slid a light glance at her daughter. "I am a very fine dancer," she said simply.

Evelyn laughed. There was not time to say more because the first set was forming and her partner had come up to claim her hand. He was a young gentleman, ill at ease as though it was not often that he was in company. Since Evelyn had met Mr. Sanders before and knew him to be a writer who lived with his elder sister in almost complete seclusion, she was not at all surprised or offended by his tongue-tied greeting.

As Evelyn took her place in the set, she glanced back to see that Lord Hughes was bending over her mother's hand. Evelyn frowned a little. She had grown accustomed to the attentions that Lord Hughes was forever playing to her mother, but she was still a little uncertain how to take that gentleman. His lordship was perfectly polite toward herself, yet there seemed always an indefinable amusement lurking in his eyes and his manner that made her uncomfortable in his presence. No, not uncomfortable, Evelyn amended, but as though his lordship knew something that she did not. It was a feeling that Evelyn disliked.

The set was a country dance, and as Evelyn came together with her partner, Mr. Sanders asked, "Is something untoward, Miss Dower? You seem rather preoccupied."

Evelyn looked at the gentleman, startled. She had not realized that Mr. Sanders was so perceptive. She would have to keep closer guard over her expression, she thought, as she smiled at him. "I am merely concentrating on the intricacies of the steps. If I do not, I make a perfect mull of it."

"I say, that is awfully brave of you to admit." In a burst of candor, Mr. Sanders confided, "I do also, you know."

Evelyn had already discovered that the gentleman was a heavy trodder. Her sore toes were proof of it, but she only smiled again. "No one would immediately guess it, sir."

Mr. Sanders was not at all affronted, but instead grinned. He began counting under his breath and miraculously his steps evened out. Evelyn nodded her encouragement, wanting to laugh but not daring to do so. "Very good, Mr. Sanders. I do believe that with a little practice you will have it down perfectly."

As the movement of the country dance separated them, Mr. Sanders threw her a grateful look. Evelyn smiled at him, thinking that the youthful gentleman was rather endearing. It did not occur to her that Mr. Sanders was actually several years older than herself.

When the set ended and Mr. Sanders returned Evelyn to her chair, her next partner was already waiting to take her out to the floor. For some time then, Evelyn was in a constant whirl as gentleman after gentleman claimed her hand for the dance floor. She laughed and parried their pretty compliments, enjoying herself tremendously.

Then she looked up to meet Mr. Hawkins's eyes as she placed her hand in his, and the crowded ballroom appeared to recede, leaving just the two of them. In the silence, they regarded one another. Evelyn had never noticed how very like a dark pool of water his eyes looked. She felt as though she were drowning in their blue depths. She drew her breath, struggling against the odd feeling. "Mr. Hawkins, I—"

He drew her up out of her chair. "It is a waltz, Miss Dower."

His quiet words sent a frisson along her nerve endings. Evelyn looked up at his face quickly, then away. She had danced the waltz before. She had danced it before with Mr. Hawkins. She did not understand why she should be so aware of him walking beside her, nor, when he turned and took her into his arms, why she should actually tremble.

It was the fault of that idiotic wager, she decided crossly. She was consciously aware of being ill at ease. It was dread of what he would demand of her that caused her heart to flutter in her throat so that she could scarcely speak. Of course that was what it was.

"Did you say something, Miss Dower?"

Startled, Evelyn met Mr. Hawkins's eyes. She realized that she must have made some inarticulate sound. The color rose in her face. "It was nothing of any consequence, Mr. Hawkins." She was acutely aware of his arm about her, that his hand pressed firmly against her waist, that she was held ever closer in the swirl of turns.

He smiled down at her, amusement lighting his eyes. "Are you frightened of me, Miss Dower?" he asked softly.

"What a question, Mr. Hawkins! Of course I am not." Evelyn gave a laugh that sounded nervous even to her own ears.

That so greatly annoyed her that she threw a glittering glance of resentment up at him. She hissed in a low voice,

"If you must know, I am wondering what you shall demand in payment of my wager."

"I see." Mr. Hawkins did not enlarge upon his reply, but merely squired her in another round of dizzying spirals about the dance floor.

The exhilarating feeling of floating proved a fine counterpoint to her anxiety. Evelyn could not stand the suspense, and breathlessly she demanded, "Well?"

Mr. Hawkins threw back his head and laughed. When he looked at her again, he acknowledged her offended tawny eyes with a shrug. "Forgive me for teasing you, Miss Dower. That was ungentlemanly of me. I have not decided what form the payment shall take . . . yet." His gaze lowered to her slightly parted lips and lingered.

Evelyn's breath caught. It was almost as though he caressed her with that long half-lidded glance. Then his eyes swept up and caught her own. She averted her face to fix her eyes on the point over his broad shoulder. "You—you have the most disconcerting effect upon my good sense. I am inclined to give you a set-down each time we meet," she said, forcing irritation into her voice.

"So I have noticed, Miss Dower."

Evelyn looked at him sharply. His voice was wry, though with an underlying current that she could not quite identify. Of all her admirers, Mr. Hawkins was the most incomprehensible. She had sent him away with a finality that must have wounded his pride, and yet he had become one of her most faithful admirers. She had shown herself at her most hoydenish, and though he had been surprised by her wagering on the outcome of the race, he did not act as though he had developed a disgust of her. He was universally polite in address and gesture, but he had often astonished her with a teasing word or warmth of gaze.

Mr. Hawkins was an enigma. Reflecting, Evelyn thought that she did not care for such a gentleman. She was too unsure of herself when she was in his company.

"Surely I am not such grim company as your frown indicates, Miss Dower?"

Chapter Twenty-one

The quiet question disconcerted her. Evelyn found that she had been staring at him and she looked away, thoroughly embarrassed. "On the contrary, Mr. Hawkins. I fear it is I who is not being particularly good company," she said, managing a credible smile. "I do apologize, sir. It is a perfectly lovely evening, is it not? The Woodthorpes always arrange grand entertainments when they are not caught up in hunting and other such sport."

"It is plain that you do not share the same interest in sport, Miss Dower," said Mr. Hawkins, apparently quite willing to follow her lead in conversation.

Evelyn relaxed, laughing a little ruefully. "No, I fear I do not. It is a great disappointment to Pol—Miss Woodthorpe, but she remains fast friends with me despite my most glaring fault."

"I had noticed that the lady was most knowledgeable. My cousin was quite impressed with Miss Woodthorpe's horse savvy. In fact, I believe that he has called on her several times since discovering that she is a kindred spirit," said Mr. Hawkins, throwing Evelyn a quick penetrating glance.

"Viscount Waithe?" Evelyn looked around for the viscount. She had vaguely wondered at his less assiduous attentions of late, having become used to his lordship's appearance nearly every afternoon in Queen Square. She located the viscount, who was at that moment seated beside Miss Woodthorpe, and from what she could discern before her view was blocked by the passing of a dancing couple, the two were in deep discussion.

Evelyn chuckled softly. Of course they were talking about horses, for she was certain nothing was closer to either heart than equines. "I am not at all surprised. It was only a matter of time before they discovered one another."

"You do not mind it, Miss Dower?" asked Mr. Hawkins quietly, still looking at her quite keenly.

Evelyn was surprised. "Why should I mind, Mr. Hawkins?"

His mouth turned upward at one corner. He met her puzzled gaze with an odd expression in his own eyes. "Many young ladies would resent losing an admirer to another young lady, no matter how friendly she was with that lady."

"Resent Pol? Of course I do not. As for Viscount Waithe, I counted him as more a brother than an admirer. But you shall not tell him that, if you please," said Evelyn.

Mr. Hawkins's smile broadened. The watchful expression in his eyes had disappeared. "Be assured that I will not, Miss Dower." He casually introduced another topic.

The set ended swiftly after that, and the orchestra indicated that there would be a short intermission for refreshments to be served.

Mr. Hawkins escorted Evelyn off the floor. They chanced to encounter Miss Sparrow and her betrothed also leaving the floor. After the couples greeted one another, Miss Sparrow said, "I am simply parched. What of you, Evelyn? Will you gentlemen be so kind as to find us refreshments?"

"Of course," said Mr. Hawkins, his expression as polite as ever. Mr. Fiddle pronounced himself quite ready to be of service to the ladies. Mr. Hawkins and the excellent Mr. Fiddle left the ladies in adjoining chairs to fan themselves.

Miss Sparrow leaned toward Evelyn, her hand up before her mouth. "My dear, has Mr. Hawkins said anything to you?"

Evelyn stared at her friend in surprise. "Whatever should he say to me, Abigail?"

"Oh, you can be so frustrating, Evelyn. You must know what I am referring to. Why, it is quite obvious to the dullest intelligence that Mr. Hawkins is smitten with you," said Miss Sparrow.

Evelyn felt heat rising in her face. "Mr. Hawkins is one of several admirers, Abigail. I do not think—"

"Pray do not think to put me off, Evelyn! I shan't be diverted, I promise you." Miss Sparrow regarded Evelyn's rising brows with a sigh. "You may as well divulge it all to me, for at least I am your friend, and not like some others I could mention who have expressed their scarcely concealed curiosity to me."

Evelyn was taken aback. "What are you talking about, Abigail?"

Miss Sparrow had the grace to look abashed. "I do not gossip, truly I do not, but one cannot help hearing what others say to one. And of late . . . I do wish you would rid yourself of that frown, Evelyn. It is not so very bad, after all. It is merely being said that Mr. Hawkins is being particularly attentive to you, and I think it is quite true. He does not waltz with anyone else, and he has not done so since he arrived in Bath. Then you were seen with him at Ned Woodthorpe's race. I know that your maid was with you, but still it appeared to some to be an indication. And the way he has of quietly discouraging some of the other gentlemen has made *me* wonder whether—I *am* sorry if I have trespassed, Evelyn."

Evelyn looked away from Miss Sparrow's anxious look. "Oh no, I am glad you have told me. I had no notion that my name had become linked so closely with Mr. Hawkins." She swung around again, her eyes quite bright—but with what emotion Miss Sparrow could not have said. "Did you say that Mr. Hawkins has been discouraging some of my admirers?"

Miss Sparrow now wished that she had never said a word. "Not precisely discouraged. I should not have said that. I-it is only that I have observed on one or two occasions that Mr. Hawkins has—has intercepted a gentleman and spoken quite civilly to him. Then it would strike me a few evenings later that the gentleman would no longer be in attendance on you."

Miss Sparrow most definitely recognized the expression that now narrowed her friend's eyes. She said hastily, "It is nothing but conjecture, Evelyn, truly. I do have an active imagination, you know that I do."

"So, apparently, do those others you spoke of, Abigail," said Evelyn evenly. She saw that her friend was quite distressed at the reception of her disclosures. Evelyn smiled brightly. "Do not concern yourself, Abigail. Of course you were right to alert me to the gossip. Now I may be more circumspect in my dealings with Mr. Hawkins."

The gentlemen returned with lemonades, and Miss Sparrow accepted hers with an air of relief. The two couples spent a few minutes in idle conversation, and all the while Evelyn held on to her smouldering temper.

She knew that Mr. Hawkins's gaze rested thoughtfully upon her several times, but she gave no indication of it. She spoke animatedly and laughed with a naturalness that surprised her and which she knew must cloak her true feelings. She did not know that the overbrightness of her eyes gave her away.

The orchestra struck up again, indicating the short intermission was over. At once, Evelyn was approached by Viscount Waithe, who bowed to her in solicitation of her hand. "Of course, my lord. I would be delighted," said Evelyn warmly, and promptly moved off with him, her head held high.

Mr. Hawkins stared after the lady, his expression unreadable. He had perceived almost the instant that he had come back with Miss Dower's lemonade that she was in a towering temper. He wondered why it appeared to be directed at him, for he had not been behind in absorbing her slitted glances when she had thought he would not notice. Mr. Hawkins turned his head to regard Miss Sparrow.

That lady, with a prudent regard for her own self-preservation, had risen hastily and importuned her betrothed to take her out onto the floor. "For it is above all my favorite dance," she said.

"But I thought the quadrille was your favorite," said Mr. Fiddle.

Miss Sparrow cast a rather hunted look at Mr. Hawkins's sardonic expression. "Oh, what does it matter which is my favorite, Mr. Fiddle, when I am able to dance with you." Much gratified, Mr. Fiddle proudly led off his wonderful lady.

Mr. Hawkins was left behind with his speculations about what Miss Sparrow could possibly have said to Miss Dower concerning him. This business of courting the lady of his choice was utterly fatiguing. One moment he seemed to be making progress and the next moment he had lost every inch of ground.

Mr. Hawkins's eyes fell on the empty glasses left by the ladies chairs. Lemonade was not precisely what he had in mind, he thought grimly. Turning on his heel, he went in search of a refreshment that was a bit stronger.

As soon as the viscount and Evelyn reached the floor, her store of witty chatter disappeared. She danced silently, almost absently. Viscount Waithe attempted several conversational gambits, to which she made answer in monosyllables or not at all.

Viscount Waithe had noticed how his cousin's eyes had followed him and Miss Dower onto the floor, and it slowly dawned on him that there could have been something more in that than casual observation. The viscount was not used to being ignored so thoroughly, and for the sake of his own ego he finally decided to press the issue. "Miss Dower, have you and Peter had a falling out?"

Evelyn raised her eyes quickly, shocked.

Viscount Waithe was startled by her response. He had not actually thought it was true, but now as he looked down into Miss Dower's face he was utterly certain that it had been so. He said earnestly, "You mustn't believe everything that is said, ma'am. I assure you that Peter is as near to being a saint as it is possible for a mere mortal to be. He would never do anything to cause the least pain to anyone."

Evelyn's eyes fell. "I know that. Mr. Hawkins is the perfect gentleman."

The viscount was at something of a standstill. He could not imagine what could have put such an expression into the lady's eyes if it had not been an argument of some sort. However, it couldn't have been a quarrel, or otherwise Miss Dower would not have asserted so calmly that she agreed with him about his cousin.

"I am useless at this, I am afraid," said Viscount Waithe. He caught Miss Dower's glance and held it with the appeal of his charming smile. "Won't you confide in me? Are we not good enough friends for you to do so?"

Evelyn hesitated, torn by her inclination to do just that and her pride, which would not admit anyone to the humiliation that she felt. She finally shook her head and with a wavering smile said, "Thank you, my lord, but I think it would be best if I did not say anything to you. It—it is something rather lowering to my self-esteem, you see, and I would prefer to work it out for myself."

With blinding clarity, Viscount Waithe thought he knew the cause of her despondency. She was obviously in love with his cousin and had shown it to Peter, either through word or glance, and had been rebuffed.

The viscount saw it all. He had always been aware of the polite barrier that his cousin held between himself and the world. He counted himself fortunate that he was one of the few people that Peter had let come close. Lady Pomerancy and Sir Charles were two others who shared that intimacy, but Viscount Waithe suspected that there were very few others. His cousin was well liked and pleasant and had a wealth of acquaintances, even some who believed themselves to be close friends, but Viscount Waithe did not think that Peter himself thought of more than a dozen or so individuals as true friends.

Miss Dower was apparently not one of those individuals.

Not very long past, Viscount Waithe had thought himself to be deeply in love with Miss Dower. Enough of those feelings remained, though more in the guise of warm friendship, than he had anticipated, and her obvious distress pained him. "Miss Dower, if there is anything that I can do, anything at all, pray call upon me," he said.

Evelyn was touched and astonished by his sincere offer. "Thank you, my lord. I shall remember that." She smiled up at him, determined to make up for her lack of manners. "I noticed earlier that you were seated with my friend, Miss Woodthorpe. I suppose that she has told you about the perfectly stunning hunter that she bought last spring?"

Viscount Waithe smiled, admiring Miss Dower's strength of spirit. He knew well that she had no interest whatsoever in hunters, but he was willing to allow her to lead him into safer conversational waters. For the rest of the dance, they chatted amiably on several topics. When the music ceased and Viscount Waithe returned her to her chair, he was able to leave her with some feeling of having done some good toward repairing her lowness of spirits.

Evelyn found that the next set on her card was reserved

for Sir Charles. Surprisingly enough, when she read the
gentleman's name it caused hardly a flutter. Her thoughts
had reverted to what she had learned about Mr. Hawkins.

Sir Charles presented himself. His dark gaze was deliberately appreciative of her appearance. "You are lovely as always, Miss Dower. I would have rushed to your side before now if I had been able to push my way through the admiring press, but alas, one must be fair to one's competitors."

Evelyn bestowed a smile upon the gentleman as she gave
her hand to him. "What nonsense, sir. I hope that I know
better than that."

Sir Charles was somewhat taken aback by her lack of
blushes at his exquisite periods, but he recovered almost at
once. Lowering his voice, he asked, "I hope that you received my humble billet?"

Evelyn nodded, and the smile that entered her eyes went
far toward alleviating his slight sense of pique. "Yes, and I
truly thank you. Your poetry is wonderfully romantic. What
lady could possibly resist such soulful sensitivity?"

"My fairest lady, I had not dared to hope that you would
perceive me half so well," he said, smiling down into her
unusual eyes. Really, she had the most beguiling eyes, like
molten gold, he thought.

She was saying something to him, a question of some
sort. Still entranced by his thoughts, he replied absently,
"Of course, lovely lady. How could one withstand the
pleading of such brilliant jewels? Miss Dower, have I told
you that your eyes are—"

"Oh thank you, Sir Charles!"

Her exclamation shook him out of his reverie.

"I really did not think that you would agree, sir," said
Evelyn confidingly. "For I do understand that your horses
are your greatest pleasure. I promise you that I shall be very
attentive to all you say."

Evelyn laughed, quite unperceiving of his startlement. "I
shall be the envy of all my friends when I tell them that you
have agreed to teach me to drive."

"What?"

Evelyn looked at him, surprised. Sir Charles was staring
at her with a most peculiar expression on his face. "Oh, forgive me. My enthusiasm has quite gotten the better of me,

has it not? It does not have to be at that early an hour, of course. I had forgotten that gentlemen sometimes prefer not to go out before luncheon. Will three o'clock tomorrow do instead?"

For once Sir Charles's famed urbanity appeared to have deserted him. "Miss Dower, I—"

The set ended, and as Evelyn stepped back, a young gentleman appeared at her shoulder. Evelyn welcomed his arrival with a quick smile. "Mr. Sanders! Sir Charles, let me make known to you Mr. Sanders."

The gentlemen exchanged polite pleasantries. Mr. Sanders reminded Miss Dower that she was promised to him for the country dance that was starting up. She agreed and excused herself to Sir Charles, who appeared strangely at loose ends. Evelyn wondered at it. She had never seen that gentleman at a loss before.

Looking back over her shoulder at Sir Charles, she said, "Three o'clock, Sir Charles?"

"I—yes, of course," said Sir Charles, defeated.

Chapter Twenty-two

Sir Charles came to call at the appointed time. Evelyn and her mother were entertaining Lord Hughes when the gentleman was ushered into the drawing room.

Sir Charles made the correct overtures to Mrs. Dower and Lord Hughes, whom he naturally knew even though the gentlemen did not run in quite the same London circles. At last, Sir Charles turned to Evelyn.

Evelyn greeted him with a warm smile and offered her hand to him. "Sir Charles, I *am* glad to see you."

He retained her hand, smiling down into her uplifted eyes. "Each time I meet you, I am astounded anew how the very sun seems brightened," he said.

Evelyn blushed. "How very gallant of you, Sir Charles."

"Indeed, I stand in awe of such adroit courtesy, my boy. I had quite thought savoir faire a fading art unto my own generation," said Lord Hughes in a friendly way.

There was a flicker across Sir Charles's face of what might be annoyance. Evelyn hurried into the suspected breach. "Sir Charles has come to take me driving."

"Ah, I *had* wondered at your attire. The bronze shade of your carriage dress quite compliments you, Miss Dower," said Lord Hughes.

"Doesn't it, though? Evelyn had been somewhat hesitant to settle on that particular color, but I assured her it was quite perfect," said Mrs. Dower, seemingly unconscious of the sudden tension.

"I should have guessed that it was your exquisite taste," said Lord Hughes, lifting Mrs. Dower's hand to his lips for a salute.

"I hold myself ready at your service, Miss Dower," said Sir Charles.

"Of course. I shall go directly up for my bonnet," said Evelyn, rising and exiting the drawing room.

When she returned, she said good-bye to her mother and Lord Hughes and tripped out the door on Sir Charles's arm.

Evelyn was handed up into the phaeton. She settled on the leather seat with high anticipation. She had been looking forward to this particular outing all morning, for Sir Charles Reginald *had* promised to teach her to drive.

Sir Charles instructed his groom to stand away from the horses. "I will not need you further. You may meet me back at the hotel," he told the servant.

Sir Charles tooled the carriage away from the curb and down the street. Evelyn turned a brilliant smile on her companion. "I have so been looking forward to this lesson, Sir Charles. You cannot conceive how much! Your awe-inspiring example during the race has persuaded me that nothing will do but to acquire a similar mastery of the reins."

Sir Charles appeared momentarily startled. Then his expression smoothed to its usual urbanity. "Of course, Miss Dower. Your driving lesson. I am always happy to be of service to a beautiful young lady," he drawled. "Pray watch me carefully while I attempt to explain the intricacies of technique in driving a four-in-hand."

Evelyn professed herself quite willing to do so and folded her hands in her lap. She was delighted when Sir Charles directed the phaeton out of the congested town into the country.

For the next hour, Sir Charles tooled the phaeton sedately over the gentle rises and drops of the tree-shadowed lanes. He explained in great detail each flick of the reins or whip, intermingling among his strictures compliments to Evelyn and poetic accolades on the passing countryside.

Evelyn enjoyed herself hugely. When Sir Charles remarked that it was time that they should consider returning to town and turned the phaeton, she began to wonder when he was going to allow her to actually take the reins. She paid less heed to his smooth flirtation as the conviction slowly grew on her that Sir Charles was endeavoring to divert her attention from her previously stated hope of driving his team.

As the minutes passed, Evelyn threw him a few keen glances. Finally she decided to put her suspicion to the test.

"Sir Charles, I am truly grateful for the patient explanations that you have offered me. I assure you, I have listened carefully to every word. I am quite ready to take the reins for a short interval."

"Er—take the reins?" Sir Charles looked unhappy, obviously reluctant to allow her to take control of his team.

"Why, certainly," said Evelyn, as though in surprise. "That is an essential part of driving, is it not?"

He tossed her a smile. "Perhaps we should put that off until a future lesson, Miss Dower. I am not at all certain that you are ready for such a momentous step."

Evelyn smiled up at her companion. The expression in her tawny eyes was friendly, but the set of her chin betrayed determination. "Oh, I must disagree, sir! I am not likely ever to be in the company of such a notable whip again, for I am aware that you do not mean to make a long stay in Bath. And how am I to test my understanding of your excellent tutelage if I do not handle the reins?"

Sir Charles allowed his smile to broaden to one of patient amusement. His tone displayed the tolerance reserved for those of simpler understanding. "My dear young lady, forgive me. But I can not think it a sound notion. You see how it is, of course. We are near enough to Bath now that the traffic must increase quite dramatically. I would not wish to return you to your dear mother shaken and disheveled from a carriage accident that can be so easily prevented."

Evelyn smiled back in her most charming manner. "I am completely confident in your skill and alert attention to prevent any evil consequences."

Gazing down at his fair companion, Sir Charles began to realize that he was neatly caught. He thoughtfully took note of the alarmingly determined glint in the young lady's eyes and mentally cursed himself for having made the careless promise. He must have been momentarily bedazzled to have uttered such mad words.

Whatever his inner feelings, however, he could not do less than give in with good grace to the inevitable. "I am complimented by your exorbitant faith in me," he said ironically, as with visible reluctance he surrendered the reins.

Evelyn accepted the leathers and with a certain delighted trepidation took over the driving of Sir Charles Reginald's prize team. Any of Sir Charles's acquaintances who might have seen them would have been struck slack-jawed with astonishment, for it was well known that Sir Charles was extremely jealous of his horses. He rarely granted the privilege of tooling them to another driver.

"Mind the off-leader, Miss Dower!" There was now an edge to Sir Charles's voice that Evelyn was unaccustomed to hearing from him. He instructed her precisely in her commands to the horses, and at his insistence, Evelyn kept the team to a sedate walk.

The gentleman's anxiety on behalf of his beloved horses while in the lady's inexperienced hands was inordinate. At any moment he expected disaster to strike and his horses to take hurt from the unaccustomed and dubious honor of being driven by a lady.

Sir Charles consoled himself with the thought that the team's freshness had already been so dulled that they would not object to being kept down to such a pedestrian speed and therefore there was little chance of anything dire actually happening.

Evelyn was quite proud of her accomplishment in driving the team. She had been somewhat nervous in the beginning, but she had always been a quick study, and she had absorbed enough of Sir Charles's explanations that the actual driving came relatively easy to her.

As she had gained confidence, she had entertained the thought of putting the team along a bit faster. She was aware of Sir Charles's tense anxiety, however, and she was extremely careful to do nothing except that which he instructed her.

After the first several minutes, it was not particularly thrilling to proceed at such a paltry pace, but she well knew that she did not dare to suggest anything livelier. Sir Charles would not only refuse, she thought, but would in all likelihood use her request as an excuse to reclaim the reins, and she was not at all ready to give over control just yet. It was, after all, quite an experience to be up behind a strong team of horses and know that it was her hands that directed them.

Flushed with her success, she tossed a laughing glance up at her markedly unenthusiastic companion. "They are beauties, sir! I had no notion what enjoyment driving such an outstanding team would be."

Sir Charles was so thoroughly enchanted by her sparkling enthusiasm that his irritation with her waned. "Indeed, it is an excellent team," he agreed.

When she flashed him another bright smile, he added with a return of warmth, "You have a very good eye, Miss Dower, and I believe an instinct for the leathers, as well."

"You are too kind, Sir Charles, for I know that I cannot hope to become a true whip in but one lesson. My keenest ambition now is to own a carriage of my own, if Mama permits me. Perhaps I might rely upon your advice in choosing such an equipage and, of course, the team?"

Sir Charles genuinely smiled. There was nothing that appealed to him more than to deal in horses and carriages. The added draw of doing so for an attractive young lady was an extremely pleasing prospect. "I hold myself ready at your earliest convenience, Miss Dower. Indeed, I would deem it an honor to prove myself of such service to a delightful and discerning lady."

His voice had assumed the caressing note that Evelyn had grown used to from him, and her heart thrilled. Just for an instant she removed her attention from the horses, her hands dropping a fraction as she looked wide-eyed up at him from around the edge of her bonnet.

There was an element in Evelyn's gaze that invited. Sir Charles was not a man to turn away from an opportunity offered. He drew a finger slowly across her mouth and felt her soft lips part on a faint gasp. When he heard the little sharp intake of breath, he gave no more thought to his horses.

" 'Tis beauty unawakened, that siren song, which man cannot resist," he breathed, and with expert fingers upturned her face for a lingering kiss.

At the first touch of his mouth, Evelyn started like a fawn. But his fingers held her captive, long enough for her to fall in thrall to the unaccustomed and pleasurable sensations the kiss was awakening in her.

Winding up and over the hills, the road was a vista of bucolic serenity. No other carriages maneuvered along it, and all about were the peaceful sounds of a country day as Sir Charles's team steadily paced forward, completely unattended by the occupants of the carriage.

Suddenly the leaders snorted, perceiving danger ahead. Nervously the horses threw up their heads. The dark haze of bees hovering above the middle of the road buzzed angrily and attacked. The horses panicked.

The carriage jerked forward, slamming Evelyn and Sir Charles against the back of the seat. The reins ran through Evelyn's slackened fingers and slipped free.

"What the devil!"

Sir Charles lunged forward and grabbed the reins.

The phaeton was pulled into the cloud of enraged bees. Evelyn shrieked as the bees hit her bonnet with solid crunches and one or two spent their stings on her cheek and neck. She clung to the seat rail with only one hand while she frantically slapped aside the infuriated insects and shook them out of her skirt.

Sir Charles cursed steadily, futilely ducking his head against attack while he tried to regain control of the maddened horses. The team thundered on, heedless of their master, and the phaeton was carried at precarious speed.

Sir Charles saw the sharp bend in the road, and in an instant recognized disaster. Renewing his curses, he pulled cruelly with all his strength on the off-leaders. He felt their belated response, even as he knew it was too late.

Wide-eyed with horror, Evelyn clutched the seat rail with both hands. She screamed as the carriage swung too wide for the bend.

An outside wheel hit a rock. The carriage lifted, momentarily skyborne. The elegant phaeton descended with bone-jarring force, and there was the resounding splintering of wood. Then all was quiet.

Evelyn lay very still. She blinked up at the blue sky. Realizing that she had been thrown clear of the phaeton, she cautiously sat up.

She was perfectly astonished to be alive. She took careful inventory. There was not an inch of her that did not protest from bruising or burn from bee sting. She was only thankful that she had not broken any bones.

It was then she thought of her companion.

"Sir Charles?"

Evelyn got painfully to her feet, alarmed suddenly by the absolute quiet. "Sir Charles! Are you hurt?"

Evelyn limped hurriedly over to the once-proud carriage. The dust-covered yellow phaeton lay on its side, its underpinnings smashed. Two wheels still spun madly in the air. Evelyn's heart thumped with fear as her imagination supplied her with an all-too lurid vision of the gentleman lying trapped and perhaps dead underneath the wreckage. "Sir Charles!"

"Here, Miss Dower!"

Chapter Twenty-three

Sir Charles's voice sounded reassuringly strong, and Evelyn hurried around the carriage, following its direction. At sight of Sir Charles, she stopped stock-still. He was carefully inspecting the legs of each of his horses, murmuring soothingly when they quickstepped as he touched a tender spot.

Without pausing in his ministrations, Sir Charles glanced around. "Oh, there you are. You are all right, then," he said casually.

Evelyn was aghast for a moment or two. She could not believe her ears or her eyes. The gentleman cared more for the welfare of his horses than he did for her safe delivery. "Thank you for your concern, Sir Charles!" she snapped.

Despite his overriding preoccupation, Sir Charles detected the anger in her voice. He glanced about again, somewhat impatiently. "Of course I am concerned about you, Miss Dower. In point of fact, it was just this sort of accident that I wished to avoid when I attempted to dissuade you from taking the reins. Now I have two horses with sprained hocks and a smashed wheel and axle and no way to get either of us safely back to town. I shudder to think what your parent may think of this misadventure, but I daresay I shall be denied the door from this day forward."

Somewhat mollified, Evelyn said, "I do not think it, Sir Charles. Mama is not at all unreasonable, you know. You may still call upon me, I am persuaded."

Sir Charles's next statement did not precisely convey the unutterable relief that Evelyn had assumed he must surely feel upon her reassurance. "You relieve my mind, naturally. Here, come hold the strap on this one. I need him to be perfectly still so that I can take a closer look at this ugly scrape."

Evelyn reluctantly complied with the gentleman's request and took hold of the horse's head. She was wary of standing so close to one of the big brutes, but the horse stood peacefully enough under her hand.

Her brows knit as she observed Sir Charles's absorbed inspection of the animal. She was filled with disquiet, for this scenario was all wrong.

The romantic hero that she had built up in her imagination would have cared nothing for the horses, but instead would have been wild with anxiety over *her* safety and *her* well-being. He would have treated her in a tender and concerned manner, and his uppermost thought would have been to see to her comfort and succor.

Instead, the gentleman that she had cast in that romantic light crooned to his horses and talked to himself while he did a careful inspection of every inch of horse leg. He had not asked if she was hurt, nor had he been concerned that the shock of the accident might have led her to feel light-headed.

Evelyn toyed with the notion of falling down in a belated faint. However, she was not at all certain that Sir Charles would notice anything untoward except that she had let go of the horse's bridle. That would be humiliation, indeed, and so she did not act upon the ridiculous inspiration.

Evelyn was slowly coming into a fair state of pique and outrage.

Sir Charles had not only taken it for granted that she was perfectly fine, but he had commanded her in the most cavalier fashion possible to participate in lavishing attention upon his horses.

Evelyn hoped that she was not unfeeling toward the poor creatures. But she did feel that she was a bit more important than a team of horses, regardless of how well matched they were or how valuable. She did not voice her thoughts, however, but instead continued to hold the horse's head steady.

Sir Charles was at last satisfied, and he straightened from his inspection. He smiled relief at his silent companion. "I do believe that with a bit of luck there will not be a bit of scarring."

"Fortunate, indeed," said Evelyn shortly. She let go of the bridle and stepped away from the horses.

Sir Charles looked more closely at her face. He was experienced enough with women to realize that she was upset. There was nothing that could make the present circumstances even more unpleasant than would a fit of hysterics, he thought, and so it would behoove him to make an attempt to be conciliatory.

Sir Charles reached out to take her hand between his own, and the tone of his voice became solicitous. "My dear Miss Dower, your nerves are naturally stretched nearly beyond bearing by this business."

Her anger melted away in the face of his attention. Evelyn looked up at him in an appealing fashion. "I—I am feeling rather shaken by it all. Never could I have imagined such a thing could come to happen," she said. She wondered what her mother would say when that lady learned how near she had come to being killed.

Sir Charles mistook her words as an apology to himself. With all of the gallantry of which he was capable, he said, "I assure you that I do not hold any ill will toward you, Miss Dower. The fault was as much mine."

Evelyn gaped up at him, amazed. That he should mention anything of blame was positively outrageous. How he could do so was beyond her comprehension. She had almost had her neck broken, all because he had chosen to kiss her at that precise moment.

Sir Charles was unaware of her gathering indignation. "You must come over to the shade. See, there is a rather large rock beneath this tree, where you may sit and cool yourself. I could not forgive myself if you were to take harm from either the jarring that you undoubtedly suffered or through taking too much sun."

Though her confidence in his character had been badly shaken, Evelyn nevertheless warmed to him once more. He was at last behaving just as he ought. Perhaps she had not perfectly understood him when he had seemingly blamed her for the accident. He would have behaved exceedingly angrily if he had truly thought she was at fault. And certainly the warmth in his eyes and in his voice was not that of an angry man.

As she accepted his proffered arm, she offered a wavering smile to him. "Thank you, Sir Charles. I appreciate your concern for my welfare."

Sir Charles seated her on the rock before leaning one shoulder up against the tree trunk. With distaste he flicked a dead bee from off his coat sleeve. "We might as well be comfortable. The time will pass more pleasantly then. I am persuaded that it cannot be long before someone passes this way and stops to take us up."

Evelyn stared up at him with renewed surprise. "But . . . do you not intend to make your way into Bath, sir, and return for me with a carriage?"

Sir Charles raised his brows as he regarded her with amusement. "My dear Miss Dower, what an idea! It is still all of three miles to town. Of course I do not mean to walk such a distance. The day is by far too warm for such exertion."

"Surely you could ride one of your horses," Evelyn pointed out.

Sir Charles regarded her with an expression that conveyed quite clearly his opinion that she was either mad or brutally callous. "Come, Miss Dower! That would be most inadvisable in light of the injuries that my horses have sustained. In any event, I could not possibly leave you unattended here on the public road. One could not know what sort of characters might come along and accost you."

Evelyn chose to overlook that he had thought first of his horses. She laughed, waving aside his consideration for herself. "I have lived here all my life, Sir Charles, and I have yet to hear of anything dire come to sitting beside this road. I assure you that I would be perfectly safe. Pray do not allow reservations over my welfare to detain you, sir."

Sir Charles Reginald eyed the young lady seated at a little distance from him with disapprobation. With determined civility, he said, "Thank you, Miss Dower. However, I am not inclined to go to such extraordinary and unnecessary effort when I am confident that we shall soon procure a lift from some passing stranger."

"Well! I do think it somewhat pudding-hearted of you," said Evelyn.

"One cannot expect a miss barely out of the schoolroom

to perfectly understand these things," said Sir Charles loftily.

The conversation languished.

Several minutes elapsed, during which each had absently slapped away insects and thought their own dismal thoughts. At length, Evelyn stood up and shook out the creased folds of her skirts. She cast a calculating glance at her companion. "Sir Charles, it is apparent to me that it will be some little time yet before our unknown rescuer makes an appearance. Perhaps matters might be expedited a bit if I were to walk back to town myself and convey the tidings of the carriage accident."

Sir Charles straightened up from his indolent posture, surprised. "Miss Dower, your zeal is commendable but quite unnecessary, I assure you. It is too far for a gently nurtured female to venture. You will be wilted by the sun before you have gained the next rise."

"Nevertheless, Sir Charles, I find that I am too impatient to remain," said Evelyn firmly.

Sir Charles raised a brow, wondering what he had ever seen in the stubborn wench that had caused him to bestow his flattering condescension upon her. Miss Dower was altogether too willful for his taste. Only consider what had come of bowing to her insistence to drive his prized equipage. Now she thought to force him to an exertion equally abhorrent to his nature. But Miss Dower was about to learn that a gentleman's sense of gallantry could be pushed only so far.

Sir Charles's disapproval was patent in his stiff voice. "As you will, Miss Dower."

Evelyn waited an instant to see whether Sir Charles meant to accompany her, but he made no move to do so. Instead, he removed a handkerchief from his pocket and carefully mopped his perspiring brow.

Angered and disappointed, Evelyn turned on her heel. Without a backward glance, she set off, striking out at a furious pace in testament to her hurt and bewilderment.

She had thought Sir Charles cared something for her, but it had become patently apparent to her that was not at all the case. She saw it now in all its stark reality. Sir Charles had been merely amusing himself by paying her court.

What an absolute fool she had been to weave romantic fancies around him.

Disillusionment set in with terrible finality. An unexpected tear slid down her cheek. Angrily, she brushed it away. She would not cry over the gentleman. He was not worthy of it, she thought. Despite her determination, a few more tears followed the first.

Evelyn trudged on. Though she was accustomed to walking, Sir Charles had been correct in his estimation about the heat. Her pace had slowed considerably under the influence of her stung emotions and the warm afternoon. Her face and neck prickled and her fine carriage dress clung uncomfortably hot against her skin. The scattered bee stings she had suffered on her face and arms raised burning welts. Evelyn thought she had never been so miserable in her life.

Yet worse than her physical misery was the taste in her mouth of bitter disappointment. She had discovered that her ideal of the romantic hero was all-too flawed. She was in genuine need of rescue, but Sir Charles had failed miserably to rise to the occasion. At the thought, a few more tears fell.

Evelyn was relieved when she at last reached a portion of Bath with which she was familiar. As she walked up the street fronted by the same shops that she had often patronized, she pretended not to notice the curious stares that her bedraggled and wilted appearance were garnering.

Evelyn had not realized before how awkward an explanation of her situation would be, but now that she had, she was too embarrassed to seek out an acquaintance in one of the shops. If only she would run into one of her particular friends, like Pol or Abigail, or even one of their esteemable parents; but neither Miss Woodthorpe nor Miss Sparrow materialized at the yearning of her thoughts.

Coming to a corner, Evelyn hesitated. She knew how much to the pence that she had in her reticule, and it was woefully inadequate to hire a cab. She thought of hailing a cab anyway and appealing to the driver's compassion, but she suspected her appearance would scarcely engender trust in her reassurances that the fare would be forthcoming once she had arrived at her destination. She debated tiredly with herself whether embarrassment from asking for help from

an acquaintance or shopkeeper would really be as onerous
as to continue the long walk, and even half turned so that
she could retrace her steps to the shops that she had passed.
But the thought of going back was awful to contemplate.

Once more close to tears, Evelyn thought longingly of
home. Never had the familiar walk to Queen Square
seemed so distant.

Chapter Twenty-four

Mr. Hawkins was finishing up his errands and was about to climb back up into his carriage when he caught sight of a familiar figure across the road. He stared hard, then swore under his breath. Dodging through the light traffic, he crossed quickly over. Gently he took the young woman's arm. "Miss Dower!"

Evelyn turned and at sight of his concerned face, she quite suddenly burst into tears. With all the naturalness in the world she buried her face in his shoulder. "Oh, Mr. Hawkins! How h-happy I am to s-see you!"

Mr. Hawkins did not think that she sounded particularly ecstatic, but he reserved the thought to himself. He awkwardly patted her shoulder, never having had to deal with a weeping female before and feeling himself inadequate to the task, when what he really wanted to do was to enfold her comfortingly in his arms.

Mr. Hawkins exerted a manful control upon his emotions. "There, there, Miss Dower. Everything will be better presently, I promise you."

Evelyn hiccupped and let go of his lapel. Her eyes averted, she requested in a muffled voice for his handkerchief. He obliged, and she wiped her eyes and blew her nose.

"I do apologize, Mr. Hawkins. I am not generally such a water—watering pot," she said in a choked voice. She held the soiled linen uncertainly, staring at it. "I shall—shall wash this for you." She wadded up the handkerchief and fumbled open her reticule to stuff it inside.

"But what has happened to so overset you?" asked Mr. Hawkins. His observant eyes had already seen the signs of previous tears and the red welts on her face. Now as he took note of the sudden tide of color into her face, his eyes darkened. His fingers tightened on her elbow. "Evelyn, are you perfectly all right?"

There was an urgent note in his voice.

Evelyn looked up quickly. The tide of color rose again in her face at the question in his hard blue eyes. "Yes, of course I am!"

She glanced around, suddenly very much aware of a disapproving stare from an unknown lady. "Mr. Hawkins, could we possibly continue this conversation elsewhere?"

Mr. Hawkins saw the sense in her request when he also realized that they were gathering curious glances. "Of course, Miss Dower. I apologize for not thinking clearly. My carriage is across the street. I will drive you home." He took her arm and escorted her over to the gig. He saw that she was seated comfortably before climbing up himself and taking the reins.

As he turned the carriage in the direction of Queen Square, he said with admirable restraint, "I do not mean to pry, Miss Dower, but I do consider myself to be your friend. Your welfare is naturally of concern to me. Won't you confide in me now?"

"I have been out driving with Sir Charles," said Evelyn. Her throat closed suddenly with the humiliation she felt.

"Sir Charles," repeated Mr. Hawkins. He kept his eyes trained straight ahead, not wanting the lady to read the fury that rose in him. He considered what bodily harm he would do to that gentleman when next he saw him.

Still not looking at her companion, Evelyn said succinctly, "There was an accident. I did not choose to remain, so I walked back into town." She threw a fleeting glance up to his profile, dreading that he would ask questions that she preferred not to answer.

"A carriage accident—*Sir Charles*!?"

The look that Mr. Hawkins threw her was one of incredulous astonishment.

Evelyn hastened to reassure her companion. "He is perfectly well." She paused a fraction of an instant. "And so are his horses."

Mr. Hawkins digested this for a moment, having sensed a strong undercurrent of emotion in her voice that he did not understand. Leaving it for the moment, he said, "How comes it that Sir Charles did not accompany you into Bath?"

Evelyn bit her lip, turning away her face. Again the humiliation burned her. "He—he did not want to leave his horses, and I was too impatient to simply wait, so I volunteered to come instead to alert someone of the accident." She looked round at Mr. Hawkins. "I suppose that you will send someone for him?"

"I will certainly do so. Your duty is fully discharged, Miss Dower," said Mr. Hawkins gravely. His mind was rife with questions arising out of what little she had said. The original conclusion that he had leaped to that Sir Charles had forced his attentions upon her was now discarded, but he gathered that it was a delicate matter nevertheless and so he was careful in his probing. "Er—how did this accident occur, Miss Dower?"

"We drove into a cloud of bees before we became aware of them. I had the reins, and when the horses bolted I could not contain them," said Evelyn shortly.

Mr. Hawkins shot her a sharp glance. "Did I understand you correctly? *You* had the reins?" It was unbelievable, if true. Sir Charles must have become so besotted with her that he had lost his senses, he thought savagely.

Evelyn straightened her spine, her heightened sensitivity having caught his astonishment. She threw him a challenging glance and said with dignity, "Sir Charles was teaching me to drive."

"I am certain that you were a very apt pupil," said Mr. Hawkins soothingly. His mouth quirked. "That is, before the descent of the irate bees."

A reluctant smile twitched at Evelyn's lips as her sense of the ridiculous finally began to catch up with her. "Yes," she admitted.

When he laughed, she said firmly, "I shall have you know that I have a natural instinct for the leathers. It is only a pity that the bees did not stand aside in admiration of my skill."

Mr. Hawkins laughed again, before saying, "I am very happy that you were unhurt, Miss Dower. Since you walked into town I must assume the worst regarding Sir Charles's equipage."

"The phaeton was quite, quite smashed," said Evelyn. She found something of cheer in the recollection. At least Sir Charles would not go completely unscathed for his perfidy in becoming only an ordinary mortal rather than the romantic hero she had thought him.

"I see." Mr. Hawkins glanced down at his companion once more. The rim of her bedraggled bonnet sheltered her expression from him, but he thought he had heard a peculiarly pleased note in her voice. He realized that there was more to the tale than the lady had chosen to tell him. However, he was too cognizant of the bounds of propriety to press her further.

Nevertheless, it was already a fascinating story. He smiled to himself. He would roast Sir Charles finely for allowing a lady, and especially one as raw as Miss Dower, the privilege of driving his prized horses. The temptation to see the destruction for himself became suddenly overriding.

As they reached Miss Dower's address, he swiftly made up his mind. He helped her down from the carriage and walked her up to the door, where he saw her into the care of the concerned footman.

"I shall leave you now to the tender ministrations of your household, Miss Dower, while I go see what can be done on Sir Charles's behalf," he said.

"Thank you, Mr. Hawkins."

Evelyn was quite self-possessed in the presence of the servant. But after Mr. Hawkins had turned away and the door was closed on his broad back, she turned and fled up the stairs. To her consternation, she met her mother on the upstairs landing.

"Oh, are you returned from driving with Sir Charles? I hope that you enjoyed your lesson, dear," said Mrs. Dower. She frowned at her daughter. "Your bonnet is quite oddly canted, Evelyn. I do not mean to scold, but it is not at all the fashion for you."

Evelyn gave a sobbing laugh. She fell straightway into her mother's startled arms and cried, "Oh, Mama! The phaeton was wrecked and Sir Charles cared for nothing but his idiotic horses. What am I to do?"

"Do, dear? Why, I suppose you should stay completely away from horses. You do seem to have the most dismaying ill fortune around the creatures," said Mrs. Dower practically. "If you wish it, I shall myself inform Sir Charles that you will no longer be taking lessons with him."

Evelyn wailed, and she pressed her face against her mother's neck. Her shoulders shook, whether with grief or laugher Mrs. Dower was uncertain.

"Evelyn? Are you quite all right?" She tried what she thought to be an inspired observation. "Do, *do* try for a little decorum, my dear. I had thought you such a sensible girl. Whatever would Sir Charles think to see you in such a state? It could very well put him off and—"

Mrs. Dower watched in astonishment as Evelyn staggered away in the direction of her bedroom. Her daughter was now definitely laughing. "Why, whatever have I said now to set you off again? Dearest, I do believe you are hysterical!"

The week following the abortive driving lesson with Sir Charles, Evelyn did not go out to any social engagements until the angry welts on her face had subsided. It was put about that she suffered from a light cold, and only her closest friends were given access to her.

Miss Woodthorpe laughed outright at the story of the cloud of bees and the subsequent misadventure. "Mrs. Dower was quite right, Evelyn, you do have the most amazing bad luck around horses. Perhaps you would do best to give them a wide berth in future. Though I must say I am glad to hear that Sir Charles's team took no permanent harm, as they are a prime bit of blood and bone."

Miss Sparrow sent a reproving look in Miss Woodthorpe's direction. "Indeed, Evelyn, I shudder to think how close you came to real injury," she said.

"Oh well, it is all done with and I am none the worse for wear," said Evelyn cheerfully as she offered a tray of biscuits to her friends.

"Truly? I noticed several lovely bouquets when I arrived. When I commented upon them to your dear mother, I was quite surprised to learn that none were from Sir Charles," said Miss Sparrow.

Evelyn colored faintly. "No, none are from Sir Charles," she agreed calmly. "Will you take more tea, Pol?"

Miss Woodthorpe smiled at Evelyn, holding away her cup. "That is a very weak ruse, my dear."

Evelyn looked from one to the other of her friends. She sighed. "Oh, very well. I shall satisfy your curiosity, for I can see that neither of you will let it go otherwise. Sir Charles has not been to visit me, nor am I particularly unhappy about it. Now, may I serve you a proper tea?"

"But I thought you quite taken with Sir Charles," said Miss Sparrow, scarcely noticing as Evelyn poured her cup.

Evelyn's brows pulled together in the faintest of frowns. She poured for Miss Woodthorpe and set down the teapot before replying. "It is quite puzzling, actually. I thought Sir Charles very much the perfect gentleman for me until I became so very disillusioned in him. I suppose that is what cured me so rapidly of those feelings that I had harbored for him."

"Otherwise you must suspect yourself to be a heartless flirt," said Miss Woodthorpe, her eyes twinkling.

"There is that, of course," said Evelyn, laughing.

"What a horrid thing to say, Apollonia," said Miss Sparrow, though she also smiled. "Of course Evelyn is not a *flirt*. She was merely mistaken in her heart."

"Then I may think myself to be merely foolish," said Evelyn wryly.

Her friends laughed with her. Miss Woodthorpe assured her that neither of them thought her any more foolish than she had ever been.

"Thank you ever so much, Pol," said Evelyn with a laughing grimace.

"Apollonia is a merciless tease so pay no attention to her, Evelyn. I am only glad that you have not suffered too much from Sir Charles's own turn of heart."

"There only remains the question of who *did* send all of these lovely flowers," said Miss Woodthorpe in her quiet way.

Evelyn opened her eyes wide. "Why, they come from my several other admirers, of course." She abandoned her innocent air to say, "And do not dare to inquire of my mother, Abigail!"

That set Miss Woodthorpe and Miss Sparrow laughing again, and Miss Sparrow assured her that she would not be so disobliging. "Though I do think it quite pinching of you to leave us in suspense," she said, pulling on her gloves.

Miss Woodthorpe also made ready to leave. "I suppose that you have heard from Mr. Hawkins?" she asked casually.

"Oh indeed; also from Lord Waithe and a handful of my other admirers," said Evelyn with a laughing look. "I have not been forgotten, it seems.'

"Of course you have not," said Miss Sparrow staunchly. "A few days' absence will but enhance the gentlemen's sincere admiration for you. You will be as popular as before."

"Thank you, Abigail. You have done me a world of good," said Evelyn, hugging her friend in farewell.

"Pray give my regards to your dear mama. I hope that the little domestic emergency that called her away so hastily before tea is swiftly resolved," said Miss Sparrow.

"I shall," said Evelyn. She turned to Miss Woodthorpe, who was regarding her with a knowing gaze. Evelyn laughed, shaking her head. "Oh, Pol! What would I do without you to tease me?"

Miss Woodthorpe shrugged negligently. "You would go on very well, I should think, except that you would have no one to give you sound advice on what to expect of particular gentlemen. After all, you do have the most amazing ill fortune with horses, which gentlemen very much resemble in temperament and character."

"Oh do go away! I shall very likely decide to end as a spinster if you keep on in that vein," said Evelyn, walking her friends to the drawing room door.

Miss Sparrow had waited so that she and Miss Woodthorpe could accompany one another out. The ladies left after repeating their good-byes.

Evelyn turned back into the drawing room. Almost absently she reached out to touch a delicate yellow rose, one of several in a Waterford crystal vase. A soft smile touched her lips, for these roses as well as a scattering of the other bouquets among the tokens sent by her admirers were from Mr. Hawkins.

Of course, Mr. Hawkins *would* be so thoughtful as to

send several offerings, along with his solicitous notes that inquired after her continued well-being. He would do no less for any lady whom he had rescued from a street corner.

She sighed, a curiously regretful sound, and left the drawing room.

Chapter Twenty-five

Evelyn's gratitude to Mr. Hawkins lasted for precisely one
fortnight before it was completely overborne by her former
anger against him.

In the excess of her gratitude she had forgotten how furious she had been to hear from Miss Sparrow that he had
hinted away some of her admirers. It was not that she
missed the attentions of those particular gentlemen. Without exception the gentlemen who dropped away from her
circle were in some respect unworthy of consideration as a
possible husband, all having been too old, or too lecherous,
or too much the fortunehunter.

What had so infuriated Evelyn was Mr. Hawkins's high-
handed, arrogant presumption. Weeding out the undesire-
ables among her admirers was a task for her mother or her
to do. It was not at all the concern of a gentleman who
could not even claim to be a family relation.

Evelyn thought she could have accepted all that Mr.
Hawkins had done, if not in a glad spirit, at least with some
semblance of dignity. She would have found a way, in the
politest manner possible, to make clear to him that his concern for her was quite inappropriate and unnecessary. He
would have realized his error, and she would have retained
his friendship.

Such as Evelyn's intention when next she had the opportunity to speak to Mr. Hawkins privately, but certain events
made that tempered resolution impossible.

When Evelyn finally emerged from seclusion, it was
quickly borne in on her that she had become the focus of
speculative glances and whispers. Uncomfortable, uncom-
prehending, Evelyn did not know what to make of any of it.

Mrs. Dower was equally as bewildered and could offer

no explanation. "I truly do not understand it, Evelyn. Several of my friends drop what I know must be sly hints of some sort, but I have no notion what it is all about. Dearest, I *am* sorry. I so wish I were cleverer at times."

Evelyn sighed and patted her mother's hand. "It is all right, Mama. I am certain it must all come clear sooner or later."

Evelyn continued to endure the unwelcome attention at the social functions that she and Mrs. Dower attended, never for a moment letting her smile falter. If she only knew what it was all about! She knew that Miss Woodthorpe would have told her, if asked, but she did not see her friend except for a few moments during an assembly. Miss Woodthorpe had been escorted by Viscount Waithe, and not for worlds would Evelyn have intimated in his lordship's presence that she needed her friend's counsel. Miss Sparrow had also been unavailable to her, having contracted her youngest sister's mumps and perforce been required to keep to her bed. It was frustrating in the extreme, for there was no one else that Evelyn could completely trust.

Then one afternoon at tea, an acquaintance inquired archly whether Evelyn had been receiving Mr. Hawkins during her convalescence. Quite suddenly, Evelyn's quick intuitive mind fastened upon the truth. It astounded her. It enraged her. She seethed with it, but on no account could she demonstrate a hint of her feelings before this lady.

With a glittering smile, she raised her brows in cool inquiry. She infused a faint note of surprise into her voice. "Why no, ma'am. Should I have? Pray, why do you ask?"

The lady fluttered in confusion. She cast a glance at Evelyn's mother. Mrs. Dower's puzzled expression only confirmed her instant and horrible suspicion that she had committed a faux pas. The lady hastily changed the topic, chattering quickly past the uncomfortable moment. Within minutes, she had taken her leave.

Mrs. Dower was astonished by their guest's hurried exit. "Gracious, whatever was that about?"

"I do believe Mr. Hawkins has been quite busy on my behalf," said Evelyn very evenly. Her hands were folded so tightly together that her knuckles had gone white.

Mrs. Dower regarded her daughter with sudden anxiety. "I *can* not like that peculiar light in your eyes, Evelyn. You—you are not going to do anything foolish?"

Evelyn smiled at her mother. The molten sparks in her eyes did not abate. "Oh no. I promise you, I shall be all that is circumspect, Mama."

Mrs. Dower let out her breath. "Thank you, dear. I should not like to see you go to the soiree this evening while you were caught up in a temper. I do not quite see what Mr. Hawkins—but never mind, do not explain it to me. I do not wish to know. Only assure me that you will not make a scene."

"I hope I am too sensible to disgrace you, Mama," said Evelyn, still smiling.

Mrs. Dower chose to overlook the martial light that still burned brightly in Evelyn's eyes. She said firmly, "We shall have a marvelous time, then. Lord Hughes has promised to escort us."

"Has he? Then I may look forward to seeing Mr. Hawkins as well," said Evelyn.

Mrs. Dower's faint uneasiness was strengthened by the silky note in her daughter's voice. But after throwing Evelyn a worried glance, she decided that she really, really did not want to know what her daughter was contemplating. The girl bore entirely too close a resemblance to her late husband when he had been taken by a high fury. "Oh, it is going to be an uncomfortable evening. I just know it is," Mrs. Dower murmured unhappily.

Evelyn tested her theory by throwing herself into the enjoyment of the evening. She laughed often and threw artless glances at all the gentlemen who courted her. She appeared at her loveliest, and even some of those gentlemen who had been glaringly absent from her circle were drawn back as moths to a flame. Evelyn was particularly pleased by that, and she made a point of flirting outrageously with the most undesirable of her suitors. Out of the corner of her eyes she became aware of Mr. Hawkins's glowering presence, but she pretended not to see him while she waited to see what he might do.

Evelyn did not have long to wonder. For the first time,

perhaps because she was acutely tuned to the possibility, she saw Mr. Hawkins at work. It was done adroitly, subtlely, cleverly. One by one the unsuitable admirers faded away once again.

Evelyn was in a towering rage. She was positively quivering. She knew, however, that it would be disastrous to show it, for that would inevitably lead to just the sort of public scene that her mother most disliked.

As she racked her brains over how she was to deliver the long overdue set-down that Mr. Hawkins deserved, she accepted an invitation to dance with Lord Hughes. Evelyn smiled at the gentleman as she rose and gave her hand to him. "Your gallantry is much appreciated, my lord," she said.

"I have always had an eye for a lovely lady. You are very much like your mother in appearance, you know," Lord Hughes said with a merry wink.

Evelyn laughed, surprised by his lordship's manner. She had not thought that Lord Hughes liked her overmuch, for he had always treated her with the slightest air of amusement. She realized as she looked into his knowledgeable eyes that he had guessed at the reasons behind her original reserve toward him. "Thank you, sir. It is a compliment, indeed," she said, a smile still touching her lips. "I know that my mother sets great store by you as well."

Lord Hughes acknowledged her oblique apology with a slight nod. Tucking her hand into his arm, he said, "I am not as young as I once was. Perhaps you will not mind it if I usher you to the refreshment table instead of joining this set?"

"Of course not, my lord," said Evelyn.

"I believe Miss Dower promised this dance to me."

The hard voice brought both Lord Hughes and Evelyn around. At sight of his grandnephew, Lord Hughes raised a brow. "Indeed, nevvy?"

"Yes," Mr. Hawkins ground out. His short glance at Evelyn's astonished face was one of thin-lipped disapproval.

Evelyn had had quite enough. With a tight smile for Lord Hughes, she said, "I am sorry, my lord. I had indeed forgotten that I had promised this dance to Mr. Hawkins. I hope that you will forgive me."

Lord Hughes swept her hand to his lips to place a lingering kiss. He was quietly amused by the hard look in Mr. Hawkins's eyes. "I can forgive you anything, Miss Dower," he said. His rich voice was a veritable caress.

Evelyn inclined her head, her smile for him less constrained. She appreciated the irony in his lazy gaze. Then she turned to place her fingers delicately on Mr. Hawkins's sleeve.

As he led her toward the floor, Evelyn hissed, "I do not wish to dance. We shall find a private room, if you please!"

Mr. Hawkins glanced down to encounter her overly bright, glittering eyes. His brows rose slightly. "Of course, Miss Dower, if that is your wish."

"It is!" Evelyn snapped.

She did not address him again as he led her out of the ballroom and a short distance down a hall. He paused to open a door and stood aside for her to precede him. Evelyn swept past him without a glance.

She found herself in a study. She did not turn until she heard the closing of the door, then she rounded on him. "How dare you, sir!" Her voice was trembling with fury. "How dare you to presume to interfere in my concerns."

Mr. Hawkins was stunned alike by her fury and her beauty. Evelyn's eyes blazed and the firelight cast molten gold over her delicately boned face and the swift rise and descent of her bosom. He had never seen her look so magnificent. He desired at that moment nothing except to pull her into his arms and make love to her.

Dragging his thoughts back to the matter at hand, he attempted to placate her. He advanced, saying in reasoned tones, "I was but thinking of your best interests. An innocent such as yourself cannot be expected to recognize knavery in all its guises. My uncle is a careless libertine. I would not have you fall prey to his seductions."

His quiet inflections served to incite her fury to greater proportions. "Mr. Hawkins, I am far less in need of protection than you assume. On the contrary, I am quite up to snuff."

Evelyn saw that he did not appear in the least convinced by her declaration. His expression of polite disbelief was the final straw. She stamped her foot. "You infuriating

man! How can I make you understand that I do not wish,
nor do I need you to play my bodyguard?"

He saw that tears glittered on her lashes and his heart
smote him. Mr. Hawkins reached out to capture her hands.
"Evelyn—"

She pulled free instantly. "Stop! Pray do not!"

He looked startled. He said stiffly, "I am sorry if I offended you. I assure you, I had no intention of taking advantage of our tête à tête, Miss Dower."

Evelyn stared up at him for an astonished moment, various emotions fleeting across her face. Quite suddenly, she
gave a low laugh that bordered on hysteria. "Yes, of course
you would not! How very like you, Mr. Hawkins!" Her
voice broke and her eyes were suddenly awash with tears.
She turned away quickly, the back of her hand pressed over
her mouth.

Mr. Hawkins stood stock-still, staring at her bowed head.
Then he moved, swiftly and surely. His hands descended
on her shoulders and turned her so quickly that she had to
catch herself against him with her hands. He pulled her
close into his arms.

Her face was pressed against his shoulder, while her
hands were folded against his chest. She fancied that she
could feel the strong, swift beat of his heart. She did not
move, not daring to believe that he was actually holding her
in so intimate a fashion.

Evelyn closed her eyes, drinking in the feel and the masculine smell of him. She loved him, she slowly realized.
She had denied it for so long. She had even hidden it from
herself behind a romantic fancy woven around Sir Charles.
Poor Sir Charles, she thought. He had never had a proper
chance at all.

Mr. Hawkins breathed in the sweet scent of the soft hair
beneath his cheek. She was in his arms at last, the warmth
of her feminine curves fitted neatly against him.

His breath quickened. He ached to do more than hold
her. It was agonizing to hold her thus when he dared not
demonstrate the depth of his passion. She was such an innocent. Even to take possession of her mouth in the manner
he so desperately craved must surely frighten her and
would undoubtedly give her a disgust of him.

They stood thus for several heartbeats while the battle raged in him. But honor, battered and bitterly hated, finally won.

Evelyn sighed and stirred. She lifted her head and smiled up at him. "I am quite composed now," she said softly.

It was an effort for Mr. Hawkins to unlock his arms from about her; even more an effort to step back and put distance between them. His hungry gaze brushed her half-parted lips before dropping to the rounded breasts so invitingly displayed by her low décolletage. Firelight created fascinating shadows with every breath she took, further stoking his imagination. Realizing the turn of his thoughts, he dragged away his eyes.

He turned abruptly toward the mantel. Without glancing again in her direction, he said harshly, "Forgive me. I have crossed over the line yet once again."

The warmth that Evelyn had been feeling evaporated with the cold indifference of his voice. Tears pricked her eyes again. He cared nothing for her. He never had. His demonstration had been naught but a ploy to divert her from her anger against him.

"I cannot bear this," she said on a half-muffled sob.

He turned.

His expression was one of such surprise that Evelyn's fury returned full-blown. Her voice shook with the force of her pent emotions. "You have attempted to keep me immuned and isolated all Season. You have warned off several other gentlemen from me, even your own friends. You cannot deny it, for I have seen that even Viscount Waithe is no longer my ardent admirer! Why, *why* have you done this?"

"I cannot answer that," said Mr. Hawkins raggedly. She had spurned him once. He could not bear for her to do so again, not now when he had so desperate a control over himself.

"It is obvious that you cannot possibly want me for yourself!" Evelyn cried, all of her hurt bursting forth. He had set her aside with just a few cold words. "You have made that abundantly clear!"

Her words struck him with the force of thrown daggers, and he jerked toward her. He stopped, his fists clenched as he stared at her. More than anything else, he wanted to protest his love for her.

Chapter Twenty-six

He did not trust himself to refute her charge of indifference, however, fearing that if he did so he would not be able to constrain himself any longer. It was safer to concentrate on her lesser accusations. "Isolated you? My dear Miss Dower, surely you do not believe that. On the contrary, I have done all in my power to insure an uncomplicated and serene come-out for you. I cannot see that you should have any complaints."

Evelyn had seen something undefinable flicker for a moment in his eyes, before his expression had become shuttered. She had felt an answering leap in her pulses, and hope beat in step with her heart. But his reply was completely deflating.

She drew herself up, stiffening against the knifing hurt that she felt in her chest. "Indeed, Mr. Hawkins! Then pray allow me to enlighten you. This last week when I have gone to tea or to attend a function, I have been asked by all the ladies of my acquaintance, with a quite disgusting archness, where my noble protector has gotten himself to. As for the gentlemen, you have made me a laughingstock with them! The boldest inquire whether I have your—*your*—leave to consort with them!"

Mr. Hawkins was taken aback as much by her vehemence as by her astonishing assertions. "I have but attempted to safeguard your reputation!"

"*Guard* my reputation?" Evelyn gave a bitter laugh. "You have all but destroyed it!"

"I was not aware that I was doing you such disservice, Miss Dower," he said stiffly.

Evelyn saw that he was genuinely bewildered and upset. "Oh, Peter." She moved close and touched his sleeve. She

said in a gentler tone, "Peter, you must stop hedging me
about. Pray allow me to succeed or fail on my own account.
If I choose my acquaintances unwisely, it will be an honest
mistake and one from which I shall learn. But I am not the
widgen you think me, I promise you."

"Your reputation—"

"Have you not been listening to a word that I have been
saying to you? If you possibly cared as much for my reputation as you aver, then you would cease to interfere so!"

Evelyn stopped and drew a difficult breath. She said quietly, "I tell you, I will not endure it any longer."

Mr. Hawkins stared at her. She was flushed, but no
longer with temper. There was a determined light in her
eyes. He recognized that she believed entirely in what she
had said, and it gave him pause.

His initial reaction was to reject her conclusions out of
hand. However, the echo of certain comments made to him
by one or two acquaintances came back to mind. He had
previously brushed aside the remarks as ridiculous, but now
they assumed new importance.

He said slowly, "Are you saying that I have caused you
public humiliation?"

"Yes," said Evelyn unsteadily.

"I see," he said heavily. His expression was stern and
deep-carven and his brows were knit as he glanced into the
fire.

Once again Evelyn's heart softened toward him. "I am
sorry, Peter. But it is true. Even the dullest slowtop has
noted that you have appointed yourself as my overzealous
guardian. I suspect that half of my admirers are so oblig-
ingly attentive only to tease you into action. That is really
the most infuriating thing, for how can I discern which are
sincere in their compliments when my suitors run hot and
cold, depending upon whether they have run foul of your
disapproval?"

She managed to summon up a smile in an attempt to
lighten the moment, which threatened to overwhelm her
again. "It positively drives me mad to wonder whether they
are all playing the same silly games."

Her weak humor fell sadly flat with him.

Evelyn sighed. "Peter, I do appreciate what you have

tried to do, truly I do. However, it simply cannot go on. Do you not see?"

He was silent for so long that she wondered whether he had heard her at all. But finally he sighed. "Yes, I do see. I profoundly regret my error in judgment, Miss Dower." He reached for her hand and briefly carried her fingers to his lips. "I shall not so trouble you again, ma'am. You have my word of honor on it. Shall we return to the ballroom?"

He offered his arm to her. As Evelyn placed her hand in his elbow, she cast an anxious glance up at his stern expression. "I—I did not want to anger you, Peter."

He laughed, but without any real vestige of amusement. "I am not in the least angered, Miss Dower. I am surely embarrassed that I did not realize for myself what I have been putting you through."

"Pray—let's not speak of it again," Evelyn begged, not liking the underlying bitterness in his tone.

"As you wish, Miss Dower."

Not another word was said between them, though Evelyn threw several glances up at his shuttered expression, wishing that he would break the heavy silence, while he returned her to the ballroom.

The set was just ending, and Evelyn's next partner approached to claim her hand. She met Mr. Hawkins's eyes, but he did not speak. He merely bowed and gave way to the waiting gentleman.

As she was led away into the forming set by her partner, Evelyn glanced back. She half hoped to see Mr. Hawkins glowering after them as he had earlier in the evening, but that gentleman had not remained to watch the dance. Evelyn looked swiftly about her, and to her dismay she saw that Mr. Hawkins, without a backward glance in her direction, was leaving the ballroom.

Evelyn turned to stare straight ahead. Though she smiled and otherwise acknowledged her partner's sallies, she did not really hear a word that was exchanged between them. Her misery was such that she wanted very much to simply sink into the floor and disappear.

But what exactly had she expected of Mr. Hawkins when she had confronted him? Of course he would step aside. Of course he would assure her that he would no longer be such a bother to her. He would do only what was proper. He was a paragon among gentlemen, head and shoulders above the rest. And was that not exactly what she had wanted from him?

Evelyn broke apart from her partner, a small sob escaping her.

The gentleman looked at her in astonishment. "Miss Dower! Have I offended you?"

Evelyn suddenly realized that others were turning their heads. More than anything else she did not want to be the center of anyone's attention. She shook her head quickly, summoning up a trembling smile for the gentleman. "Oh no! No, nothing of the sort. I—I have the headache. I tried to ignore it, not wishing to spoil the pleasure of this d-dance. I *am* sorry!" She put her fingers to her temples, which had genuinely begun to throb.

The gentleman took her elbow, looking down at her in concern. "You've gone all pale, Miss Dower. It is the heat, I daresay. I should have seen it at once. Come, I shall take you at once to your mother."

Evelyn was inordinately grateful for the gentleman's forbearance. He returned her to her mother's safekeeping and then went off to summon their carriage while Mrs. Dower exclaimed with soft distress over Evelyn's wilted figure.

Evelyn managed to smile and straightened in her chair. "I am sorry, Mama. I do not mean to be a nuisance. I shall be perfectly all right once I am home. Why do you not stay and enjoy yourself?"

"Of course I shall not stay!" said Mrs. Dower indignantly. "I would be the most selfish creature alive were I to do so. No, I shall return with you. I am certain that Lord Hughes understands the necessity."

"Of course, Amanda." Lord Hughes spared Evelyn a sharp, penetrating glance. He was apparently satisfied. "I will do the proper with our hosts if you wish to take Evelyn straight out."

"Thank you, Horace. I knew that you would understand," said Mrs. Dower gratefully. She placed her arm about her daughter's waist and was very astonished when Evelyn actually leaned on her. Concern rippled over her face, but she said in a light voice, "Come, my dear. A cup of chocolate and a cold compress will undoubtedly do you a world of good."

Evelyn allowed herself to be led out, too spent to notice the glance that Lord Hughes and her mother had shared before his lordship went off to make their excuses to their hosts.

The headache that she had excused herself with had become a full-blown reality. Pain assaulted her with every heavy heartbeat and her eyes ached from the force of the tears that were dammed behind them. She was scarce aware of it when Lord Hughes returned, nor that Mrs. Dower relinquished her to his lordship's support.

However, Evelyn did raise her head at the sound of Mr. Hawkins's voice. She had just emerged into the entry hall on Lord Hughes's arm, her mother on her far side. The headache momentarily receded, so that Evelyn saw with perfect clarity that Mr. Hawkins stood with Viscount Waithe, Miss Woodthorpe, and Sir Charles. Lady Pomerancy was seated in her chair, the footman standing attentively behind ready to push it once the maid had finished tucking a wrap over her ladyship's narrow lap. They were apparently preparing to leave as well.

Miss Woodthorpe came across to Evelyn at once. Her green eyes were shining with a surprising degree of happiness as she reached out to take Evelyn's hand. "Oh, you are going home early, too? I shall come to call on you tomorrow." She lowered her voice. "I have something rather exciting to divulge."

The softened smile that she directed in Viscount Waithe's direction, and his response to it, was all that Evelyn required in order to guess what had transpired. Tears trembled on her lashes as she smiled. "Oh, Pol."

Behind Miss Woodthorpe's shoulder, Evelyn met Mr. Hawkins's hard, shuttered glance. His expression was devoid of anything but polite interest, and suddenly Evelyn had the overwhelming urge to strike him. She wanted to see his face crack and see something—anything!—in his eyes but that close-held civil mask.

Evelyn deliberately closed the distance between herself and Lord Hughes. She turned a brilliant smile to that gentleman and said, "I, too, have something to tell you, Pol."

There was a gasp, to be quickly covered by a sharp curse.

Evelyn did not look around, but stared rather desperately at Lord Hughes.

Lord Hughes had started visibly. He glanced down at Evelyn's white face, his lids drooping abruptly to hide his expression. He raised his free hand to place it proprietarily over hers where her fingers rested on his arm. "It is quite an extraordinary evening," he said smoothly. He bestowed a jovial smile on the young lady who clutched his arm so tightly.

At last, Evelyn turned her eyes on the company. She met the astonished gazes of Miss Woodthorpe and Viscount Waithe, while Sir Charles stood frowning into space. Dawning horror of what she had done was beginning to seep into her senses. Evelyn steeled herself to look at Mr. Hawkins. She should have been satisfied, she supposed vaguely. He had gone white under his tan, and there was a pinched, stricken look in his eyes. "I should like to go home now, please," she said in a low voice.

"Of course, my dear. I will escort you to Queen Square, but do not think to invite me in. Your mother will wish to talk with you, no doubt," said Lord Hughes in a faintly ironic voice.

Evelyn cast a fleeting glance into his lordship's face, understanding at once. Her heart sank into her slippers. She did not dare to turn her head and meet her mother's eyes. She was afraid of what she might see. "Yes, my lord." The headache had returned, more viciously than before, and it was all Evelyn could do but to cling blindly to Lord Hughes's arm.

Lord Hughes ushered Evelyn and Mrs. Dower through the entry hall and outside to the waiting carriage. Uncharacteristically, Mrs. Dower had not said a word of parting to those left behind frozen in the entry, but her lapse was probably not noted because Lord Hughes kept up a steady stream of amusing tittle-tattle.

Solicitously Lord Hughes aided Mrs. Dower up into the carriage, then Evelyn. When the ladies were seated, he followed, shutting the door behind him. The carriage started away from the curb.

From the dark, Lord Hughes's voice rolled out rather grimly. "Now, young lady, you will explain how it is that I have come to find myself betrothed to you."

Both of the Dower ladies burst into tears.

Chapter Twenty-seven

Mr. Hawkins had hoped to avoid Lord Hughes by going down early to breakfast. However, when he entered the breakfast room he saw that the viscount had also risen early. Lord Hughes had his full attention centered on his plate and did not immediately notice his grandnephew.

Mr. Hawkins paused the barest second before making his presence known. "Good morning, my lord." He walked over to the sideboard to serve himself.

Lord Hughes glanced up and a wicked gleam entered his world-weary eyes. " 'Morning, nevvy. A fine morning, indeed! It is not every morning that a gentleman wakens with the gratifying thought that he is shortly to be wed," said Lord Hughes expansively.

"I suppose not," said Mr. Hawkins shortly. He stared at the kippers and steak that he had put on his plate. He found that he was not as ravenous as he had assumed.

"Certainly it is an unusual feeling for a gentleman such as myself. I have never been one to give much thought to the betrothed state, and I do not assign it overmuch importance even now. But it is intriguing, nevertheless. Do you not think it intriguing, Peter?"

"I have not had that salubrious experience so that I cannot judge," said Mr. Hawkins coldly. He sat down opposite Lord Hughes, unnecessarily clattering his plate on the tabletop.

Lord Hughes laughed as though at a huge joke. "Aye, and likely never will have it, my boy! What a cold fish you are. M'sister has seen to that. I fancy you do not know the first thing about how to make up to a woman."

His lordship leaned back in his damask-covered chair to study his grandnephew critically. "However, you are a

handsome enough devil. There have been a few caps
thrown in your direction, I'll warrant. The question is, what
did you do with them when you caught them? Dare I specu-
late that a fine time was had by all?"

A muscle worked in Mr. Hawkins's jaw even though he
had not as yet had a single bite of breakfast. "I do not discuss any lady with such disrespect, my lord."

Lord Hughes's glance was shrewd. "No, of course not. It
is beneath you, whilst I have no difficulty whatsoever in
discussing the ladies at length and in the most intimate detail. Shall I tell you of my last little bird of paradise? A
truly delectable morsel. She possessed a skin of velvet and
a provocative bottom that made one's—"

"Enough!" Mr. Hawkins shoved aside his untouched
plate and stood up. His eyes smouldered with disgust and
contempt. "Have you no shred of decency, my lord? Can
you not even pretend some finer feelings? You are betrothed to a true lady! You should be thinking of her, not
dwelling on past peccadillos."

Lord Hughes's lids drooped over his eyes. "You wrong
me, boy. I do indeed think of the lady. Since the betrothal I
have thought of little else but our wedding day. Or more
precisely, the wedding night. My blood runs hotter even at
this moment. The lady has much to offer a man of experience and jaded tastes. That lovely hair—spread like so
much molten fire over the white pillow, for instance. I do
indeed think of my bride to be, believe me."

Lord Hughes's words conjured up a vision so unbearable
that Mr. Hawkins shot over the table to catch hold of his
great-uncle's throat. He shook the older man. Crockery
shattered onto the floor, but neither man heard it. "You bas-
tard," he enunciated softly, his vivid blue eyes twin blazes.
"I should throttle you this instant for defaming the lady in
such a base fashion."

Lord Hughes looked up into his grandnephew's cold
eyes. His smile was disdainful. Not by a flicker of an eyelid
did he acknowledge the bruising power of Mr. Hawkins's
hold. "Such a display of emotion, nevvy! One could suspect you of being a disappointed lover."

The door to the breakfast room opened. Viscount Waithe
entered, addressing Sir Charles over his shoulder, and so he

did not immediately witness the same startling tableau as that other gentleman.

"Good God!"

Upon Sir Charles's horrified exclamation, Viscount Waithe whirled around, and an equal look of astonishment came over his countenance. "Peter! What are you about, man!"

Mr. Hawkins let go of Lord Hughes, a rush of color staining his lean cheekbones. He said stiffly, "I shall not stand by to bandy words with you, my lord."

He turned on his heel, brushing past his astonished friends. His hand was already on the doorknob when his grand-uncle's mocking voice stopped him.

"No. You are definitely miscast as the jealous lover."

Viscount Waithe and Sir Charles stood rooted to the spot, appalled. Their eyes went from one to the other of the gentlemen.

Lord Hughes gave a low laugh. His gaze was fastened on his grandnephew's stiffened back. He said contemptuously, "It would never occur to you that that same passion, played to a woman, would make her heart flutter with delicious desire. No, you're too much the idealistic fool! You'll never learn that most valuable lesson—all is fair in love and war." His voice dropped to a silky purr. "And I assure you, I am a past master of the first, as my lovely lady shall discover."

Mr. Hawkins yanked open the door and left the breakfast room. He strode swiftly down the entry hall toward his study, barely checking when a strong hand fell on his shoulder.

"Peter! Hold up, cousin."

Swinging about in the open doorway, Mr. Hawkins shook off Viscount Waithe's restraining fingers. "Leave me be, Percy. I am in no fit mood and so I warn you."

"So I can see, so you needn't glare daggers at me. But Charles and I are your friends. If there is anything that we might do—"

"There is nothing. It is a private matter between myself and Lord Hughes."

Viscount Waithe shrewdly regarded his taller cousin's granitelike face. "I'll lay a monkey that it has to do with that preposterous announcement last night. However that could have come about is anyone's guess. But I do know this. You have been head over heels in love with Miss Dower for weeks. We have all seen it, so you needn't deny it."

"Percy, what my feelings may or may not be for Miss Dower are none of your concern, nor anyone else's."

Mr. Hawkins's voice was cold. It was apparent that he had erected a barrier and would not be brought to acknowledge either the cause of his fury or his friends' concern.

"Now, gentlemen, if you will excuse me—" He turned to cross the threshold into the study.

The fist caught him full on the jaw and set him staggering back.

"What the devil!" Viscount Waithe whirled to stare in shocked disbelief at Sir Charles, who was coolly flexing his hand. "Are you *mad*, Charles?"

Sir Charles did not spare him even a glance. He followed Mr. Hawkins into the study. His narrowed eyes were trained on the gentleman, who was shaking the daze from his head. "Not at all, Percy. Ah, just as I thought."

With a roar, Mr. Hawkins rushed at Sir Charles. The two connected with a crash of bone and muscle.

The next few minutes were confusing ones. Viscount Waithe looked on with appalled fascination while his two best friends brutally slugged one another without regard to the finer points of the pugilistic sport.

A scream captured his attention, and he glanced around with an irritated frown to discover several servants gathered at the study door. Perceiving clearly his duty, Viscount Waithe pushed them all out and closed and locked the door. He dropped the key into his pocket.

When it was all done, the combatants dropped exhausted into wingback chairs. Viscount Waithe solicitously supplied each with a glass of wine. He grinned as he saw their twin grimaces that the wine burned their cut lips. He replaced the decanter and waited with great interest for the other two gentlemen to speak.

"Thank you, Charles," said Mr. Hawkins finally. His bloodied mouth twisted as he gingerly examined a bruised cheekbone with cautious fingertips. "I think."

"Not at all, dear fellow." Sir Charles grimaced down at his torn and bloodied self. "I do detest exertion of this sort."

"Your sartorial splendor is no more," Mr. Hawkins observed.

"I don't know when I have seen a better turnout," said Viscount Waithe, settling himself on the corner of the desk and swinging his booted foot.

There came a hesitant knocking on the study door. The butler's voice was plainly recognizable. "Sir? Do you care for anything?"

Raising his voice slightly, Mr. Hawkins said succinctly, "Go away."

"Very good, sir." The disembodied voice conveyed disapproval.

Inside the study, the gentlemen laughed. Viscount Waithe withdrew the key from his pocket and held it aloft. "Shall I unlock the door?"

"As you wish, Percy."

"I shan't, then. I don't fancy a lot of curious faces popping in with one excuse or another," Viscount Waithe said, dropping the key back into his pocket. He looked over at his cousin. "I suppose that there is nothing that I can do?"

Mr. Hawkins shook his head, his lips twisting in a humorless smile. "Thank you, Percy. But unless you might somehow call back Miss Dower's declaration of yesterday evening, I do not think that there is anything to the purpose."

"Damnation! Why did that court card ever come to Bath?" muttered Viscount Waithe with a scowl, staring at his toe.

"It is certainly odd that his lordship should suddenly take it into his head to journey to Bath, and especially during the Season," Sir Charles agreed. "Lord Hughes is a gentleman given over to the pursuit of his own pleasure, and he is known rarely to leave London."

"What is odd in that? We came down to Bath," Viscount Waithe pointed out.

"But we came down for the fisticuffs and then remained because our friend showed us such excellent entertainment," said Sir Charles. "I hardly think that the cases could be said to be the same."

Peter had been listening to the idle argument with a gathering thoughtful attention. "You have the right of it, Charles. Lord Hughes had a specific goal in mind when he made this pilgrimage, and there is something that yet holds him here."

"Perhaps it is Lady Pomerancy?" Viscount Waithe suggested tentatively. Before his companions could remark on it, he himself rejected the notion. "I cannot believe that is true, for they do not seem to like one another above half, do they? In point of fact, I would lay odds that Lady Pomerancy would be delighted to hear of his lordship's shaking the dust of Bath from his feet."

"No one with sense would accept that wager," said Mr. Hawkins humorously.

Viscount Waithe and Sir Charles laughed.

Viscount Waithe shook his head, still grinning, and said, "Lord, did you chance to see her ladyship's face when Lord Hughes acknowledged that he was betrothed to Miss Dower? She started to say something, then snapped shut her mouth. I feared she would have apoplexy on the spot."

Mr. Hawkins's gaze sharpened. "What did my grandmother say?"

Viscount Waithe shook his head. "I did not quite catch it. It did not make a bit of sense. It sounded as though she said she should have known that he could not be trusted."

Mr. Hawkins was silent for a long moment. When he looked up again to meet his friends' eyes, he managed to smile. "It appears that I should speak with Lady Pomerancy. She might be able to enlighten me on certain points."

"I do not believe that her ladyship would work in any way to your harm, Peter," Viscount Waithe said.

"Perhaps not. However, she would go to great lengths to establish what she perceived to be best for me." Mr. Hawkins sighed, running his hand gingerly over his battered face. "It has all grown so complicated. I don't know what to think about any of it anymore. I thought I was going about it the right way to win Miss Dower's affections. Throughout I have acted to the best of my honor. Instead of winning my lady, I have lost her to Lord Hughes, who is a libertine and a patently selfish character."

"Females are odd creatures at best," commented Sir Charles. "One only has to look at how they place such emphasis upon expressions of affection to realize it. I imagine that Lord Hughes played upon Miss Dower's romantic sensibilities in just such a fashion."

"A lady as unsophisticated and unspoiled as Miss Dower could not hope to prove a match for one of his lordship's wide experience in the art of seduction," Viscount Waithe agreed with melancholy.

"What you are telling me, Percy, is that *I* could not prove a match for Lord Hughes and his tactics," said Mr. Hawkins slowly.

Viscount Waithe looked taken aback, and said hastily, "I never meant any such thing, Peter. Why, you are a fair dab with the ladies yourself. Always popular. Anyone could tell you so."

Mr. Hawkins threw up his hand. "Never mind, Percy. I know you meant nothing of insult by it. It is a valid observation, however. Certainly you have set in motion an original train of thought." He stood up, setting aside his wineglass. "The key, Percy. You both have come for breakfast and I have been a negligent host. However, I should like to clean myself up after that little bout before I join you at table."

"And I," said Sir Charles, rising indolently to his feet. He grimaced down at himself. "My man will fall to weeping when he lays eyes on this coat. It was quite his favorite."

Viscount Waithe unlocked the door, chuckling while he did so. "He may give notice on the instant."

"I trust not. One cannot hope to put up a decent appearance without the ministrations of a talented valet. I suppose I shall be forced to bribe him to stay," said Sir Charles. He considered a moment and sighed. "Undoubtedly I shall have to bribe him. What a deuced nuisance."

The gentlemen left the study, Mr. Hawkins and the viscount laughing.

Chapter Twenty-eight

The assembly was much like any other that Evelyn had attended in Bath. The company was agreeable and willing to entertain and be entertained. The ladies were gowned elegantly and the gentlemen appeared sophisticated in well-tailored evening coats and breeches.

Evelyn herself laughed and talked and danced, as had always been her wont. Despite her apparent spirits, her heart was heavy. She had not slept well for several nights, tossing and turning on her pillows as over and over her tired mind grappled with the horrid coil that she had inexplicably gotten herself tangled up in. She could scarcely believe that she had entered into a betrothal with Lord Hughes.

When she had risen, her eyes had felt grainy from lack of rest and tears. She had endured each day as well as she could, and though she was aware that she had been to several functions, none now stood out in her memory. She had listlessly begged off receiving callers, and her mother had not pressed her.

Evelyn closed her burning eyes momentarily against the brilliance of the numerous lighted candelabras. When she opened them, she saw Peter Hawkins enter the ballroom. She had been waiting for sight of him, and her heart gave a painful leap at his appearance. His leonine blond head was bent courteously to the shorter gentleman who had claimed his attention. Mr. Hawkins's lean virility was set off to distinction by his dark evening clothes, bringing a fluttering pulse to Evelyn's throat.

She waited hopefully for him to come over to speak to her, even not knowing what she might say to him. As the evening wore on and he did not make an attempt to greet her, hope withered and died in her breast. He despised her, she thought numbly. It was a further blow to her state of mind.

She tried to dismiss the depression that settled like a gray pall over her and threw herself into the dancing and outrageous flirtations. Her circle of suitors stirred with admiration of her vivaciousness and beauty.

Sir Charles was perhaps not quite as attentive as he had been heretofore, but Evelyn scarcely noticed. She danced with the gentleman and smiled dazzlingly at his whispered compliments, but she hardly heard what he said. When he handed her back into the care of her mother and took his leave, Evelyn felt obliquely relieved.

Viscount Waithe was also in attendance, and Evelyn accepted his invitation to dance with gratitude, certain that with him at least she could relax and not pretend to a lightheartedness that was becoming increasingly difficult to maintain.

However, Viscount Waithe was not the uncritical partner that she had assumed that he would be. He spoke disapprovingly of her betrothal, saying, "That fellow is old enough to be your father, and his reputation is raddled to boot. Whatever possessed you, Evelyn?"

"Percy, please let us not argue," Evelyn begged. Her head had begun to ache, the pain settling grimly behind her burning eyes.

"Of course we shan't," he said stiffly. "It is just that I cannot accept the thought of such an ignoble match for you when Pe—when there are any number of others."

"Oh, let me be, Percy!"

But Viscount Waithe was intent on pursuing his course and ignored the warning signals in her flashing eyes. He was determined as a friend to bring her to her senses. "Evelyn, you cannot know what a bounder Lord Hughes is. He will make you the devil of a husband, I promise you. My advice to you is to jilt the fellow before it is too late. No one would think the worse of you. Why, everyone knows what his lordship is like and—"

Evelyn drew away, breaking step. "That is quite enough, my lord! I think that I should like to be returned to my chair," she said coldly.

Viscount Waithe was momentarily taken aback by her glacial rebuff. Then his expression smoothed and he said, excessively polite, "Of course, Miss Dower. I shall be more than happy to do so." Without any deference to protocol or convention he instantly whisked her back to her seat.

Evelyn sank down on the chair with a smothered sigh. She nodded in response to Viscount Waithe's rigid bow, but she did not watch as he took himself off. Instead, she closed her eyes for a moment, her hands pressed to her temples.

Mrs. Dower was still seated in her own chair. She had not danced once that evening. She did not acknowledge her daughter's return, but pleated the folds of her skirt between her fingers.

When Evelyn turned to her, she saw that her mother's normally placid expression had been replaced by one of unusual strain. "Mama, you do not appear in the best of spirits this evening."

Evelyn was astonished and hurt by her mother's instant rebuff.

"Pray do not address me. I am still extremely upset with you, Evelyn, and I do not wish to be here."

Evelyn felt the tears crowding behind her eyes. Her mother had been very quiet ever since that disastrous evening, but she had not been actively unkind before. Evelyn said unsteadily, "I am sorry, Mama. I did not realize that you were so out of curl. If I had known, I would not have suggested that we come tonight. Why did you not tell me that you would have preferred to remain at home?"

"If you must know, I am only here because you require a chaperon and I know my duty." Mrs. Dower searched for her handkerchief and dabbed at her eyes. "But I do not have to like it, nor do I intend to do so. How you could be so thoughtless and provoking and—and—" Words appeared to fail her. She turned her shoulder on her daughter.

Evelyn sighed. She was tired and her head was coming to pound abominably. Nothing was right. Unhappiness pervaded her thoughts. She had lost Peter Hawkins, entered unintentionally into a distasteful betrothal, driven away her friends, and made her mother cry.

Evelyn watched the dancing and heard the laughter and congenial buzz of conversation. The stark contrast between the frivolity of the gathering and what she was feeling was nearly unbearable. It was a horrible evening. It was quite the horridest time that she had ever had.

Evelyn refused the next few dances, pleading the headache. The inexorable pounding soon crowded out any desire to put up a sociable front.

Several minutes before, Mrs. Loweling, a friend of Mrs. Dower's, had seated herself beside Mrs. Dower, and the ladies had entered into conversation. Evelyn quietly broke in to inform her mother that she had decided to go home early. "I have the headache and so I am not in a particularly festive frame of mind," she said, attempting a smile.

"You do appear pulled, Miss Dower," said Mrs. Loweling, sympathetically regarding her overly pale countenance.

"Of course, Evelyn. I shall accompany you at once," said Mrs. Dower coolly.

Evelyn stopped her mother from rising. She did not think that she could stand the cold civility with which her mother was treating her. "Oh, you must not cut short your own enjoyment on my behalf, Mama. There is no need, for I mean to go straight off to bed. I shall send the carriage back for you."

"If you are certain, dear," said Mrs. Dower.

Evelyn assured her that she was, and her mother acquiesced. Mrs. Dower turned back to Mrs. Loweling to pick up the thread of their conversation. Evelyn wavered, feeling curiously bereft. Then, swiftly, she turned away. She did not see that Mrs. Dower's eyes followed her.

Evelyn sought out her hostess to make her brief apologies and then left the ballroom. Outside, the night air felt wonderful on Evelyn's heated brow, and she paused a moment before going to summon the carriage.

Suddenly a woolen cover was thrown over her head. She gave a choked cry, but was quickly silenced when a rough hand clamped over her face, pressing the cloth suffocatingly close over her nose and mouth. She was lifted off the ground, her mouth covered and her arms held pinned to her sides, and carried helplessly to an unknown destination.

Evelyn was tossed unceremoniously into a carriage onto the seat. The door was slammed. The carriage jerked forward as the horses were whipped up, and Evelyn tumbled onto the floor.

Evelyn tore off the blinding woolen hood. She scrambled over to the door and tried to open it, but it was latched from the outside and would not budge despite her frantic attempts. She banged on the door, screaming for someone to release her. But it was all futile. Next she tried the windows, but they, too, had been fixed not to open from the inside.

Evelyn curled up tightly on the seat in one corner. Unheeded tears coursed down her cheeks. She was stunned and terrified. She could scarcely believe it was all real, that there had not been some ghastly mistake, or that she would not waken safely in her own bed from a very bad dream.

But she did not waken. The terrible nightmare went on and on, the din of hooves and wheels the only accompaniment to her anguished thoughts. As time passed, she knew with despair that she was being carried away from Bath, away from her mother and her home.

Once, then twice, the carriage slowed. Each time, Evelyn sat up straighter, stiffening with fear as she expected one of the doors to be wrenched open. But both occasions were false alarms, which left her already stretched nerves quite shattered.

Evelyn bitterly regretted now having so emphatically rejected Mr. Hawkins's self-appointed protection. *If only! If only!* her thoughts chanted in rhythm with the carriage wheels. But Mr. Hawkins would not come to her rescue. She had pushed him away and he no longer even liked her. Somehow that was worse than all the rest. She fell over onto her face on the seat and wept.

Evelyn did not know how long it was before she felt the carriage come to a stop. She sat up, hastily wiping her eyes and cheeks. She would not give her abductor the satisfaction of seeing her in tears.

When the door was opened, she was sitting composedly

on the seat. Not a word was spoke but a gloved hand was held out to her in command.

Evelyn rose. Disdaining to accept the proffered help from the carriage, she ducked out and stepped down to the ground. She had a fleeting impression of moonlight and that the shadow of a building was before her. Then another hood came down over her head. She cried out, her hands rising to thrust off the terrifying blindness, but her wrists were caught in a hard grip and she was flung over a wide shoulder.

She kicked and struggled, but to no avail. In the darkness of her cloth prison she heard a door open, low voices, the swift thud of her captor's boots as she was carried into the building.

Another door was opened.

Suddenly she was dropped onto something yielding. Stunned, she heard her carrier step away, the sharp closing of a door. Evelyn sat up and ripped off the hood. She looked about her wildly.

Her surroundings were sinisterly familiar, which but made her situation all the more fearful. She was sitting on a silk-covered settee in a tastefully furnished private parlor. A fire was lit on the hearth and cast somber shadows over expensively papered walls. Walls that were discordantly bare of pictures or mirrors or other decoration.

Evelyn stood up slowly, absorbing the atmosphere. It was obvious that she had been brought to a house owned by someone of her own social class. Conjectures fleeted through her mind. She could not imagine who among her acquaintances could have betrayed her in such a fashion, but the fact that her abductor was of her own social class displayed an enormity of callous disregard for all convention and taboo.

Her heart beat hard with dread as she began to fear more than ever discovering why she had been abducted.

Evelyn stepped toward the door. Even though she knew the door must be locked, she intended to try the knob.

A rustle of sound behind her whirled her around. Her heart was in her mouth and her breath was shortened. Her horrified eyes discerned now a tall dark figure standing in the shadows next to the heavily curtained window.

"Who are you? What do you want?" Her voice was hoarse.

The man stepped fully into the firelight. Recognizing him Evelyn took an inadvertent step back.

"The door is locked, Evelyn."

"You!" Evelyn was stunned. She could only stare across at him while her thoughts stumbled, unable to grasp the truth. Of anyone she might have conceived to be capable of such villainy, never would she have suspected that most proper gentleman of all, Peter Hawkins.

"Yes." In a moment of silence, he studied her face and the tense manner in which she held herself. His expression was unreadable. "You appear overwrought and tired. A glass of burgundy will do you good." He turned to the side table to pick up a decanter, glancing again at her as he did so.

Evelyn stayed where she was. She did not know what to do. She could not believe even with the evidence of Peter Hawkins's presence that he could possibly be the author of this ghastly experience.

He came up to her, offering the glass of burgundy. Fumbling a little, numb in spirit and body, she took it. She did not resist when he took her elbow and guided her back to the settee.

It was only after they were both seated that she spoke. In a low trembling voice, she said, "I do not understand."

Mr. Hawkins smiled slightly, but there was nothing of humor in his eyes. "I hope that you will come to, however. You are shivering. Drink the wine. It will help to warm you."

Evelyn obediently touched the glass to her lips. She took too much and strangled on it. She choked and coughed, sending some of the wine spilling from her glass. The glass was taken from her, and strong hands held her for the duration of the paroxysm.

Her eyes were still streaming when Evelyn struggled away from his impersonal hold. "Pray—! Let me go."

At once, he did so. He leaned at his ease against the back of the settee and rested one arm along it. "I am glad you are recovered. Perhaps now we might proceed to the reason why I have had you brought here."

Evelyn was very aware of his size. She had never before thought of him as the possessor of an intimidating presence, but so she found now. She was aware also of the proximity of his hand, where it rested close to her shoulder. Holding herself stiffly, she said with as much dignity as she could muster under the circumstances, "Yes. I should like an explanation." Her voice was still hoarse and betrayed her fear.

Mr. Hawkins looked away, a frown gathering his brows. "It is not what I wished."

She felt the thud of her pulse deep in her throat. "Then perhaps it is all a mistake. Perhaps it would be best if you returned me to Bath."

He looked at her for a long moment. He sighed. "I am sorry, Evelyn. It is no longer so simple as that. I have already embarked on this course, and I cannot call it back. I cannot allow you to return home until I have made you understand certain things. It is unfortunate that it has come to such a pass as this. If there had been any other alternative left to me, believe me, I would never have thought of subjecting you to such distress as you are now laboring under."

Evelyn felt an insane desire to laugh. His expression conveyed regret and he had actually apologized to her, as though he had committed a mere solecism. "My dear sir, I assure you that what I feel is in no way assuaged by your words. On the contrary! I am even more filled with foreboding. Am I incorrect in my instinct?"

She was surprised by her own daring in so addressing him, when obviously she dealt with a madman. She supposed it was because his manner and his apology were so much in character with what she had come to take for granted of him. For a fleeting moment, she could almost believe that she was bandying words with him in her own sitting room.

But then he smiled. It was a smile of such grimness that the tiny surge of confidence that she had felt was completely banished, to be replaced by fearful dread.

Chapter Twenty-nine

Evelyn shrank away from him. That was a mistake, for she came in contact with his hand, which dropped onto her shoulder. Evelyn instantly flinched, but his fingers tightened, stopping her instinctive movement. She could not free herself from his hold without wrenching herself away, and she feared his reaction if she dared to do so. Evelyn froze beneath his hand. "Will—will you unhand me, sir?"

"I think not," he said quietly. His other hand slid up her bare arm. He drew her closer and a strong arm slipped about her shoulders. His fingers tangled in her hair and caressed the back of her neck.

Evelyn's eyes were huge pools. She trembled with the odd sensations that he was arousing in her. She was frightened and confused. He was still Peter Hawkins, the gentleman she had thought would deal honorably with her over an impulsive and stupid wager. But he had also become someone she did not know. He had become a wicked seducer. "Peter—" she whispered. "Do not."

His expression was unreadable. He did not reply. Instead, lowering his head slowly, he sought her lips.

It was a slow, exploratory kiss, quite different from what Evelyn had dreaded from him in this stranger's guise. A sob strangled in her throat.

When he released her, Evelyn swiftly leaped up from the settee. As she crossed over to the draped window, she heard his step behind her. She turned, feeling herself to be at bay. "Why? Why have you done this? Is this the payment you exact for my lost wager?" she cried.

He had come to stand so near to her that the toes of his boots touched her hem. He did not need to reach out for her to feel his leashed power. She stared up at his face, but his back was to the fire and she could not easily make out his expression. Yet she could have sworn that she saw a flicker of distress cross his face.

"The wager? Hardly that. Simply, I could think of no other way to persuade you that you should not marry Lord Hughes," he said quietly.

Evelyn stared up at him, disbelieving. Incredulity lacing her voice, she asked, "This is simply another one of your machinations to rid me of a suitor that you deem unworthy?"

"As bizarre as that sounds, yes."

Evelyn slapped him with all the pent-up fear and strength of which she was capable. He staggered with the shock of it.

Tears glittered on the ends of her lashes. Her voice trembled with fury and grief. "Damn you, Peter Hawkins! You have succeeded. Lord Hughes will want nothing to do with me after this night, nor will any other respectable gentleman. Your misguided notions of propriety have finally compromised me beyond repair."

"It was not my intention to ruin you!"

"Was it not?" Evelyn managed a brittle laugh. "You have a difficult task of proving it otherwise, my dear sir."

"I have only one way to prove it," he said grimly.

Before Evelyn quite grasped his intention, he caught her up roughly into his arms. The kiss that he pressed on her was savage. His mouth wholly possessed hers. She gave an inarticulate mewl in her throat and tried to twist free. But her arms were caught and pinned, while her body was held immobile by the strength that he demonstrated.

Evelyn felt herself drowning beneath the assault of his mouth. It was no longer brutal but strove to melt her with its heat. His arms loosened from about her, but she no longer struggled to be free. Instead, her arms slid up about his neck. His lips left hers to travel the length of her throat until coming to rest on her frantic pulse. His teeth delicately nipped the flesh.

In a haze, Evelyn felt his arms sweep around her, lifting her so that she was cradled high against his chest. His mouth claimed hers again.

When he at last broke the kiss, she dimly realized that

they had somehow come to be back on the settee. She was half reclining in his lap, her head pillowed on his shoulder. She felt his harsh breath against her brow, and when she placed her palm lightly against his shirtfront she could feel the quick thud of his heart. Wonderingly, she looked up into his face.

His mouth was quirked in a smile, but his eyes were shadowed. "I have succeeded in sweeping you off of your feet at last, Miss Dower. Will you marry me?"

Evelyn blinked. "What did you say?" she breathed.

"I asked whether you would—"

"Not that." Evelyn sat up as indignation took spark in her eyes. "You discussed me with my mother. And *she*—!" Evelyn could not even properly articulate her outrage and disgust.

Mr. Hawkins cleared his throat. Somewhat shamefaced, he said, "Well, yes. I believe she might have mentioned, just in passing, that you had a penchant for romance novels. I solicited her advice in how to win your hand. She told me to sweep you off your feet and carry you off. Thus this highly unconventional episode, which was made very much easier when you left the assembly alone."

"Mama knew!" Evelyn saw now that her mother had been unusually amenable to her going home alone. She clenched her fists. "Oh! How *could* she!"

Evelyn tried to scramble away, but he prevented her by the simple expedient of tightening his arms. Evelyn, realizing that to struggle must only make her look even more ridiculous, glared at him. In her coldest voice, she said, "Pray let go of me this instant!"

He shook his head regretfully. "I fear that I must risk your further displeasure, ma'am. You have not yet answered my question, and"—he grinned with surprising wickedness—"I am finding this a most intriguing circumstance."

"I loathe you with every fiber of my being," Evelyn stated with disdain.

He reached up to gently smooth back a curl that had fallen across her brow. "I do not think so, sweetheart," he said softly, almost marveling. "And I suspect that you know it, too."

Evelyn swallowed. Her heart had given a considerable jump at his endearment and was even now betraying her with its quickened tempo. She took refuge in bravado. "I do not know to what you are referring, Mr. Hawkins."

"Marry me, Evelyn. I am wholly in love with you, you see, and even though that might frighten you now, I promise that I shall not—"

"Frighten me!" exclaimed Evelyn. "Why should I be frightened of what I have wished to hear from you for positively years?"

Mr. Hawkins shook his head, bewildered. "I did offer for your hand," he pointed out.

"But I believed you did so because Lady Pomerancy ordered you to," said Evelyn. "And even when I discovered that wasn't so, I thought you motivated solely by propriety and duty."

"You thought *what*?"

Evelyn had the grace to flush. "It—it was the way Mama explained it to me, you see. I was already half in love with you; but then I became so disillusioned. I thought you naught but a mawkworm and worse."

Mr. Hawkins threw back his head and shouted with laughter.

Evelyn tossed her head, a reluctant smile curving her lips. She fiddled with his coat lapel. "Of course it sounds ridiculous now, but at the time—and then, when you never gave any sign of wanting me, why, I—"

"Not want you?" A distinct glitter entered his eyes. "My dear Miss Dower, obviously you can have no notion what Herculean efforts I was put to in order to stop myself from snatching you up and so thoroughly kissing you that you would never recover."

"Why didn't you, then?" Evelyn asked, blushing under his look.

"I did not wish to frighten you off."

"Peter!" She leaned as far as the limits of his arms would allow to stare up at him. "I am not such a chucklehead as that."

He sighed. With deliberation, he said, "I feared that any excess of passion on my part would give you a permanent disgust of me."

Evelyn shook her head. She put up her hand and with her fingers gently, delicately, traced his strong jawline. "You stupid, idiotic man." A disturbing thought strayed into her mind.

His expression altered, and his arms tightened about her once more. "I tend to agree with that assessment," he said and started to lower his head.

Evelyn's hand shot up between their lips, forestalling him. "You have forgotten, sir. I am betrothed to Lord Hughes." She said it with a smile, but she was perfectly serious. The recollection was a lowering one and effectively dispelled her giddy happiness.

However, Mr. Hawkins did not seem to share her downcast feelings. He shook his head. "On the contrary. It is your mother who will become Lady Hughes."

"What?!"

He laughed at her expression. "Is your nose quite out of joint, my love? It seems that Lord Hughes and your mother had already come to an understanding when you made that ludicrous announcement. I do not believe any who were present have since touted it about, but to cover any public confusion, we shall put it about that in the throes of your excitement you garbled the news of your mother's engagement so that it *sounded* as though it was you who had been the recipient of the honor."

Evelyn drew a deep breath. Some things had suddenly become very much clearer. "I am so glad. Lord Hughes is not precisely what one prefers in a stepfather, of course, but I know that he will be good for my mother. He will not demand such of her except that she go on entertaining and shopping. As for Mama—"

Evelyn chuckled suddenly. "I suppose that she will lead his lordship a rather lively dance. He may even find that he does not have the energy to make up to any other ladies."

"So would I assume," Mr. Hawkins agreed. He regarded her with the quirk of his mouth that was so familiar and dear to her. "I shall ask you but one more time. Evelyn, will you consent to become my wife?"

"I suppose I must since you have ruined me," said Evelyn on a mock sigh.

He was suddenly very grave. "I have not, actually. We

are at this moment in my town house in Lansdown Crescent. The door is not even locked. If you so wished it, I would call out a carriage and request my grandmother's maid to chaperon you home."

Evelyn regarded him in astonishment. "But the carriage drove for ever so long. I was certain that I had been carried out of Bath."

"You were only meant to think it. I had the coachman drive around for an hour before coming back here. I would never have purposely placed you into a compromising position," he said.

Various emotions crossed Evelyn's face, indignation and amusement among them. Finally she said, glancing down at her position in his lap, "On the contrary! I am in just such a compromising position."

He opened his mouth, but she swiftly covered his lips with her fingers. "Do not dare apologize, my paragon," she warned. "Or I shall refuse your suit yet again. Pray try to pretend, for a few moments at least, that you are the wickedest flouter of convention in England."

"I am at your command, my dearest lady," he said, and proceeded to prove it.